THE MARTIAN CONSPIRACY

JOHN A. READ

Cover Art by Steven James Catizone

Editing by Editworks
www.editworksusa.com

Final Copy Edit by Johnnie Mazzocco

Formatting by Heidi Sutherlin
http://www.mycreativepursuits.com/

Angels and Airwaves lyrics used with permission from the artist.
High Flight poem by John Gillespie Magee, Jr. is public domain.

Interior artwork:
"Electro Glider over Yosemite" and "Mayflower Over Mars" are works by the Author.

Follow me here:
www.facebook.com/TheMartianConspiracy
Twitter: @JohnAaronRead
Google: plus.google.com/+JohnReadAuthor/

Contents

Acknowledgements

It all started when my parents bought me a used copy of the October 1981 issue of *National Geographic*. On the cover was the Space Shuttle Columbia launching into space for the very first time. From that point on, I was hooked on space.

First, I'd like to acknowledge my childhood heroes Julie Payette and Chris Hadfield. As a child growing up on Prince Edward Island, these two Canadian astronauts were my window to the cosmos.

I'd like to thank NASA Engineer Robert Frost and NASA Astronaut Clayton Anderson for being an endless supply of knowledge on the dynamics of space travel. Your dedication to teaching the public through your participation on Quora.com has been instrumental in helping keep this book as scientifically accurate as possible (my apologies for the artistic liberties included in these pages).

A huge thank you to James and Claudia Altucher, your "ten ideas" strategy hatched the creativity between these pages (including the idea for this book in the first place).

To all the brilliant folks at SpaceX and Orbital ATK for bringing the human exploration of Mars closer than ever. I truly believe the work you do will open the door for human exploration of the solar system.

I would also like to thank Tom DeLonge and all the members of Angels and Airwaves. Many ideas in this book came to me while listening to your albums.

To the cover artist, Steven James Catizone: May your amazing artwork continue to inspire budding space enthusiasts around the world.

To John Harten, the editor: Your guidance, patience, and wisdom have taken this book to a level surpassing my wildest expectations.

A huge thank you to the beta readers: Erin Patel, Jennifer Read, Debbie Nadler, Jim Read and Susan Peters. These amazing individuals weeded through several unedited drafts, making hundreds of suggestions that added enormous depth to the story.

Special thanks to Graeme Shimmin, author of *A Kill in the Morning*, for writing the blurb for the rear cover and also for your blogs, especially your post on story archetypes, which helped drive this story to where it needed to be.

Finally, to my wife Jennifer and sons Isaac and Oliver: I couldn't have done this without your love and support.

Prologue

July 2068 - Moffett Field, San Francisco Bay Area

It took me five years to rebuild the vintage Katana. I sat in a timeworn leather seat and threw the red master switch. The cockpit came alive with the hum of whirling gyroscopes as the instruments came online. A key rested in the ignition and I turned it clockwise two clicks. The engine coughed several times, sputtered, and rumbled to a steady idle. Air washed into the cockpit, carrying with it the smell of hot tarmac and engine oil. I reached up and closed the canopy, put on a classic green DC headset, and fixed the microphone to my chin.

I taxied to Moffet's runway, got clearance from ATC, and took to the sky. The airstrip disappeared below me, replaced by the murky shoreline slough. The Rotax 912 engine tugged at the air, pulling the Katana higher into the California sky. I flew over San Jose's rusted desalination plants and continued north toward San Francisco. On my right, windmills on the East Bay's skyline carved the atmosphere with three-hundred-foot blades.

Sailboats with colorful spinnakers littered the bay, but the skies over San Francisco were empty. It was just me and the seagulls this morning.

I flew over Bernal Heights, where my wife and I were about to move. Marie had dreamed of renting one of the Victorian flats that peppered San Francisco's historic neighborhoods. We had made that dream a reality, signing the lease the previous Friday.

Passing the Golden Gate Bridge, I banked right, heading toward wine country. I checked my watch. *Forty minutes until I have to land.*

The southern tip of Napa Valley had airspace dedicated to aerobatics. Would the controllers let me use it? The Katana was agile but by no means a stunt plane. I decided to give it a try. "Sonoma Tower, this is Katana two seven niner foxtrot, requesting permission to enter practice area Charley over."

"Copy Katana two seven niner, Charley is empty, you are clear for aerobatic flight up to six thousand feet."

"Roger that, tower, six thousand feet, Katana two seven niner out." I grinned.

With the throttle punched in, I cranked the stick to the left, rolling into a steep left bank that pressed the airframe to its structural limits. Adrenaline pulsed through me, or was that just the G load? It was probably both. I dove, gaining speed as altitude dwindled. A hundred feet from the swamps of Skaggs Island, I pulled up, shooting back into the sky. As the aircraft bled off speed, I kicked the rudder to the right, throwing the Katana into a hammerhead. I'd never be able to do this again. *Better make it count!*

I exited the hammerhead into another dive, and then leveled out, thinking of Marie. On that note, I kept my distance from the ground. *Marie would kill me if I died*, I thought.

After a few more wingovers and attempted loops, most of which ended in stalls, I'd had all my stomach could take. I radioed Sonoma Skypark and requested permission to land. After a single circuit around the airport, I set the aircraft down and taxied toward the hangars.

A man in his mid-fifties waited on the tarmac and waved as I taxied by. He was getting a fully rebuilt Katana, a plane he'd surely enjoy for years to come.

The Katana came to a stop. I pulled back on the mixture control, switched off the master and pulled out the key. I unclipped the four-point harness and flipped up the canopy, tossing my headset onto the copilot's seat.

We shook hands and I handed over the oil-stained registration.

I never thought I'd sell my aircraft. But two weeks earlier, we had discovered Marie was pregnant. We did some math, drawing up a budget. Rent in San Francisco and a child, we could afford, but hangar fees and aircraft maintenance would put us in the red.

The Katana had to go.

That night Marie and I stood on the deck of our apartment and took turns looking through a telescope she had given me for Christmas. As a boy I had been fascinated with space, leading me to my dream job as a NASA engineer. But since I'd probably never have the chance to visit Mars or even the lunar colony, I got my pilot's license. It wasn't the same, but flying had provided me an authentic joy.

Marie looked into my eyes, took my hand and squeezed it. We had prepared ourselves for a new set of adventures and were eager to experience them together.

PART 1

Chapter 1

2071 - California

July 20th, 2071. This was the day NASA started a war.

I stepped out of the car in San Francisco to the familiar smell of fresh coffee and homeless people. A musician sat on a bucket playing a saxophone, his music echoing between the buildings. I walked down Market Street toward the Embarcadero, grateful for the chance to stretch my legs. It can be a long drive from NASA's Mountain View research center, and driverless vehicles always obey the speed limit.

I glanced up at the Ferry Building, fog hovered around the clock tower. The sun would burn it off soon. San Fran's mornings were always a bit chilly. I stepped into a café, grabbing a coffee. When I left the shop, I walked back to the musician and passed my wristwatch over his case, transferring a few dollars.

Three blocks away, the Transbay Transit Center's glass facade twinkled as the sun broke through the clouds. I walked there, enjoying the hot coffee while pigeons dodged my feet. Usually, I'd stroll through the station's five-acre rooftop garden, but not today.

I jogged down the escalator and boarded a train. Cameras inspected my eyes, billing me for the ticket as metallic doors clanged shut behind me. My body pressed into a cloth seat as we rocketed out of the Bay Area. I held my coffee in the air to prevent it from spilling.

My tablet clung to the seatback like a magnet on a fridge. I was about to start working when my phone chimed. It was my wife. She called every day around the same time, the calls so routine I took them for granted.

Marie and I had met at George Washington University when she was a junior and I a senior. We took a film studies class together, spending our evenings together watching classic sci fi movies and falling in love. When the semester ended we watched three movies a week until the day we were married, three years later.

I slid the phone from my wristwatch and my son's face filled the display. "Hey dude!" I said. Branson was two and a half years old. His brown hair was a mess and needed to be trimmed.

"Dada!" he replied. Branson struggled in my wife's arms as she pulled him back from the camera. "Dada on loop!" he said, looking up at his mother.

"That's right buddy!" I said, leaning forward and smiling. I had left for work before either Branson or Marie had woken up. "Did you brush your teeth this morning?" Branson nodded enthusiastically. He loved the hyperloop and laughed every time we rode the super-fast train. I guess he thought of it as an amusement park ride.

I had driven to L.A. twice since we moved to California. Driving to L.A. is kind of a pain, and takes about six hours. The fastest route used to be Interstate 5. But, since the Cartel expanded in the Central Valley, I tried to avoid that route, not wanting to be mistaken for a government official or the DEA.

"Sword!" Branson said holding an action figure in one hand and an oversized plastic sword in the other. The figurine had huge eyes, dark skin and wore a turban. The toy was from his favorite Disney movie, *Mongol,* the one about the boy who was tired of pillaging.

"Johnny, come home early as you can." Marie's voice sounded soft and pleasant but also tired. She'd taken time off from teaching genetic anthropology at UC Berkeley and got cabin fever from being at home while I was away. Marie grabbed my son's hand to prevent him from pulling out her braids. She had done her hair in loops like Princess Leia in *The Empire Strikes Back.*

"I'll try, but it could be another late night."

Marie frowned then covered it with a smile. She wasn't looking forward to another evening watching Disney characters dance around the holovision.

"I'll make it up to you. On my next trip, you can join me in L.A. and we'll go to Griffith Park together. We'll take Branson to the observatory. It'll be great, I promise." This seemed to satisfy Marie, at least a little.

After ending the call, I opened the blueprints for Destiny Colony, currently under construction in Earth orbit. The name symbolized humanity's future as a space faring species. I twisted my hand in the air, rotating the view on the screen. The design had been a staple in science fiction, a two-mile wide rotating ring. It was time to make the dream a reality.

Construction of a space station is as much about accounting as engineering. Launching from Earth is the most expensive method, so this was kept to a minimum. The aluminum was mined on the moon, while other raw materials, various silicates, carbonate, and oxides, came from Mars.

Six months ago, a spacecraft named the CTS-Bradbury had been in orbit above the surface of Mars. The Bradbury, an unmanned cargo vessel the size of ten Carnival cruise ships, was loaded with enough material to complete Destiny Colony. The ship, and its massive payload, blasted towards Earth at fifty thousand miles per hour, accelerating further as it fell deeper into the sun's gravity well.

Today, six months after leaving Mars, it would arrive.

Stepping out of Union Station in Los Angeles, I took in the blue sky and breathed the fresh air. I could hear the gentle hum of electric cars racing along the San Bernardino Freeway. In the distance, the skyline was laced with the vertical farms that provided California with an effectively unlimited supply of food. Almost half of L.A.'s population was freeliving and it was obvious wherever you looked. It was the middle of a work day, and dozens of the non-working middleclass people sat outside Union Station, enjoying the sun.

I jumped into a car with Nicolas, a young engineer from Houston. Nicolas was fairly new to NASA, fresh off his internship. He had been assigned to me to help with logistics. I was an electrical systems engineer by trade, but NASA required its engineers to do a stint in logistics.

Nicolas was a quintessential engineer. He wore a short-sleeved white shirt with a pocket protector for his phone. He always wore slacks, even though most of us wore jeans. And he wore glasses, a recent retro trend, and as far as I could tell, his only concession to style.

The car sped north on Highway 101. Palm trees lined the freeway and the Hollywood sign loomed in the distance. The original sign had been replaced after the 2042 quake and a new and bigger sign sat in its place.

Nicolas ignored the scenery, concentrating instead on the bumper to bumper traffic speeding along at seventy miles per hour. He had a childlike curiosity, studying the algorithms the auto-cars used to optimize the traffic patterns, allowing us to travel anywhere in central L.A. in less than ten minutes.

"Do you think you'll get to go into space?" Nicolas asked as we approached NASA's Spacecraft Operations Center.

"Probably not, but I've always wanted to." I had a pilot's license, was an engineer, and worked for NASA. In a sense, my resume suited me for a job in Earth orbit or the Martian colony. "How about you?" I asked.

"Nah," he responded, "Never thought of myself as an astronaut." This surprised me. I pictured him in space, staring out in childlike awe from Destiny's control room.

"You know they don't call anyone who goes into space an astronaut," I said. "Thousands of people have been to space."

Nicolas gave me a serious look. "And so few understand how amazing that is."

I nodded my agreement.

We left the car in northeast Los Angeles near Pasadena and headed into the lobby of NASA's Watney building. The car drove back onto the boulevard in search of its next customer. We rode the elevator to the control room on the thirteenth floor.

The elevator's window granted us an outside view. Griffith Observatory rested on the hill in the distance. I imagined holding Branson up to the eyepieces of the historic telescopes.

We stepped out of the elevator and walked through a set of double doors into Mission Control. A confident looking man wearing a white vest welcomed us as we walked down the aisle between the stations.

"Today's the big day, John," Norman said, smiling and patting me on the back. Norman Kim, the flight director, stood well over six feet tall. He had to be over sixty, but rumor had it he could still dunk a basketball and was savage on the court. This was our second time meeting in person. The fact that he remembered my name was moving. "We get this shipment in orbit and you guys can get to work."

"It's about time," I joked. The shipment was on schedule, down to the nearest second. I introduced Nicolas and Norman. Norman always made an effort to inspire NASA's young engineers. He asked Nicolas how he had gotten interested in space, and how he ended up at NASA. The two of them continued to make small talk as I settled into my station.

I looked around the room and realized that everyone was smiling. In fact, they were almost giddy. Everyone was excited for the supplies to arrive from Mars, but even more excited to finish building Destiny Colony.

Today's plan was simple. The CTS-Bradbury would park in

geostationary orbit. Once there, the logistics team, which included me and Nicolas, would take over. We were in charge of ferrying the supplies from the CTS-Bradbury to Destiny's construction site, thirty-six thousand kilometers above the Galapagos Islands.

We watched the projection at the front of the room. A telescopic camera in a high orbit gave us live images of the spacecraft as it approached the orbital insertion burn point.

"Excuse me," Norman said, as he and Nicolas ceased their conversation. He brushed past us and headed to the front of the room. From there, he gave a quick pep talk.

"Ladies and Gentlemen!" he began. "Since the days of Isaac Asimov, engineers like us have dreamed of the day we could construct the first rotating space station. Today, we are poised to make that dream a reality." He paused, letting the gravity of our mission sink in. "Once the CTS-Bradbury settles into orbit, I will start this clock." He pointed to a digital countdown clock on the wall that read, *1,095 Days, 00 hours, 00 minutes, 00 seconds.* "Three years from today, we will open the airlock to a new chapter in human history."

The room erupted into cheers, but Norman held up his hand to silence it. "People of NASA, contractors, and friends, let's make history!"

At that moment there was a hustle and bustle as engineers tapped away on their consoles. Additional screens flicked on, showing immense amounts of data.

For the next hour, we worked through dozens of checklists. Norman read from a tablet, requesting the status of each system. After each request, someone in the room would shout, "Nominal!"

The time came to inject the Bradbury into Earth's orbit. There was a countdown, which included another checklist, but instead of responding with, "Nominal," everyone responded, "Go Flight." It was time.

"Retro rockets firing," said an engineer. An animation on the screen showed four jets of rocket flame shooting from the giant spacecraft's engines.

"Trajectory nominal," said a female voice. I glanced at another display which plotted the path of the ship into Earth's orbit. "Pitch... nominal... Attitude... nominal."

"Navigation...wait..." said a man seated in the row ahead of me. He sat at a radar station. I looked at his screen, trying to see what he was looking at. This was a critical moment in the flight, and my heartrate quickened.

"Wait... There's something on the radar. It's small, about the size of a baseball." I still couldn't see what he was looking at. The engineer pushed his head closer to the screen, trying to get a read. At the speeds that these spaceships traveled, debris of any size was a threat. But space is very empty, and spacecraft rarely hit anything larger than a grain of sand.

"Switch to dorsal camera," Norman ordered. The views on a half dozen screens showed the top half of the freighter. We all saw it, a piece of space junk streaking through space at incredible speed. We watched as the object grazed both the liquid oxygen and liquid hydrogen tanks.

I didn't realize it, but I was standing. Nicolas put a hand on my shoulder, guiding me back into my chair. "It'll be alright, John," he whispered, always the optimist. I tried to wrap my mind around it. NASA monitored most of the space junk in the Earth's vicinity. The trajectory calculations always took debris into consideration.

"Zoom in on that fuel tank," Norman ordered, pointing at the room's primary display. The screen zoomed in, revealing a small impact hole with hydrogen leaking out. The gas appearing to glow as it streamed out into space, trailing ahead of the craft as the main engines slowed down the giant spacecraft.

"Can we shut down those tanks?" Norman asked.

"Affirmative, Flight, tank shutdown complete, increasing flow from the remaining tanks," someone reported.

I spoke up. "We should shut down the thrusters until the gasses disperse!" I yelled, hating myself for not speaking up sooner.

"Do it!" Norman yelled, but it was too late.

The live views of the spacecraft turned white. I stared in disbelief. Something had overwhelmed the cameras. Error messages flashed over all the displays.

"We're still getting data," someone said, "but it looks like we've had an explosion. I'm patching in another video feed now." We watched as millions of pounds of fuel erupted in pulsing spheres of blinding light.

I slunk down in my chair and pinched my temples, using my hand to hide my tears. I'd poured my heart and soul into this mission. I'd worked long hours, time I could have spent playing with my son. And for what, a thirty-second firework show? I felt worthless. This was compounded by the fact that there was nothing for me to do. If this mission failed, I had no reason to be here.

"It's off course," the telemetry engineer said. On one of the large screens we watched a simulation showing the hunk of spacecraft veering off its projected course by two degrees.

"Estimated trajectory?" the flight director whispered to the telemetry engineer. This was an important question. I perked up, trying to hear, dying to know where the unguided spacecraft was headed.

"Calculating now, Flight," she replied. "Give me two minutes."

"Engines?" Norman asked the room.

"Offline," said an engineer. "We're not getting any readings from the fuel tanks. My guess is that we lost the fuel in the explosion."

"All of it?" Norman asked.

"All of it, Flight."

"Cycle the cameras," Norman ordered. "Let's see if there's anything good on the spacecraft."

Someone in the room cycled through the Bradbury's cameras like a slideshow. A large cloud of debris surrounded the spacecraft. Burned chunks of metal floated around it in an expanding sphere. Through the debris field, we could see the bulk of the spacecraft from a high vantage point, probably from a mast camera of some type. The majority of the spacecraft's mass seemed relatively unaffected by the explosion.

"Do any of the thrusters work?" the flight director asked.

"We have two functioning starboard thrusters and three port thrusters. However, without the main engines, we can only change our orientation, not our trajectory."

"Understood," he responded. "Okay, everyone, is there any chance that we can salvage this?" Norman had my full attention again.

"Sir, if the Bradbury enters a stable orbit, we'll be able to dock with it using a tow-shuttle, and eventually pull it back into the correct orbit," suggested one of the engineers. For a moment, I felt a glimmer of hope. I looked over at Nicolas. He was seated, resting his head on his hands as if listening to a fascinating speech. The young engineer's eyes glistened. I'm sure he and I felt exactly the same way.

"That's not going to happen," the telemetry engineer said, using a hand to brush her hair behind an ear. "We're not going to get a stable orbit."

"What's the result, Alaina?" Norman said, using the engineer's first name, a rare event in mission control.

"Well sir, the Bradbury is, well, it's headed straight for the Earth."

Chapter 2

IMPACT

"Dammit!" Norman muttered. "Any chance it will miss?"

This changed everything. It was a silly question. The telemetry reports were never wrong. If Alaina said the spaceship was headed for Earth, you could be damn sure it was going to hit the Earth. I felt like I was going to die, as if the spacecraft was going to land right on top of this building.

"No, sir," Alaina said. "Probability is one hundred percent, updating visuals now." Everyone looked to the front of the room. The primary display showed an animation with the path of the spacecraft leading straight to Earth.

"Mr. Collins, bring up the procedure for self-destruct," the flight director ordered. Several people in the room gasped and there were tears in people's eyes.

"Self-destruct sequence on your mark, Flight," an engineer at the back of the room said.

"Mark," Norman said.

Nothing happened.

"Mr. Collins, update please."

With the debris field dispersing, the Bradbury's superstructure came clearly into view. If you weren't looking closely, you almost couldn't see the damage.

"Sir, we're not getting a response from the detonators."

"How about a workaround?" Norman asked, pacing up the hallway between the workstations.

"I don't think so," Collins said. "It looks like the main bus was destroyed in the explosion, sort of like Apollo Thirteen."

"Shit," Norman swore. "Lock the doors."

During most emergencies, the "lock the doors" command is the first command given after a disaster. It had been so long since the last major incident in space, I guessed he just forgot to say it.

His expletive did not do the situation justice. The CTS-Bradbury was a giant hunk of steel, ten million tons in mass. It was about to hit Earth traveling at tens of thousands of miles per hour.

We knew one thing for sure. The spacecraft was going to hit this side of the planet. We had timed the arrival so that it would be over North America. This reduced communication lag. All geostationary orbits are over the equator, so it would probably hit the tropics, with a margin of error of thirty-something degrees. This put a potential impact zone within the continental United States.

When the news leaked, there would be panic. The standard procedure in a NASA emergency was to halt communication with the outside world. This gave the communications team time to align on a consistent message.

I slunk down in my chair and pulled out my phone, shooting a text to my wife.

Epic disaster with spacecraft,
Impact with Earth imminent,
Get out of SF, drive north.
Tell no one, just go. I love you.

Marie knew the risks. I discussed my work every day over dinner. She knew the ramifications of a rogue spacecraft better than most. She also understood that when the news got out that a spaceship was going to land on their heads, people would panic and act irrationally.

The phone dinged, a text: *I love you.*

Norman looked over at me and frowned. He walked to the back of the room and picked up a trashcan, dumping the contents on the floor. A half empty coffee cup rolled under my workstation, leaving a helical pattern of cold coffee on the floor. "Mr. Johnson," he said, and held out the trashcan to the security man. He raised his voice and said, "All right, people, the doors are locked. You know what it means."

Johnson walked from workstation to workstation, and people dropped their phones, tablets and watches in—anything that could call or message out.

"Thank you, everyone," Norman said, pacing between the workstations. "Time to impact?"

"Forty-five minutes, Flight"

"I need a location, Alaina."

"Hard to say." Alaina had a habit of speaking quietly. Norman leaned in to hear her better. "Twenty minutes at the least." When Alaina spoke, the whole room quieted down, but like everyone else in the room, she was one of the best.

"Flight, I'm getting dozens of emails from the press," said a voice from one of the stations. "The live feed *was* broadcast on NASA 3D."

"Wonderful," Norman said.

"What should I tell them, sir?" said the communications director.

"Tell them we've had an anomaly onboard the spacecraft."

"That's it?"

"That's it," Norman replied. "Let's just pray it comes down in the water somewhere."

"And if it hits near a major city?" someone asked, speaking without formally addressing the director.

"Then God help us," Norman responded.

For twenty minutes, the room reverberated with the sounds of a dozen engineers debating vectors and the other directors coordinating with the Air Force. Ideas flew around the room like sparrows trapped in a chimney.

"Shoot it down?" I heard someone say.

"Can't launch a missile without accurate telemetry," said another.

"Wouldn't matter anyway, this thing is just too damn large."

"Shut up, everyone," someone yelled from the front of the room. "Everyone, shut up!"

The room went silent.

"We have an impact site and it's confirmed," Alaina said.

"Let's hear it," Norman ordered.

"Thirty-six point eight degrees north," she said. "And...one hundred nineteen point seven degrees west."

No one spoke. A bead of sweat trickled down the engineer's face.

All eyes turned to the map. "Northern California," Norman said.

"Just north of Fresno, Flight. Right in the middle of the Central Valley."

Only two hundred miles from here, I thought. Fresno had, what, a half million people? *Jesus.*

"Jerry," Norman said and motioned to the communications director. "Spread the word."

As news of the impending collision spread around the world, a holovision on the left side of the control room played the news. "CTS-Bradbury Expected to Impact Fresno, California," was the headline.

A reporter from ABC news paraphrased our press release. "This ship, containing billions of pounds of material, will ram into Earth at sixty thousand miles per hour. According to NASA, shockwaves could travel for hundreds of miles, reaching San Francisco and even Los Angeles."

We were in serious trouble.

"Nick," I whispered, "Hey, Nicolas!" he looked over. "We need to get the hell out of here!"

"We're locked in!" Nicolas whispered back. He was right, we were stuck in there. Most of the people in the room had a job to do. They had an obligation to stay, to keep working the problem. All I wanted to do was get to my family.

I read the ticker displayed beneath the commentators. "Subterranean rail and hyperloops will be halted in thirty minutes in anticipation of massive earthquakes." I figured they would send most of the trains away from the cities while they had time. I definitely wouldn't want to be *on* a train when the spaceship impacted.

Another headline: "Traffic Insanity – Drivers override vehicle automation systems causing major congestion." I thought about this for a moment. After thirty years of automation, there was an entire generation who had never learned to drive. Did Marie have enough warning to get ahead of the congestion? I didn't know.

"Flight, can we have our phones back?" I asked, desperate to get ahold of Marie. I looked around the room, noticing other people sitting around with nothing to do.

"Johnson, give them back their phones," Norman said.

I reached into the trashcan and grabbed my phone. In a panic, I sprinted to the back of the room and called my wife. She had been listening to the news reports and knew almost as much as I did.

"How bad is it?" she asked, and without waiting for an answer said, "There are car accidents everywhere!"

"It's bad," I said, "and we don't know how bad. The blast radius could be anywhere from fifty to three hundred miles and we expect earthquakes, big ones."

"Oh, John, how could this happen!" she said.

"Let's just focus on the problem," I said. "Where are you?"

"Santa Rosa."

"Marie, we need to make a decision," I said. "You can stay on the highway and risk the drivers, or you can head west into the hills and try to avoid the blast that way."

"I'll think I'll head into the hills," she said.

"When this is over, we may not have working cell phones. San Francisco and Los Angeles will be a mess. If we lose contact, meet me in Las Vegas, at I don't know, how about the Bellagio? The mountains should protect Las Vegas. Can you do that?"

"I'll do my best, I love you," Marie said.

Someone in the room patched in video from ground-based observatories and satellites in geostationary orbit. The spaceship's hull started to glow as it entered the atmosphere. There were no windows in the control room, but we were informed that the spacecraft could be seen from Los Angeles and that the entire population was outside, looking up.

Someone yelled, "Open the God damned doors!"

Several people had gathered at the back of the room where a row of doors led to a hallway on the north side of the building. Norman flicked a finger at the guard and nodded his head. Johnson pulled out his keys and opened each of the doors, allowing natural light to stream into the room.

I ran to the window and looked up. Earth had a second sun. The CTS-Bradbury appeared as a giant orange orb in the sky, with a tail of debris stretching out like a comet. It descended lower and lower and eventually passed out of sight behind the hills. The news stations showed live views of the crashing spaceship. There were holovisions in the hallway, and every network had camera crews following the doomed craft. Suddenly, all of the news feeds winked out, and the broadcasts returned to the commentators at their home stations in faraway cities.

Nicolas stood beside me, shaking. He was more afraid than I was. Perhaps he understood the implications better than I. Nicolas was slightly overweight and reminded me of a kid on the playground after he'd been bullied. "We gave the world twenty minutes notice," he said. "Twenty minutes to gather your things and run. But it's not going to matter, is it? People are still going to burn."

If the spacecraft had impacted where telemetry had predicted, the San Joaquin Valley was a crater. I looked back at the data screens in the control room. We had live satellite images of the impact zone. The spacecraft didn't impact with a ball of flame like I would have imagined. It was a reddish brown cloud, a giant plume of opacity, billions of tons of sedimentary rock thrown up into the atmosphere. An air shock rippled the clouds as it traveled north up the valley and toward the ocean, to the place where my wife was fighting the traffic.

No No No! I thought of Branson, he must be so scared. No, he was too young to understand what was going on. He probably even enjoyed the ride as they raced through the Northern California hills. I knew my wife. She was a strong woman and could compose herself in the most stressful situations. I pictured her in my mind's eye, focusing intensely on getting to safety, making me proud to be her husband.

I refocused on the display in the control room. The shock wave was headed our way too.

Live data from the United States Geological Survey projected onto the screen. The data showed earthquakes all over the United States. Red numbers in yellow boxes representing the Richter scale popped up in an expanding ring around the impact site. There were eights, tens, and even a few elevens, the highest possible number on the scale. This scared me more than anything had in my entire life. Sometimes it's not the event itself that's terrifying, but the anticipation.

We felt a shudder go through the building. A P-wave, the first sign of an approaching mega quake. The building's earthquake early warning system roared.

"Everyone OUT OUT OUT!" Johnson yelled from the nearest stairwell. He held open the door as people rushed out.

Nicolas and I rushed into the stairwell as the power went out, stumbling down the thirteen floors in the dark.

Chapter 3

SHOCKWAVES

We made it to the lobby as the first shockwave hit L.A. The sky darkened as debris filled the air. There was a loud boom and the sound of shattering glass resonated through the building. We stayed in the building until the glass stopped falling.

Nicolas and I struggled to maintain our balance as an earthquake shook the lobby. People from the control room pooled around us as we rushed to get outside. On the street, traffic was at a standstill. Members of the press were waiting for us, ready to bombard NASA employees with questions. Another earthquake hit, and we used the distraction to avoid the press. Outside, people were running away from any structure that might collapse, avoiding burst water mains and broken glass.

Another tremor rocked the ground, this one much more intense than the last. I looked back from where we'd come. The pillars of NASA's Watney building swayed to the left, then to the right, before snapping like matchsticks. The building crumbled to the ground.

We ran towards the hills a mile away, hoping that the lack of infrastructure would provide safety from the collapsing buildings.

Maintaining balance was tricky as we ran across the shaking ground. The earth continued to shake and giant cracks formed in the road. I was a runner, but my legs ached with the extra effort. I had Nicolas by the arm and was dragging him forward. Chunks of roadway the size of busses collapsed into the sewers, while dirt and grime shot into the air. The structures on either side of us shook off their foundations, and the rubble continued to shake.

We ran up the hill and reached the Roosevelt Golf Course. The irrigation lines had burst, and pools of water covered the fairways.

Another shockwave hit, an air shock and earthquake all at once. The air shock blew me off my feet and onto my back. I slid across the green, looking up in time to see Griffith Observatory blown to pieces. The three astronomical domes flew into the air while the bricks, mortar, dirt and debris blew down off the hillside towards us.

I leapt to my feet, surrounded by sinkholes as pieces of the observatory rained down.

"Nicolas!" I yelled.

People scattered all over the fairway. Nicolas lay nearby, stunned. I grabbed his arm, using all my strength to raise him to his feet. We continued our sprint across the greens as chunks of the observatory rained down, leaving basketball-sized holes in the muddy ground.

I saw it out the corner of my eye, but it was too late. A cinder block punched Nicolas in the back at two hundred miles per hour, driving his body deep into the mud. He disappeared into the sludge. I tried to pull him out, digging with my hands as mud and gunk pooled in around my knees.

My arms ached, but I kept digging, reaching into the muck trying to grab an arm or piece of clothing to drag his body to the surface.

The debris no longer rained down. I looked about, realizing I was up to my waist in dark brown water. Nicolas was gone. I could feel the adrenaline shooting through my veins. I'd never witnessed anyone die before, and I was surprised that I didn't feel grief, only anger.

I looked around at all the people. Some had serious injuries, while some carried their injured friends. Some just looked stunned. I unclicked my phone from my watch. The screen was caked with mud. I tried my best to wipe it clean, dipping it in the water. The phone was waterproof, but I had no bars. I put it back.

I climbed northward, higher into the hills. Tears streamed down my face. I turned around to face the city, slouched down and took in the view. The sky was a pinkish brown, with patches of black. Smoke billowed from a thousand fires and the air was thick with the smell of burning plastic and raw sewage. A gas line burst into flames and then fizzled out. I could see Los Angeles International Airport in the distance. A pile of double decker A380s and part of the terminal lay jumbled at the bottom of a sinkhole.

Not a single building stood more than a few stories high in all of downtown L.A., and Santa Monica was underwater. The city resembled a trash heap in a third world country. I watched as fires burned only to be extinguished by rising sewer water. A siren blared in the distance and then stopped. For the moment, all was silent in Griffith Park.

I looked at my watch. It was only six p.m. and sunset wasn't for a few more hours, but the sky had grown dark. I contemplated using my phone's flashlight, but I wanted to conserve power on the off chance we got signal back. I paced around the park near the observatory, trying to work out my options. Going back down into the city was far too dangerous. Several people were already on the hill, probably tourists visiting the observatory and freelivers who had been enjoying their ample free time in the park.

I walked from person to person, asking if anyone needed help, and administered first aid where I could. Most people just wanted to be alone.

I slept, or at least took shelter that night in the remains of the observatory. What else was I supposed to do?

I awoke early the next morning to the sound of horns blaring in the distance, the sound a ship makes when it comes into port. I got up and looked towards the ocean. Aircraft carriers lined the shore. They must have arrived from San Diego. A squadron of helicopters and other vertical takeoff and landing aircraft swarmed over the city, picking people off mounds of rubble, taking the survivors back to the ships. I could see thousands of men and women in military uniform searching through the debris.

A large military helicopter landed on the plateau where Griffith Observatory used to be. I recognized the helicopter; NASA had a few of them for recovering spacecraft that landed at sea. The helicopter was the Sikorsky Super Stallion, which, in its current configuration, could carry seventy-five passengers in airline-type seats. I boarded the helicopter with about fifty or sixty others through the large hatch at the rear.

I went to the front and leaned into the cockpit, the co-pilot's seat was unoccupied. *They must be short on pilots*, I thought.

"Hey," I said to the captain. "I'm a pilot. Mind if I join you up here?"

"Have a seat, boss," he said. "Commander Avery Garcia, call me Avro." He reached out and shook my hand. He looked to be younger than me by five or six years, and though he was seated, I guessed he was a few inches taller as well, but maybe that was just the helmet.

"Avro," I said, repeating the call-sign and committing it to memory. "John Orville."

Avro then leaned out of his seat, looking back into the cabin. His straps were loose and wires dangled from his helmet. The wires connected his radio transmitter and helmet-mounted heads up display to the console. He pressed a black button on the control stick, activating the helicopter's PA system.

"Find a seat and strap the hell in," he said over the PA. He then hit another set of switches. The tail ramp retracted and the helicopter's turbofan engines spooled up. The sound of gyros filled the cockpit as the instruments came online. A second later, the first rotor whooshed overhead. After another rotation, the rotors spun so fast they were invisible, and the sound of the gyros was replaced by the *chop, chop, chop* sound that gave helicopters their nickname.

"Here's the deal," said Avro through the PA system. "I'm taking you to the aircraft carrier USS Enterprise III. From there, you'll get a connecting flight to Denver, Seattle, Phoenix, Dallas, or Las Vegas.

"Once we land, go to one of the computer terminals on the deck and log in. List any family members you believe were on the West Coast. The computer will select the destination where you will most likely be reconnected with any survivors. You can either take the computer's recommendation, or choose one of the five cities on your own. Please direct any questions to the officers on deck when we reach the Enterprise."

Avro clicked off the PA as he piloted the aircraft toward the sea. "So where are you from?" he asked.

"Washington, D.C. I've been working at AMES near San Francisco."

"NASA. Shit man, you're not going to be very popular."

"No kidding," I responded. I needed to remind myself to stop telling people that. Maybe I needed an alternative identity. Maybe I could say I sold life insurance? No one, absolutely no one, wants to hear about life insurance. "My wife and son were in San Francisco, I told them to drive north. Do you have any idea how hard that area was hit?"

"Smart," Avro said, "San Fran's in worse shape than L.A. There's trouble up north, I can tell you that."

"What kind of trouble?" I asked, feeling a lump in my throat.

"The Cartel thinks the impact was intentional, like it was a government plot or something. The rescue helicopters are taking small arms fire. We've been able to approach the downtown cores of L.A. and San Fran, but we're taking hits from everywhere else."

"I thought the Cartel was contained—I had no idea they had influence near the coast."

"They didn't until now. Conspiracy theories are powerful things," Avro said. "I guess they mobilized a number of sympathizers and are paying folks to stick around and act as human shields."

I knew the Cartel had money and lots of it. The government had reinvigorated the War on Drugs, driving up the market price of street drugs. This provided a massive influx of cash for the Cartel. Governments never seem to learn from history; this was exactly how the Cartel got started back in the twenty-twenties.

"I told my wife to meet me in Vegas."

"Log in like everyone else, buddy. You'll be in Vegas later today. Your family will meet you there."

"Thanks," I said, not convinced it could be so simple.

"You said you're a pilot?" Avro asked.

"Private pilot," I said. "IFR rated."

"After you connect with your family, call me," Avro said, "We could use your help with SAR."

"I will," I said, pretty sure I was out of a job.

CHAPTER 4

EDDIE RIZZO

After a two-hour flight on a large military jump jet, I arrived in Vegas. A data terminal at McLaren Airport indicated that Marie hadn't checked in. I leaned against the wall, staring at the floor and frozen with grief.

"Hey," said a voice over my shoulder. "There's an app for that."

"Huh?" I responded, turning around to see a young man in a blue vest. The man must have been an airport employee.

"An app, for connecting with your family," he said. "FEMA set it up. Same database as those terminals."

"Thanks," I said. Looking at my phone, I realized it had a signal again. I told it, "Download FEMA app." The Federal Emergency Management Agency's logo appeared on the screen. The application asked permission to access all my social media accounts, including location identifiers. I said, "Yes" to the all the messages.

The app contained more information than the kiosk. It let me know that my wife had not accessed social media and was not using her phone's location services. I stumbled towards the wall and slid to the airport floor, my gut wrenching with grief and worry. Other people sat along the walls crying. Some just walked down the aisles as if it were a normal day at the airport.

Airport security walked the halls, telling people to "move along." I had to get to the hotel anyway, so I followed orders.

The auto-car system in Vegas functioned without issue and I

summoned a ride to the hotel. Leaving the airport, I realized that Las Vegas was relatively unaffected by the impact. Granted, they had experienced earthquakes, but nothing over the sixth magnitude. I noticed large cracks in the roadways and dozens of broken windows, but this was Vegas; it could have been like that before the impact.

I looked out the car's window and saw the theme park over the New York, New York Casino. It reminded me of Branson. This was another place I'd promised I'd take my family someday. I stopped looking outside and I tried to focus on something else. In my head, I estimated how many people had escaped from L.A. There were hundreds of helicopters and a few dozen jump jets, but L.A. had millions of people. It was clear that this disaster was the worst in the nation's history. I gave up on the calculations as the car pulled up to the Bellagio.

I'd been to Vegas before, and stayed here at the Bellagio once with Marie. The lobby was exquisite, with grand arches and contemporary art. I was surprised the staff let me in. I looked like shit, mud caked all over my body. Fortunately, I wasn't the first evacuee to come looking for a hotel room.

"Sir, Sir?" said a bellboy, "Can I help you?"

"I…" I almost said no. "I could use some clothes. Here." I handed him two hundreds. "Thirty-four waist, medium shirts."

The bellman took the bills and looked at them. I kept them in my wallet for emergencies. No one used cash anymore, but it was still legal tender and stores had to accept it.

At the front desk, I asked the hotel manager if he'd seen my wife. It was improbable that she had arrived before me, but I asked anyway.

I tapped my phone on the desk and booked the last vacant room.

I sat down on the bed and pulled off a shoe. The bellboy appeared at the door carrying a bag with "GAP" printed on the side.

"A hundred eighty dollars," the young man said.

"Keep the change," I said. Twenty dollars wasn't much of a tip. The kid probably didn't make much more than a freeliver's wage. What was that, fifty bucks an hour? At least twenty could buy him a beer. The bellboy nodded thanks, excused himself and walked back down the hall.

I opened the plastic bag and pulled out the first item, a shirt, still warm from the printer. Its light blue coloring and oriental design was moderately tasteful. A navy blue sports jacket and blue jeans completed my new wardrobe. In the bottom of the bag, I found two pairs of socks and two pairs of underwear. The items smelled of hot polyester so I placed them on the bed to air out while I took a shower.

After the shower I sat on the bed and transferred the phone's FEMA application to the hotel's holovision. There were no recent notifications; Marie and Branson were either still driving, or they were... I couldn't finish the thought.

Thirty-eight million people were listed in the database, with only twenty million people accounted for. Of these, two hundred thousand were listed as "deceased."

Two hundred thousand. *Good God,* I thought. I searched for Nicolas Francis. A relative had listed him as missing. I selected "Edit" from a menu and entered the following information:

Last known location: Roosevelt Golf Course, East Los Angeles.

Last known health status (drop down box): *Deceased.*

Cause of death: Sub menu (drop down box): *Blunt force trauma.*

Relation (drop down box): Co-worker

I closed Nicolas's record, hoping someone would recover the body. I reloaded the previous menu, watching as the casualty count creeped upward. I wanted to throw up. I wondered if my mother had checked this. If she did, she'd find out that I was alive, but that Marie and Branson were missing. Mom was still pissed I'd joined NASA, an organization she believed was a waste of her tax dollars. I didn't bother calling her. I was already too pissed off.

Google owned several satellites that provided high quality images of Earth. The images were live, but as I zoomed in to California, thick brown clouds rendered the images useless.

The news coverage was sporadic, but one report showed a steady flow of helicopters taking survivors out of San Francisco.

It was painful to surf social media. Without cell coverage in the affected areas, the posts were limited to people in the same situation as me. People posted photos of missing loved ones, or images of their evacuation, but that was it. #NASASFAULT was trending.

I spent an hour looking for updates from Sonoma County. This was my best guess as to where Marie and Branson were at the time of the impact. From what I gathered from people's location tags, most of the roads were impassable due to avalanches and sinkholes. If Marie and Branson were on their way to Vegas, it wasn't by car.

By evening, cell coverage had returned to some of the affected areas and there was a new trend on social media. The Cartel was preventing people from leaving, preventing them from evacuating. People posted videos of armed men standing in rows across stretches of crumbling pavement.

My depression turned to rage.

My body started shaking from the anxiety. I was angry with NASA for screwing up the mission. I was angry with myself for being a part of it. Most of all, I was angry at the Cartel for being, well, the Cartel, for being stupid enough to think this catastrophe was intentional and for putting my family's lives in danger. Was there anything I could do?

I remembered what Avro had said; they needed search and rescue pilots. I sent him a text.

"No sign of family. Sign me up for SAR."

When he texted back, the message read. "Meet me at Nellis AFB tomorrow at 0730. BYO aircraft."

Bring my own aircraft? I thought. *Shit.*

I called Henderson airfield and asked if they had aircraft for rent. It was late and a Turing operator took my call. Officially, all the aircraft had been rented. But the operator said I could stop by the flight club and talk to the pilots, so I grabbed an auto-car and headed to the airfield.

Several pilots sat in the flying club's lounge. When I approached the group, they were talking about California.

"It's a mess," said a female pilot. She looked exhausted. The four bars on her shoulder meant that she was captain. Another pilot seated nearby wore a similar uniform with three bars; he must have been the copilot.

"Past Death Valley, ain't nothing but death," said an older man seated at the lounge's bar. I told the room I was looking for a plane. Everyone stopped their conversations to listen to my plea. It was embarrassing. I felt like a beggar on the metro telling some sob story and asking for cash.

The old man at the bar motioned for me to talk to him. Apparently, a prospector named Eddie Rizzo owned an electro-glider he'd used for surveying. Electro-gliders are like flying hybrid-electric cars. But while hybrid cars recharged their batteries while braking, electro-gliders recharged while descending or by flying through rising air. Eddie stored the aircraft in a hangar nearby and if I bugged him, he just might let me borrow it, for a fee.

The man showed me to a door and pointed to Eddie's hangar. It was dark, but the building was illuminated by the parking lot's lighting. A sign hung over the hangar's door and read: "WE BUY GOLD."

I found Eddie Rizzo sitting in a cubicle-sized office behind a stack of a dozen broken tablet computers. He smoked a long silver electronic cigarette, which I could tell had some kick; his office stank of real cigars. He wore a weathered brown leather jacket over a faded white t-shirt.

Eddie spoke with a strong New York accent. "So you're looking for an aircraft. Going to join SAR are ya? Ya wanna be a hero."

"That's the plan," I said, taking short breaths to avoid tasting the office's stench.

"Here's the deal, buddy. I've got the only aircraft west of Colorado that wasn't messed the hell up in today's apocalypse. If you want my baby, you better have the dough." When Eddie said the word baby, my eyes shot to his grotesque gut. It looked like Eddie was about to have twins.

"How much?" I didn't believe him that it was the only aircraft available. It was a classic sales pitch: tell the client you have the last product in town, buy it now, or forever hold your peace.

"Well, seeing as this here's the last plane, I'd say demand is quite high. The plane is rather valuable. Ya know what I'm sayin'? But not as valuable as the shit on the other side of those there mountains."

"What do you mean?" Eddie's comment caught me off guard, another salesman trick? No, he wanted something more than money and I worried I was getting in over my head. This was Vegas where desperate people get extorted.

"Well, it seems to me that Cali's population has declined and the leftovers are up for grabs. So here's the deal: the plane is yours for one hundred thousand a month. But you gotta do something for me. You're gonna use this equipment," he pointed to the pile of junk on the table, "and survey every square inch of the Golden State. If there's a gold ring in someone's dresser, my scanners will find it. And if you see a corpse with a Rolex, or an abandoned Royce, you let me know and I'll send my boys in to pick it up."

"One hundred thousand is a bit steep," I said. One hundred thousand dollars would max out my savings. After that, I'd be living on charity. Eddie probably figured that a SAR operation would operate in grids. He was probably right. This would provide the optimal data set for his survey. He needed someone like me.

"I'll tell you what. You flag some good shit, I'll give you a finder's fee of one percent." I began to see Eddie as the typical pawn shop owner. They start by throwing out a highball figure to see if you bite. If you're a good negotiator, you don't. You let them talk themselves down, keep them hanging.

"I want to see the aircraft."

Eddie gestured with his thumb to a wooden door behind his desk. I squeezed past a four-foot-tall pile of magazines, holding my breath as I got a whiff of Eddie's sweat and cigar funk.

The door led to the hangar where I found an aircraft covered in canvas. I pulled the cover off the Electro-glider and ran my hand along a faded white fuselage. The name "Moneta" was stenciled just below the canopy. The plane had to be thirty years old, a classic, but it seemed to be in workable condition. Made by AgustaWestland, its stingray-like design had been influenced by the bicycle makers of Cascina Costa in Northern Italy. This also gave the aircraft its nickname.

The Stingray had two large thrust-regen fans imbedded in the root of each wing. Each fan had three blades that were at least eight feet long. They provided thrust, yet could also act as windmills, generating electricity to recharge the battery when the aircraft descended.

I grabbed the maintenance record. It was still the law that each aircraft must carry a printed copy of the maintenance records. Even in the digital age, old laws die hard. The fact that this aircraft *had* a maintenance record was a good sign. It meant that Eddie Rizzo, as rough as he looked, still obeyed the law, and his plane had been cared for, at least according to the log.

I flipped through the reports and noticed that the plane had a ninety-kilowatt battery. This battery made up the bulk of the aircraft's weight at about three hundred pounds. I had flown electro-gliders before, but none with this much power.

The Stingray had other interesting modifications, like a charge port on the roof. I'd heard of these before, but never suspected they were actually used. The port was designed for in-air supercharging.

I stuck my head into the cockpit and hit the master switch, activating the displays. All the instruments were digital, but they represented the standard "Six Pack" of any small aircraft. The top three instruments showed the airspeed, altitude, and attitude, while the bottom three showed the turn and bank, heading, and vertical speed.

I looked at the airspeed indicator. The *Velocity to Never Exceed*, or VNE, was three hundred ten knots; this was fast, fast enough to keep up with a military helicopter. The green zone, or cruising speeds, ranged from forty knots to two hundred fifty knots. As the crow flies, Las Vegas and San Francisco are three hundred miles apart, so it would take just over an hour to get from one city to the other.

I walked back into in the office and let Eddie Rizzo know we had a deal. He didn't even ask to see my pilot's license.

The next morning I headed back to Henderson airfield. It was strange, waking up alone, getting into a car, and driving somewhere. It felt like a business trip or the first day of school, when you have no idea what to expect, but instead of nervousness, there was dread. I worried at any moment I'd receive horrible news.

I filed a flight plan at a kiosk in the flight club and waved at the dispatch lady who buzzed me onto the tarmac through a single door.

It was sunrise when I opened the hangar. I didn't see Eddie Rizzo, which didn't surprise me. The guy came off as a night owl. I found the survey equipment, two aerodynamic wedges shaped like a ship's radar. I grabbed the devices and slid them into place. They fit under the wings like missiles on a fighter jet. Once attached to the aircraft, they booted up. A small display on each device registered "Auto Sequence Start," indicating they were ready to go.

Eddie's request to have me survey California made me feel dirty, like I was invading someone's privacy. I even wondered if the SAR guys would take issue with me using the equipment. They probably wouldn't even ask. It wasn't any different than a prospector with a metal detector or a scuba diver looking for shipwrecks.

Grabbing a tow bar, I dragged the aircraft out onto the tarmac. One wing rested on the ground, a rusty skid protecting the wingtip from the concrete. The other wing rose into the morning sky.

After returning the tow bar to the hangar, I climbed into the cockpit. I closed the tinted bubble style canopy and checked the controls. *Rudder left, rudder right,* I said to myself, stepping on the foot pedals and looking over my shoulder to see the twin rudders moving freely.

I checked the ailerons, swinging the control stick to the left and right. Using my left hand, I extended the dive brakes, making sure they could be fully deployed and fully retracted. All the controls seemed in good shape. I hit the master, activating the displays and watched the dials move silently into place.

Activating the turbofans sent a whirring noise through the cockpit. As the volume increased, I grabbed the headset from behind the seat and pulled it over my ears. The headset smelled like Eddie's office. I'd be used to the smell in a few minutes, so I ignored it.

The Stingray leveled itself as the motors pulled air over the wing roots. The frequency of the motors canceled each other out, leaving a smooth hum like riding a Cadillac on freshly lain concrete.

I flipped on the radio and tuned in to the airport's frequency.

"Henderson Tower, this is EG-niner request clearance to taxi to runway seventeen left," I said.

"EG-niner, cleared to taxiway Foxtrot for takeoff on runway 17L."

The aircraft coasted across the tarmac as I adjusted the pressure on the throttle. I brought it to a stop at the button, the line that separates the taxiway from the runway.

"Henderson Tower, EG-niner is ready for takeoff."

"EG-niner, cleared for takeoff runway 17L. At five hundred feet, turn to heading three four zero," replied the tower.

"Copy three four zero."

I pushed in the throttle and felt the acceleration generated by the electric motors. The plane went from zero to sixty in under five seconds and was airborne after two hundred feet. The city of Las Vegas sank down below me and I admired the colorful lights that littered the strip. For a moment, just for a moment, I forgot why I was here and marveled at the wonder of human flight.

I thought of a poem written by RCAF pilot John Gillespie Magee, Jr:

Oh! I have slipped the surly bonds of Earth,
And danced the skies on laughter-silvered wings;
Sunward I've climbed and joined the tumbling mirth
of sun-split clouds - and done a hundred things
You have not dreamed of - wheeled and soared and swung

High in the sunlit silence. Hov'ring there,
I've chased the shouting wind along, and flung
my eager craft through footless halls of air.

Up, up the long, delirious burning blue
I've topped the wind-swept heights with easy grace,
where never lark, or even eagle, flew –
And, while with silent, lifting mind I've trod
The high untrespassed sanctity of space,
Put out my hand and touched the face of God.

The second to last line struck me today. *The high untrespassed sanctity of space.* We had trespassed on the sanctity of space, a place previously reserved for exploration and wonder. We had brought a piece of space down to Earth with horrific consequences.

John Magee died in his Spitfire days after penning that verse. I wondered if he knew that, in the end, there was no sanctity.

With that thought, I banked my aircraft to heading three-four-zero, climbing high in the sunlit silence. The Stingray's hybrid-electric engines cut out; they were no longer needed. With the turbine blades feathered, I glided silently all the way to Nellis.

Chapter 5

SEARCH AND RESCUE

When I landed at Nellis, ground control directed me to the Search and Rescue hangar. The electro-glider bumped along the old taxiways and I could feel every crack in the pavement through my seat. To save weight, the plane didn't have a tricycle landing gear like a traditional aircraft. Instead, a single gear extended from below the cockpit, while a small tailwheel hung off the rear. An airfoil behind the turbo fans stabilized the aircraft, but it still felt like riding a unicycle.

The SAR squadron wasn't hard to find with its insignia painted forty feet high on the hangar door. Parked outside the hangar were ten heavy lift helicopters. Three other vertical takeoff aircraft, all third generation Ospreys, sat nearby. There were also two civilian tail draggers parked off to the side, both Cessna Bird Dogs, scouting aircraft used as far back as the Vietnam War.

I parked the Stingray in an electric-aircraft-only parking spot and climbed out. Opening a small hatch in the tarmac, I pulled down the Electro-Glider's charge cord and plugged into the base's power supply.

As I walked toward the hangar and the helicopters, I saw three people who looked to be in the middle of a briefing. One person excused himself and walked toward me. The man walked with military confidence, his jet-black hair cut to military spec. It was the first time I had seen Avro without his helmet. He hadn't shaved that morning, which accented his square jawline. If it weren't for the flight suit, I'd swear I was looking at a professional soccer player.

"Johnny! Glad you could make it."

"Glad to help." I was anxious, nervous and scared, but knew I was where I needed to be. "I'm still wondering how I'll be of any use."

"Let me dispel that confusion," Avro said, shaking my hand. "There were two rescue squadrons on the West Coast. The 129th Rescue Wing at Moffat field…"

"I used to eat with those guys in the cafeteria at AMES."

"The other was stationed at Edwards. We lost both squadrons. Those women and men were the best of the best."

"I'm sorry," I said.

Avro accepted my sympathies with a nod, "So here's the plan. Each rescue helicopter is getting a civilian wingman. Your job will be to tag prospective targets for evacuation or termination."

"Termination!"

"You heard me right," Avro said. "The helicopters are armed and we'll have drone support. This is a war zone, John, and attrition is part of the strategy."

"So you need us as decoys?"

"We'll be adding an electronic countermeasures package to your aircraft. You'll be fine." I looked back at my plane, which from this angle, looked very much like a stingray. I wondered how it would hold up under fire. It was definitely maneuverable enough, but I'd need to rely heavy on countermeasures if I was going to be dodging bullets.

"When do we start?" I asked. "Shouldn't we be at that briefing?"

"That's not a briefing," Avro answered. "Those pilots are waiting for their wingmen."

"But what about those civilian aircraft? Where are their pilots?" I asked, glancing over at the Bird Dogs.

"The other pilots didn't show. We're having trouble finding pilots to fly into an area full of Cartel loyalists who think the government just tried to bomb them into oblivion."

"Oh," I said.

"Come with me. Let's grab your SAR computer and countermeasures and get in the air."

Metal shelves ran along the walls of the hangar. The shelves held devices of all sorts stacked in cubbies. Avro walked over to the wall, picking up a tablet and something that looked like a pipe bomb. *That must be the countermeasure package,* I thought.

"You got piss bottles?" Avro asked. "It's gonna be a long day. Tomorrow we'll get you a catheter."

I nodded. "Yeah, I've got piss bottles." I had water bottles in the cockpit that would do.

Avro tossed me a sharpie. "Label them, so you don't accidently, well, you know."

"Thanks for the advice." I pocketed the sharpie.

Avro nodded, "All right boss, let's get you set up."

Back at the electro-glider Avro handed me the SAR flight computer. I took the device and walked towards the cockpit. The SAR computer had a flexible arm with a screw-clip on its end. I secured the tablet to the airframe inside the cockpit.

Avro headed to the tail. Using specialized quick-ties, he fastened the countermeasures device to the empennage.

"This is a good set up you've got here," Avro said, running a hand along the wing.

"How so?" I asked, feeling ashamed to have shown up with an electric aircraft. Like early electric car owners facing questions about range anxiety, I worried there would be a similar stigma around electric aircraft.

"Most light aircraft top out at a hundred sixty knots. You can go north of two hundred. Also, other aircraft have to refuel about every three hours."

"Technically, I need to quick-charge every three," I said.

"Technically," said Avro, "But we'll be flying across the mountains where you can expect plenty of updrafts. That's free gas for you."

"True," I said.

"And," Avro said, "I can release a thousand volt mag-line behind the chopper. I notice that supercharger port you got on the roof."

"You do, eh," I said with a slight smile. "I think you know something about electro-gliders."

"I do, actually. I sold this one to Eddie."

Avro and I took off from Nellis and headed west. We were quite the pair, him in his Super Stallion, a beast of a machine, and me in my little Stingray. Avro's helicopter would be heard for miles and shook the ground as it approached. My aircraft was barely audible. For a moment I felt unworthy, but as we climbed into the sky I realized the electro-glider was much faster than the Stallion. Any anxiety I had about being a drag on the operation drifted away.

We climbed up and over the red rocks to the west of Vegas, getting our first view of the mountains that had protected it from the air-blast. My engine cut out and switched to regeneration mode as the electro-glider soared along the windward side of a mountain range like a surfer on a wave.

We reached cruising altitude and completed our radio checks. To our left and right, snowcapped mountains rose beyond my aircraft's operating ceiling. "Take the lead, Johnny," Avro said over the radio. His voice came through my headset with perfect clarity. "Head north through Death

Valley, then cut west at Yosemite. Rendezvous north of Sacramento. Let me know if you run into any trouble."

"Roger that. See you on the other side." I could see Avro in his cockpit on my starboard and I gave him a quick salute. He saluted back, and I wondered how he saw me through the tinted glass. I pushed my throttle forward and accelerated ahead of the lumbering chopper.

I swooped down over the remains of Yosemite Valley. *Oh my God,* I thought, looking at the devastation. Half Dome had broken off, embedding itself in the valley floor, while El Capitan had split in half like a V. A dozen multicolored tents near Glacier Point caught my attention. There was movement between the tents. I banked the aircraft around for a closer look. Six brown bears milled about between the campsites; three of the bears had their heads in coolers. By the look of it, the survivors had already been rescued, so I continued on.

I flew down from the mountains and into the foothills. The area reminded me of Pompeii: a city frozen in time. Cars were burnt to a crisp and several dead bodies lay nearby. I gagged, but held it in.

The landscape improved as I flew north. I let the throttle idle, the aircraft's long wings allowing me to cruise at under forty knots. Besides the earthquake damage to the roads and buildings, the natural landscape looked unaffected. Birds circled in the breeze as if it were just another beautiful day.

As I cruised low over a highway, I noticed flecks of light zipping by out of the corner of my eye. Moments later I heard the crack-crack-crack of the muzzle blast, the noise delayed by the speed of sound.

I'm being shot at! I realized. I watched two men taking cover behind a beat up Ford pickup. The truck's red paint had faded after years in the California sun.

I hit the transmit button on my radio. "Taking small arms fire here," I said, trying my best to sound calm.

"Don't worry about it," Avro replied.

"Don't worry about it?" I yelled back into the radio.

"Yeah, don't worry about it. I'll be there in ten minutes, over."

I glanced back at my attackers and realized that they were covering their eyes. I looked closer; they appeared to be painted in a blinding green light.

The SAR computer displayed a message. "Arms suppression activated."

"Oh God!" I said. Apparently, the countermeasures that Avro installed on my aircraft included suppression lasers. When the sensors detected small arms fire directed at the aircraft, the lasers locked onto the assailants, temporarily blinding them.

"Dammit Avro, you could have told me I'd be blinding people," I yelled.

"Wait for it…" Avro said.

"Wait for what?" I asked, in a panic.

"Are you still watching the bogeys?" Avro asked.

"Yeah, why?" I asked, banking the aircraft to maintain visual contact.

"Wait for it," Avro said, I detected a smile in his voice.

Something caught my eye and two streaks of light whizzed down from the sky towards the attackers. I watched as the streaks sliced the men in half from head to groin, their bodies exploding outward, leaving two red stains on the golden California grass.

"What the hell was that!" I yelled into the radio.

"Predator drone, guided bullets," Avro said. "The lasers on your aircraft guide the bullets to their target."

"That was brutal!" I said.

"This operation has a zero tolerance for civilian casualties. Absolute zero. This method also helps reduce the enemy's reliance on human shields."

"What if they shine a laser back at me?" I asked.

"Your aircraft's canopy reflects laser light. Just get out of there would ya?" Avro instructed.

I pushed the throttle to full and climbed past one thousand feet and continued my sweep of the area.

"Avro, John here," I radioed on our shared frequency. "I see people waving their arms at me. Looks like about twenty people."

"Hang tight, Johnny," Avro radioed back. "There's a wide scan option on your SAR display. Check them for weapons and explosives. I don't want any bombs on my chopper."

I tapped the display and a live video feed of the area appeared. The video divided into grids. "Select target zone," said the computer. On the display, I watched the people waving their arms and selected the zone containing the people.

"Fly a circuit around the target area," the computer instructed me in a calm tone. I cut the throttle and extended the dive brakes, descending in an arching path.

"Scanning. Scanning. Scanning," the computer announced. "No arms detected."

"They're clean," I announced to Avro.

"Alright. Coming in for extraction."

I watched as the giant helicopter raced in from the south, sounding like a thousand lawnmowers. Avro flew past the survivors, pulled back on the cyclic and reduced the throttle, effectively hitting the brakes. The chopper pitched up and descended. Avro chose a level stretch of road to make his landing. As the Super Stallion approached the pavement, a donut-shaped cloud of brown dust rose into the air around it. The helicopter's rear hatch opened.

People ran towards the helicopter, some protecting their heads, and others covering their ears. Once they were aboard, Avro closed that hatch and lifted back up into the air.

"Where now?" I asked.

"Beale Air Force Base," Avro replied, "fifteen miles north of here. The National Guard is holding the base, but it's a hot zone. We'll drop the civilians off and refuel. If you see anyone who needs rescuing along the way, we'll pick 'em up. I've got a few empty seats here."

"Roger, see you at Beale," I said, selecting Beale Air Force Base on my GPS.

We switched our radios from a private frequency to the general search and rescue channel and Avro radioed the base, letting them know we were coming.

Beale Air Force Base hustled and bustled with activity despite the cracks in the runway, some large enough to drop a tank into. The hangars had significant earthquake damage and the wooden barracks were completely flattened. Even the control tower was a pile of bricks.

On the plus side, there were third generation Ospreys ready to airlift the civilians out of California and medical tents set up in a staging area. I noticed eight helipads mapped out in bright orange spray paint, each a thirty-foot painted square with an "H" in the middle.

For a moment, I was seriously concerned that there would be nowhere for me to land. Fortunately, I only needed a few hundred feet of runway. I did a low pass over the tarmac and found a place with enough undamaged concrete.

I lined up for my approach, deploying my spoilers and dive brakes. I pulled back on the throttle, setting turbofan regeneration to full. This slowed the aircraft to thirty-five knots. Within moments, I was on the ground. When I came to a complete stop, a soldier in an orange vest marshaled me toward a parking spot.

The airbase had emergency generators on site. I retrieved the power cord from the plane and within minutes had a full charge.

Avro landed nearby and was out of his helicopter in seconds. He began helping get the evacuees to a waiting Osprey. The Osprey's twin rotors were already spooling up as the people transferred from one aircraft to another.

After the Osprey departed, Avro and I met on the tarmac. "How're you doing, boss? Ready to do it all over again?" he asked. I nodded. "Great." He had to yell to be heard over the sounds of the nearby generators. "I've asked the team to throw some sandwiches and coffee into our cockpits. We'll stay in this area tonight and head back to Vegas tomorrow. After this, you'll want to keep a small suitcase with you. We'll be spending quite a few nights in the field."

I nodded again, looking to my left as a corporal dropped off the food.

"Rock and roll," Avro said. He held up his hand for a fist pump. I returned the gesture and walked back to my aircraft.

We rescued over two hundred people that day, turning in shortly after midnight. We slept in a military green GP tent along with other members of the SAR squadron. The next morning we sat impatiently in the tent while a tech repaired Avro's Stallion. It had taken a hit from a single guided bullet.

Avro reached for a bottle of water. It crinkled as he squeezed the container, shooting the last drops of liquid into his mouth.

"Do you think we'll be assigned to the North Bay?" I asked. Avro knew what I was asking, I wanted to search the area where I had lost track of my family.

"Hey, Lieutenant," he yelled to a young pilot who was still in bed. "You're assigned to San Fran, right?"

The pilot slid into a seated position, dangling his legs over the bed and letting the blankets rest on his lap. "Yeah, place is messed up." A duffel bag sat at the end of his bunk. A nametag that read "Jamison" was sewn into the green canvas.

"Who's got that sector now?"

"Captain Gimply's got it," Jamison replied.

"Gimply. Dammit!" Avro shook his head at the floor. He looked up, his eyes widening, and the corners of his mouth curved up, giving him a mischievous look.

"Who's Gimply?" I whispered. "You sound like you don't get along with the guy."

"Gimply's not a guy," Avro said. "She's my ex-wife."

I didn't know what to say, so I just stared at the green wall of the tent. The tent had six windows made of transparent plastic, which didn't provide much visibility but let in the morning light. I looked over at Avro. He was concentrating.

"Any chance we can trade sectors?" I asked.

"Yeah, we can ask, follow me. It'll be fun." Avro stood up, wrapping a small white towel around his boxer shorts.

I pulled on my jeans, which made me look out of place, and chased after him.

Avro marched into the only hangar that was still standing. He ducked under an Osprey's propeller and walked along a row of offices on the far side of the hangar. Names and ranks were written in sharpie on each door. He checked the names until he found the one he was looking for. I stood back, not knowing what to expect.

Avro knocked and a woman in full military dress opened the door. When she saw Avro, a look of pure unadulterated rage crossed her face. And out of her mouth shot the longest stream of obscenities I'd ever heard, ending with, "You-god-damned-cheating-son-of-a-whore!" The woman's black hair was tied back in a bun, and her pale round face reddened as she swore.

Avro held up his arm as she tried to slap him. Avro was over a foot taller than the stout woman, and most of the blows impacted on his forearm, but some struck his bare torso. "I told you not to ever ever ever ever come see me again!"

Avro backed away to the middle of the hangar floor. A mechanic working under a nearby helicopter slid from under his aircraft on a creeper and just stared.

Captain Gimply gave Avro one final blow to the ribs, stormed back into the office and slammed the door.

Avro stood in his towel, and even with his tan-colored skin, I could see the bruises.

"That's your ex-wife?" I said, my plans for switching search zones fading fast.

"Ah, yeah, sort of, I guess. It's a long story. No, it's a very short story actually."

I walked with Avro back the tent. I looked towards Avro's helicopter in the distance. The tech was finishing up a weld on the patch.

"Well?" I prompted.

"Okay, Johnny, but you keep this a secret, okay?" Avro stopped walking, facing me.

"You got it," I said. We continued walking, picking up two individual meal packs—IMPs— on the way back to the tent.

"Gimply was my senior officer. But in SAR, we try not to take rank too seriously. We were stationed in Vegas and hit the strip four times a week, at least. Gimply and I became a killer blackjack team."

"You counted cards?"

"You keep that a secret, too." Avro pointed at my chest. I nodded and he continued. "Anyway, it was her birthday and everyone bought her shots. We ended up on the dance floor and before we knew it, everyone else had gone home and it was just her and me. Boy were we wasted! We left the club, and stumbled past a little chapel off the strip, found a rabbi dressed as Elvis and got married."

"I awoke the next morning in the Altucher suite, Vegas's most expensive Airbnb. I had a searing headache and Jane Gimply was gone." Avro took a large bite of blueberry muffin before continuing. "I got texts all that day, like 'What do you want for dinner honey,' and 'I'll be home soon my love,' which I thought was hilarious, so I played along. She was my senior, so we couldn't reveal what we'd done. I figured it would stay a secret, you know, forever. What happens in Vegas, right?"

"Right," I repeated.

"That night, the guys went out on the town again. Captain Gimply was still out on a mission. I had a few too many, again. Hit the dance floor, again. I played wingman for one of my fellow pilots. Before we knew it, we were making out with two beautiful brunettes. Well, his was beautiful, anyway."

I laughed.

"Gimply, returned from her mission and came looking for me. When she didn't find me in the barracks, she accessed my military RFID chip," Avro held up his left wrist, pointing to a scar, "to track me down. The woman is bat-shit crazy. She found me, hauled me out onto the street, and gave me this scar." Avro pointed to his temple. "And this scar," he said, pointing to his jaw.

"You didn't hit back, did you?"

"Hell no, Johnny, I just stood there and took it! The next day there were two sets of documents, hidden in my bedsheets. The first informed me that I'd been transferred to another CO." Avro took another bite of his muffin.

"What was the other document?" I asked.

Avro snorted, and then answered, "Divorce papers."

Chapter 6

RECRUITED

It had been a year since impact. My family was still missing and the Cartel continued its guerrilla war against the U.S. government. The SAR squadron had lost eight pilots out of the thirty back in the beginning.

I had originally planned to return to NASA once I found my family. But within a month of the disaster, Congress dissolved NASA after an independent panel determined that due diligence could have prevented the whole thing. After losing a class action lawsuit, there was no money left to continue, and I was left with a toxic organization on my resume.

Eddie Rizzo made a steady profit off the data I provided. He was one of many people looking to cash in on unclaimed California resources. To me, Eddie was nothing more than a desperate scavenger. When I saw him, which wasn't often, he tried to tell me where to fly, so I avoided him as best I could.

After the Impact, I spent a month living in a rundown Super 8 motel. After that, I rented a furnished studio apartment near the base. I also bought a motorcycle so I could get to my aircraft before dawn each morning, which beat having to wait for an auto-car to pick me up.

On the first anniversary of the impact, I showed up at Nellis at the usual time. Avro met me in the alley between two hangars where I parked my bike. Before I shut off the motorcycle, I knew something had changed.

"Hey, Johnny," Avro said.

"Hey," I said, stepping on the kickstand and dismounting the cycle. The enclosed space between the hangars suddenly felt claustrophobic.

"I just got word from my CO. They're calling off the search," Avro said. "We're being redeployed."

"Calling off the search! What about my family?" I could feel my face reddening and my stomach tightening as my body entered a state of fight or flight. I felt the anger surge though me and I turned and punched the seat of the bike. I stood, leaning over the motorcycle with my back to Avro.

"John, we haven't rescued anyone in weeks!" Avro said. "We've had a dozen teams in the air every day, putting their lives on the line. There's no one left."

I turned around, yelling now, "So, what, now we're just supposed to go home? Go home to what?"

"No one's going home. We've been redeployed," Avro said. "I've been redeployed," he corrected himself.

"What do you mean, you've been redeployed? Redeployed to where?" I said.

"San Diego. I'll be stationed on the Enterprise. They're sending in more ground troops to fight the Cartel and we're to provide support. The civilian rescue mission is officially over."

"Dammit!" I swore. I had no idea what to do next, not only in that moment, but with my life.

"You're a fine pilot, Johnny, and a good wingman," Avro said. "Don't do anything stupid."

Doing something stupid was exactly what I needed to do. "I'm going out there," I said and stormed off toward the hangar. Avro followed.

"Don't do it, John," he said, grabbing my shoulder. I shook him off. "Don't go out there alone, not without drone support."

The hangar door was open. I walked in, snatching a tow bar off the wall and connecting it to my plane. Avro didn't stop me. He just stood there as I dragged the Stingray onto the tarmac.

"You need to get out of Vegas and start over. Go back to D.C. if you have to."

I chucked the tow bar into the hangar. It clattered against the floor, and slid into the side wall. I threw open the canopy and hopped in, activating the twin turbines as soon as my ass hit the chair.

Avro backed away as the props sucked the air.

"Goodbye, Avro," I yelled over the sound of the fans. "It's been a pleasure." I slammed the canopy shut, leaving Avro alone. Hitting the throttle and not bothering to taxi to a runway, I took to the sky. The air traffic controllers would write me up for that stunt, but I didn't give a damn. *To hell with Nellis.*

With the throttle at full, I cruised towards San Francisco at full speed. I'd developed a habit of listening to music while over the mountains, becoming addicted to an old band Marie had turned me on to, Angels and Airwaves. I'd listen to the same songs over and over. The songs made me angry but in a good way. I was angry at the hate I felt, and one particular song seemed to justify that, so I turned it on.

But those words from your mouth they are scary,
and the hate that you have, that you carry,
it will grow, it will grow, till we're buried.
And there will be nothing left except sadness,
and a scar without words, without anything
cuz we've done this before, this is madness.

This was madness, what I was doing. I'd been risking my life every day, and for what? My life was a purposeless repetition. This was my last flight. After today, my search was over and I'd never return to California again.

I reached San Francisco and flew north over the remains of the Bay Bridge. The bridge's piers remained, but the roadway had fallen into the bay. Treasure Island was under water, only a few foundations rising up above the waves. On my right, two red towers were all that was left of the Golden Gate Bridge.

I flew low over the water, between the towns of Sausalito and Tiburon, then around Mount Tamalpais and Point Reyes Station. I was looking for a camp or some civilian holdout we might have missed. Maybe there were still people here; maybe they were hiding.

Regrets poured through my head. Did we try hard enough to negotiate with the Cartel? Should we have met their demands? They had demanded the execution of everyone involved with the impact. No. We did the best we could and Avro was right. The area wasn't just cleared of civilians; it was cleared of everyone.

I was getting low on power, so I flew along the shoreline, catching the updraft as the sea breeze blew inland. The electro-glider was light and the mildest winds would push it higher in the sky. But I didn't need altitude, just power, so I tilted downward into the airstream and let moist air flow up through the turbines, recharging the batteries.

I was soaring along the ridge back near Point Reyes when I was hit. Whack! I looked out to see a four-inch hole in the underside of the wing, halfway between the turbines and the wingtip. Shards of carbon fiber flew up in to the sky. *Bam,* another hit somewhere behind me. I pulled back on the stick and let the updraft carry me high into the sky. I hit the throttle, rocketing the Stingray to three hundred knots. Streaks of light whizzed past.

"Countermeasure failure," said the computer in her usual pleasant tone. *Oh boy.* This wasn't the first time it had happened. The Cartel was getting increasingly advanced. Like our drones, they had bullets that curved to hit their targets.

Avro had been right. I shouldn't have come alone.

I hit the rudder and yawed the aircraft thirty degrees to port, skidding around like a fish turning upstream. I looked over my shoulder, trying to catch a glance at whoever was shooting at me. Two men were huddled in a bunker. They must have been guarding the shore, using the bunkers built during World War Two.

They took another shot, and a bullet ripped through the cockpit, missing my leg by a hair's width. The bullet passed up though the floor and out through the canopy, making a coin-sized hole in the glass. For a moment I panicked, continuing to fly higher and higher at full power.

When the shock of the attack wore off, I was at twenty thousand feet and back over San Francisco. The computer inundated me with alerts: "Battery Low. Recharge. Recharge," she said. "Oxygen required. Oxygen required. Battery Low. Battery Low."

I addressed the oxygen alarm first. At this altitude, a person risked passing out.

Reaching down, I unlatched a small oxygen tank from its holster and put the mask on.

I tested the aircraft's controls. They all worked. The bullets had missed the control lines and the battery. The holes in the cockpit made whistling noises as wind rushed passed the gaps. I had a roll of duct tape under my seat, and I placed a single strip of tape over each hole.

On a good day, an electro-glider with a dead battery has a glide ratio of thirty to one. The aircraft's computer calculated my current range. At twenty thousand feet I could glide a hundred twenty miles. This did not, however, take into account the hole in my wing. I suppose I could have radioed for help, little good that would do, but pride kept my finger from the transmitter.

I was angry, but not angry enough to let myself die. "Work the problem," I said, searching my GPS for a safe hillcrest that could provide enough updraft for battery regeneration. I considered Mount Tamalpais first, but that was only a few miles away. I needed to get further away from my attackers.

I considered Mount Diablo and the Altamont Pass to the east. Windmills covered these hills for a reason. *I have a windmill on each wing,* I thought, but I'd just be a target for Cartel in that area. I continued to study the map. Every hillside within two hundred miles was under Cartel control. There was nowhere to hide, and nowhere with enough updraft to recharge the batteries. If Avro were here, he'd just drop a line from the chopper and let me supercharge off the Stallion's alternator.

I looked at the family photo I had taped to the canopy. *You're still alive,* I told myself, concentrating on my son's eyes. I realized there was a place that was not on the map, a place that had one hell of a hillside and would create the perfect updraft.

The impact crater.

I typed FRESNO into the GPS. The city, or what remained of the city, was one hundred fifty miles away.

According to the computer, I'd hit the ground thirty miles shy of the ruined city. But the impact crater was ten miles north of Fresno. That left a gap of twenty miles. The crater itself had to be huge, so I took off another five miles. That was close enough. I turned the aircraft southeast and began my glide towards Fresno.

After fifty miles, I realized that there was one thing I hadn't considered: the sea breeze. Warm air in the valley rises during the day and pulls cool air in from the Pacific. This is why San Francisco is cool during the summer. It would be close, but the sea breeze would give me the range to make it to the crater.

No one went near the impact zone, not even the Cartel. It was an area of total devastation. In every direction, boulders covered the scorched earth. Even if I wanted to land, I couldn't without hitting the rocks.

Near the crater, the earth was different shades of gray and black. For the last few miles I could feel the thermals under my wings. Columns of rising air like smoke from a campfire buffeted the aircraft like a Land Rover rumbling over uneven terrain.

Without engine power, I wasn't really flying, I was soaring. Soaring is what birds do when they cruise around without flapping their wings. With the turbines feathered and most of the electronics turned off to save energy, it was quiet in the cockpit. The sound of the wind rushing around the airframe was white noise after spending so many hours in the sky.

I had only a thousand feet of altitude when I reached the rim. I approached from the west, estimating my ground speed by banking perpendicular to the wind and watching my sideways movement over the ground. I estimated the wind speed at twenty knots.

Imagine the crater as a toilet flushed upside down. Ground level winds from the west poured down over the rim, following the curve of the crater until spiraling up into the sky. My goal was to get swept up into the sweet spot, the drain of my imaginary toilet.

I brought the aircraft over the rim. It felt as though I was being flushed as the winds hurled my aircraft toward the crater floor. I had to make it to the other side, where the winds climbed the crater walls on the eastern edge.

When I reached the floor, I was moving at over two hundred knots. When an aircraft flies low over the ground, drag is reduced substantially. Air rushing over the wingtips connects with the ground, preventing vortices that otherwise tug on the aircraft. I used this phenomenon to coast to the eastern edge of the crater.

Then I found it! I found the updraft of a glider pilot's dreams!

Whoosh! The updraft kicked me in the butt, sucking the aircraft skyward in a vacuum of current. In seconds, I leapt out of the crater, thrown higher and higher by the vertical airflow.

The updraft exceeded fifty knots! I steered into the draft and unfeathered the turbines, letting the wind press against the fans. I watched as they began spinning, slowly at first, then faster and faster until they disappeared completely into a semi-transparent blur.

I turned to my displays, watching the battery levels. For two minutes, the levels remained unchanged. "C'mon, C'mon," I said to myself. I got the first bar when the battery's charge reached one percent.

The next hour was tedious, holding my position within the updraft. On a good day, I'd need a sixty percent charge to make it back to Vegas. But with multiple holes in my aircraft, I figured I had better get a full charge.

After ninety minutes floating above the crater, I'd completely charged the battery. I hit the throttle, switching from re-gen mode to full power and headed east.

I landed at Henderson airfield, thinking I could patch the aircraft in Eddie's hangar without him finding out. That didn't happen. He was waiting for me when I landed.

"You son of a bitch! What the hell did you do to my aircraft!" he yelled as I taxied to the hangar. Eddie's face was red and seething with rage. His fat jiggled as he cursed.

I thought he was going to punch me. "I was shot dammit!" Eddie didn't touch me.

"Shoot yourself!" he said, following me to the hangar. "You damaged my aircraft, didn't get any surveys, and you haven't paid me in weeks."

"Listen," I said, stopping and turning to face him. I stood six inches taller than him, and as pissed as I was, I felt seven feet tall. "I flew over the crater today. I flew over all the areas I couldn't when I was with SAR."

I looked over at Eddie's survey equipment, still hanging from the wings.

Eddie and I just stared at each other for a moment. I was the first to break the silence. "We're even."

"Get the hell out of here," he muttered.

I left the airfield and waved down a car.

After retrieving my bike from the air base, I slumped into my apartment and grabbed a beer, convinced I would drink myself unconscious and pass out for a day. Tomorrow, I'd ride east and leave it all behind.

A message flashed on my holovision. I hadn't had a personal message in months.

What the hell. I thought. Holographic messages were personal and no one I knew anymore was *that* personal.

I played the message.

It began with a video of the electro-glider taking off. The video had been shot from the end of a runway at Nellis. It showed me on my bike, taken from a security camera. *This must be some sort of sick joke,* I thought.

The Red Planet Mining Corporation logo flashed in front of me, and a corporate jingle rang out though my speakers.

I wanted to think someone was screwing with me, but pulling footage from a security camera on a military base argued against that.

"Hello John," said the message. A man appeared in front me. I stood up with my beer in hand to see that he was about my height. The holovision gave the impression that a person was standing right in front of you, and the effect was convincing.

"As you can tell, we've been watching you," he said.

"No kidding."

"Red Planet is recruiting and we need pilot-engineers. Because of our mission to cut costs, we need folks willing to relocate, people who have no immediate family, so they can concentrate on their work, without distractions. That makes impact survivors like you perfect candidates."

"Convince me."

"Work for us for fifteen years. On top of your salary, you'll be given a full retirement package including the home of your choice in one of the Red Planet executive resort communities."

Images of the resorts flashed up on the screen as well as a description of the amenities: indoor ski hills, beaches, and so on.

"Just board the next transport to Mars, and everything will be taken care of. You won't even need a ticket." The video paused, leaving an awkward silence.

In a negotiation, silence is a winning tactic. It causes the other person to talk, filling the dead air. I looked at the beer in my hand, wondering if there was beer on Mars.

"Well?" I said to the holovision. The image had paused.

I took the last sip of my beer and tossed the can across the room into the recycle sorter. For a moment, I stood there wondering what would happen if I jumped into it, wondering how it would sort me. Was I garbage? Or could I be recycled into something new?

Sure, Red Planet mined the minerals that had crashed into Northern California. But it wasn't their fault the CTS-Bradbury crashed. It wasn't their idea to build a Destiny Colony just to boost the economy, giving engineers like me something to do.

"Screw it. I'll do it," I said just above a whisper.

"Thanks, and we'll see you on Mars! Your contract will arrive momentarily."

My phone dinged.

Chapter 7

MY LAST DAY ON EARTH

"When's the next transport to Mars?" I asked my watch.

"The next Martian transport shuttle departs from Sky Harbor International Airport at eleven a.m. tomorrow."

Located in Phoenix, Arizona, Sky Harbor was America's newest gateway to space. It also housed several military units, including the Air National Guard. The long runways and southern latitude made it an ideal launch site for the Western United States.

Prime launch windows to Mars occur every two years. The fact that there was a transport the next day was more than a coincidence. Mars-based organizations schedule as many missions as possible during each launch window. The timing of the recruitment message was strategic, no doubt given at the last minute so that applicants had limited time to think it over.

Everything I needed fit in two motorcycle saddlebags. I loaded a chip with a month's rent and left it on the counter with a note: *Gone off planet. This is my 30-day notice.*

I sent Avro a text: *Going to Mars. It's been a pleasure.* He didn't text back. I guessed he was busy.

Phoenix was a five-hour drive. I suppose I could have flown or taken a hyperloop, but I wanted to experience Earth one last time, and there's no better way to do that then on a motorcycle.

So at seven o'clock that evening, I left Las Vegas and drove south on

Highway 95, passing the crumbled remains of the Hoover Dam on my left. The last sunset I would see from Earth was a rainbow of colors over the rugged terrain. I hit the accelerator and felt the adrenaline as the bike raced between rocky hills and I crossed the border into Arizona.

Sometimes when a person dies people say they are "leaving Earth." I didn't know if I would be back, and for now, it felt like dying. I was okay with that. For the first time, I allowed myself to think, *My family is gone. They've left Earth.*

Soon, it was dark and a gibbous moon rose into the sky from the east, lighting the landscape in a strange and alien way.

Then, for the first time in a long time, I felt alive. Screaming through the night at ninety miles per hour, through an alien landscape, I felt like I was already on Mars. Tomorrow would be a new day, where I would meet new friends, learn new things, and head toward a new world.

Instead of taking the flat route through the desert, I detoured east towards Flagstaff, through the national forest. From Flagstaff, I took Highway 89 south, a road filled with hairpin turns and a lot of up and down. Fifty miles past Flagstaff, I detoured to the top of a canyon. I sat down on the cold earth. The moon was higher in the sky now, and I could see for miles. I closed my eyes and let the cold wind whip around me. I looked up at the stars and moon, and then I searched for Mars.

If you love astronomy, you know there are only a few bright red stars in the night sky, one of which is Antares, which literally means anti-Mars. There's also Beetlejuice in Orion, and Arcturus, so by simple process of elimination, I was able to find my new home.

I set a timer for five hours and did something I hadn't done since I was a kid. I lay down on the ground and fell asleep under the stars.

Five hours later, my watch woke me with a beep. I climbed back on my bike and raced down to the canyon floor. Soon after, the first light of the new day shot up from the east. The sky turned from deep purple to a bright pink and I saw my last sunrise from Earth.

It was the most beautiful thing I had ever seen.

I pulled into Phoenix at eight and pawned my bike for a fraction of its worth. The Martian colony used U.S. dollars and I could probably use the cash.

Checking in at the spaceport wasn't much different than catching a flight. Behind the counter, a logo read "Commercial Orbital Transportation System." I went through security and followed the signs to the Strato-Launch terminal, which looked just like an airport terminal, but with only one gate. About a hundred people sat around, waiting. I tried to look at each face, seeing if I knew anybody. I didn't.

Walking over to the window, I came face to face with the nose of the shuttle. It hung from the Strato-Launch System, a carrier aircraft with two fuselages, each the size of a 747. A winged booster behind the shuttle held the rocket engines that would propel us into orbit. The shuttle would deliver us to the Mayflower, a third-generation Martian transport.

Boarding time arrived and we lined up at the gate. A female COTS agent in a blue vest made several general announcements and handed out anti-nausea patches. She then opened the gate, ushering us down the jetway and into the shuttle. I took a seat near the front.

Inside, the automated spacecraft looked like a Boeing 787. Instead of a cockpit, a large screen displayed our speed and altitude. It read: "Altitude: 0.34KM" and "0.00KPH."

When the last passenger took their seat, the agent stepped aboard. She gave a brief safety message, and instructed us on how to use our five-point harnesses. This included the "crotch strap." A term that made most everyone chuckle. When the agent finished, she stepped outside and sealed the hatch.

We pushed back from the gate right on schedule. I could feel the Strato-Launch aircraft's six turbofan engines spooling up. Deep rumbles reverberated through the piggybacking vehicles. For the most part, it felt like any normal flight.

The flying launchpad lumbered onto the runway. It inched forward with a low groan as the engines spun up to full throttle. The acceleration of takeoff pressed me into the seat, and soon we were airborne, becoming the largest flying machine on the planet.

At forty thousand feet a notification came over the PA: "Booster ignition in ten seconds." My hands gripped the armrests so hard my knuckles turned a pale white. The spacecraft made pulsing electronic noises, like an electric car hitting the accelerator.

"Eight, seven, six, five," my stomach shot into my throat as the shuttle dropped from its airborne launchpad. I watched in awe as the carrier aircraft pulled up and away.

"Four, three, two, one, booster ignition." The spacecraft shook as it came to life and the luggage in the overhead bins rattled. G-force pressed me deep into my chair as the shuttle went supersonic.

Holy shit! I thought, as the altitude and velocity readings increased at an impossible rate. I turned my eyes slightly to glance out the window, my head glued to the seat from the acceleration. The sky darkened as we approached the edge of the atmosphere.

Almost there, I thought, staring back at the Earth. Out my window I could see both Texas and Florida. These states represented the heart of the American space program. I imagined all the NASA buildings in Houston and at the Cape empty. With NASA disbanded, the dust would finally settle on over one hundred years of brave exploration.

I looked back to the screen. We were traveling at twenty-eight thousand kilometers per hour. Our altitude was four hundred kilometers above sea level. The statistics disappeared and the acronym MECO showed up on the screen.

Main engine cut off. We were in orbit (or "on" orbit as they said in the industry). I let my arm float up from the armrest, turning my palm toward my face. As I stared at my hand, I let the realization kick in. I was in space!

Looking out the window, I could see the Atlantic Ocean and the Caribbean Islands where Columbus had set up his first colony in Santa Domingo. The two others in my row leaned over, trying to get a glimpse out the window, too. It was a big window, but I leaned back to let them have a look. For a few minutes, it was silent. I guess space has that effect on people.

There was a ding and the seatbelt sign switched off.

The nausea patches didn't work for everyone, and I heard a few people losing their breakfasts. I held it in.

The shuttle had five bathrooms and I needed to go. Posted on the bathroom's wall were three sets of instructions: male number one, female number one, and universal number two. Despite the technological advances, space toilets don't allow for number one and number two at the same time. I followed the instructions for "Male number one."

Back at my seat, the two folks from my row floated together, pointing at the Earth below. They noticed me and pushed back from the wall, introducing themselves. They were married, both research scientists from the European Union and experts on in-situ resource utilization. Apparently, Red Planet Mining was pushing to make Mars completely self-sufficient.

For the next hour, more and more people introduced themselves. I hadn't thought about it before, but I was about to spend the next six months with these people on our way to Mars.

Like me, many didn't know their Martian job assignments. But based on our backgrounds we could make an educated guess. Half the people seemed to have mining backgrounds, everything from strip mining to fracking. Some were scientists, but there were also meteorologists, communication technicians, and mechanical engineers.

The shuttle's display instructed us to collapse the seats into the floor, though many of the passengers had done this already. This left a lot more room to float around inside the spacecraft.

I spent my time on the shuttle staring down at the Earth. It surprised me that we spent most of our time over oceans. The Earth is seventy percent covered by water, but you don't think about that when you imagine looking down from space.

We had gone one full orbit when we got our first look at the Martian transport. *Wow,* I thought, my eyes widening, enjoying the view from a window. The cruiser looked like a large nuclear submarine, except white and covered in portholes. A blue accent stripe circled the hull. Near the bow, the name *Mayflower* interrupted the stripe. Solar arrays the size of football fields jutted out from the sides like wings.

Steel trusses extended from the rear of the spacecraft. Attached to this were the engines and the orange fuel tanks. Each tank was larger than our shuttle.

The Mayflower contained just enough fuel to complete a Hohmann transfer orbit, named for the German scientist Walter Hohmann. The trip to Mars requires two engine burns. The first burn drags the spacecraft out of Earth's gravity well and into a solar orbit. The second slows the spacecraft once it reaches Mars.

Our shuttle neared the Mayflower's bow, and I could see the docking ring with its probe assembly ready to latch on to our shuttle. Green lights blinked as we drew closer and closer. Silence returned to our spacecraft, only broken by the occasional hiss from the shuttle's thrusters. The cruiser engulfed us in shadow and our cabin went dark except for the LEDs along the ceiling.

Made primarily of a titanium alloy, the Mayflower had been printed in a manufacturing facility outside Atlanta. When it came out of the printer, it had all its wiring, all its plumbing and all its hatches. The spacecraft was painted and upholstery added before engineers loaded it onto a BFT (Big Freaking Rocket) and launched it into space.

The shuttle groaned and creaked as the Mayflower pulled it in. This was followed by a series of loud clicks. *Docking port,* I thought. There were some hissing sounds and my ears popped.

There was a knock at the hatch. The door opened and a man floated in.

He opened an access panel and retrieved a microphone.

"Good afternoon!" he said with a smile. "My name is Jason. I'd like to welcome you to the Mayflower! How is everyone doing today?"

The crowd groaned a mixture of "good" and "okay." *Oh God,* I thought. *I hope we're not stuck with this guy for six months.*

"I said, how is everyone doing today!" he repeated, somehow even more enthusiastically.

"Good," we all spoke in unison, louder this time.

Then someone yelled "Shut up!" in a slow and sarcastic tone. This elicited a chuckle from several of the folks onboard, myself included.

"Well," he said, "you'll be happy to know that I won't be joining you on your journey."

"Woo hoo!" came the voice from the rear of the shuttle, followed by more chuckles.

Jason continued undeterred. "I'll be going back to Earth on the shuttle. I have, however, prepared the Mayflower for her journey and will be here for the next hour to answer questions. In the meantime, let's go over some housekeeping items."

Jason held up a tablet and started reading a checklist. "Please collect all your belongings before you exit the shuttle, as it will be returning to Earth this afternoon. For those of you with checked bags, you will find your luggage on level one."

"For the first week of your journey, you may access real-time Earth communication from your room's computer system. However, this system will be turned off after a week, as real time communication will become impractical due to the communication lag."

"As you probably know, the Mayflower is controlled from Earth, and the ship's crews are just mechanics. If anything breaks, tell them. If you are too lazy to make your own breakfast, call a drone."

"And finally, please, be respectful. It is a small ship and you need to get along, at least until you get to Mars. Any questions?"

There was a dull murmur but no one spoke up.

The agent turned, gesturing to the hatch. "Welcome aboard."

The hatch opened into the forward section, which appeared to be the main common area. I floated in, and paused to look around. People floated past me on all sides like a school of fish.

The area looked like a movie theater. But where you would expect the holoscreen, there were windows. Fifty windows across and twenty windows tall, each pane the size of a car's windshield. Also like a movie theater, there were rows of seats, except these seats had seatbelts.

A schedule of the day's events was posted on holovisions around the ship. The trans Mars injection engine burn was set for four p.m. ship time. At a quarter to, the ship's PA ordered everyone to the theater.

I grabbed a seat near the back, hoping no one would sit near me, but the Mayflower had one seat per passenger, and not a seat more. I'd soon have a neighbor.

Holovisions beside the windows showed us how to use the seatbelts. Above the windows, a countdown ticked down to the engine burn. I fastened the seatbelt and looked out into space. The Earth occupied the bottom third of my field of view. I could see the terminator between night and day approaching as we traveled east over the planet. A minute later, the room went dark as the spacecraft passed into the Earth's shadow. I kept staring, letting my eyes adjust to the dark until I could see the stars.

I zoned out. It was a thing I had been doing a lot lately. When the things you didn't want to think about took up most of your thoughts, zoning out was the only answer.

A brawny man in his mid-twenties floated near me. Jaw-length dirty blond hair twisted in space as he shifted his orientation. He had a confident look, a half grin on his face. He floated effortlessly towards his seat, grabbing a handrail on his way down. Doing a zero gravity chin-up, he sent himself on a flightpath that forced his hair towards the ceiling, but landed him in his seat. It looked like he had done this before.

"Drink, mate?" he asked, holding out a flask in my direction.

For a moment, I just looked at it.

"I've got more," he added, his accent clearly Australian. I nodded and took the flask.

"You know, alcohol and space can mix in interesting ways," I said.

"That's the point. There's wine in the galley. But the computer limits each person to one glass a day. They don't want us hit'n the turps, if you know what I mean." The man took another swig, floating now about six inches above his seat.

The countdown showed sixty seconds.

"You better buckle up," I said.

"Ro-ight!" He said, pulling himself back down, grabbing his seatbelt. He held out a hand. "Leeth."

"John Orville." He grasped my hand in a firm grip.

Alarms blared, as thirty seconds remained on the clock.

A loud announcement came over the PA: "Trans Mars Injection in thirty seconds. Please check your seatbelts and put your head on the headrest."

"Another?" Leeth asked, leaning out of his chair.

"Sure," I said. I drank again, but mostly to be polite.

I handed the flask back as the countdown ended.

The Mayflower buffeted as it roared out of Earth's orbit, pressing us into our chairs. Another countdown appeared, indicating the seven minutes remaining in the engine burn.

For the duration of the burn we remained in the Earth's shadow. It was dark in the theater and we could see stars through the windows. The spacecraft began pitching up and away from the planet and more stars appeared.

Everything shook making it hard to maintain focus. I saw something in front of my eyes. For a moment, I couldn't tell what it was. I was focusing on the windows, and it bounced up and down in the foreground.

It was the flask. Leeth was holding it out for me again. I reached out and grabbed it. The flask was bound by a strip of brown leather. *Kangaroo hide,* I thought.

I looked at Leeth. A big grin spread across his face. It felt like he was trying to heal me, trying to lift me from my funk. I watched the Earth getting further away every second and took another drink.

Chapter 8

THE NURSE

With the engine burn complete, we were traveling at fifty thousand miles per hour. It didn't feel like it though, since we were weightless again. The engines would not ignite again until orbital insertion, when we reached Mars.

The Mayflower's holovisions displayed a looping slide show of useful information. The spaceship's clock used twenty-four hour days, but when we arrived, our schedules would switch to twenty-five hour sols. There were directions on everything from how to recycle our meal packets, to how the day/night lighting cycles worked on the spacecraft.

The galley, located at the top of the theater, allocated each person three meals a day. There were also stations around the transport that would dispense snacks and energy bars.

Leeth unbuckled his seatbelt and turned to face me. "Hey mate, I have a really important question to ask you," he said, his half smile never leaving his face. "Do you play tennis?" With Leeth's accent, *Tennis* sounded like *Tea-nis*

"Tennis?" I asked.

"Yeah, tennis!" he said. "I read up on the Mayflower. The tennis simulator is first rate. I used to play tennis every day back in Melbourne."

"You're kidding," I said.

"I'm not spending two hours a day on a treadmill."

"I hear the Tour de France simulator is very convincing."

"Yeah, well, I'm not French," Leeth joked. "C'mon then, change your clothes and meet me in the gym."

Leeth didn't wait for an answer. He pulled himself into the port-side passageway, grabbed a handrail and catapulted himself towards the staterooms.

I unbuckled my seatbelt and rose out of my seat. Most people had moved to the windows to watch the Earth sink away. I grabbed a handhold and pulled myself into the open space above the chairs. After floating in place for a moment, I pushed off the rail with my feet, feeling like a superhero as I flew across the room.

The starboard side corridor formed a half hexagon, with staterooms on the three shorter sides. It ran from the theater to the gym at the rear of the spacecraft. I floated to the entrance, stopping myself from crashing into the wall by grabbing a support beam.

I pulled hard on two support beams, propelling myself down the hall. I floated quickly at first, until the air resistance slowed me down. I passed a hatch marked "Sun room." I looked inside and saw what looked like a holographic beach, complete with wind, sand and seagulls. The room used a large picture window to bring in natural sunlight. A sign on the door read: "Don't worry about cancer, we can cure that." I rolled my eyes.

About seventy-five feet down the hall, I arrived at my stateroom. A sensor on the door scanned my eyes and the door clicked open. I grabbed a handrail, tucked my legs in, and spun in place before opening the door and going inside.

My stateroom was about the size of a bedroom closet. It had a single porthole the size of an airplane window with a shade pulled halfway down. A cozy sleep-sack was attached to the floor and the ceiling. Across from the sleep-sack, taking up half the wall, was an interactive display for connecting to SpaceNet.

Almost every surface of the room contained a storage unit. There were drawers for shoes, drawers for clean clothes, and drawers for dirty clothes. Most of the room was covered in Velcro.

I found the Oculus headset tucked away in a slot. The room also contained resistor arms as part of the room's VR system. This was interesting, but I'd figure all that out later.

My bags floated freely in the room. Using a clip, I strapped one bag to the inside wall and opened it. As I reached in, clumsily grabbing a shirt, the rest of the clothing floating out, spreading around the room.

"Dammit!" I said, but laughing at myself. I opened a drawer, picking clothes out of the air and throwing them in. When it was just my gym clothes left floating in the air, I put them on.

Even getting dressed was awkward. I wanted to lean down to pull up my shorts, but nothing happened. Leaning "down" made no sense. I pulled my legs toward me instead and started to spin. By the time I had made two revolutions, I had my shorts on.

With my personal belongings stashed away, I left the room and headed for the gym.

At the end of the hall, I got my first look at the exercise facilities. A sign posted by the entrance read: "Two hours a day keeps the doctor away! Follow your exercise program for optimum health."

A man in blue track shorts whooshed past me. I followed him with my eyes as he ran up the wall, along the ceiling and back again. The track rotated, giving him even more speed. He was probably doing at least half a G.

The gym was larger than the theater and had just as many windows. I could see the Earth, the whole Earth, over thirty thousand miles away.

I looked "up," noticing a "ceiling" covered in cycles. Five of the cycles were already occupied, and everyone wore VR headsets.

The sports simulators reminded me of a car factory, a cluster of mechanical arms. These were located in the back of the gym. I found Leeth in this area programming something into a terminal.

"Glad you could make it! Took you long enough," Leeth said.

"Ah, yeah," I said, not wanting to explain my suitcase debacle.

"Anyway, does Wimbledon work for you?" Leeth asked.

"Sure."

"Crowd?"

"No crowd."

"Smile."

"What?"

"Smile," Leeth repeated. "I'm making your avatar."

I smiled and Leeth hit a button, scanning my profile into the computer.

"This is terminal fifteen," he said, pointing to four mechanical arms in a mesh cage. "You can take any terminal on this level. I'll meet you in the game."

The terminals were designated by numbers stamped into the scaffolding. The mesh prevented people from hitting each other with rackets, or hockey sticks, or whatever other sports gear they were using.

"This one will do fine," I said, pointing to number sixteen nearby. Leeth strapped his running shoes into the resister arms. He connected a harness around his waist and over his shoulders. Once this was in place, he reached down grabbed a VR headset, resistance gloves, and tennis racket from a cubby in the floor.

I did the same in my terminal. Once I pulled the virtual reality set over my eyes, my entire perspective changed. The English sky was bright blue, accented by a few wispy clouds. As requested, the stands were empty, and I could see Leeth stretching on the other side of the tennis court.

"Ball," Leeth said as a white ASIMO robot jogged across the court.

"Ball!" Leeth repeated, throwing up his hands. The robot shrugged, it must not have understood his accent. Leeth scrunched up his face and said, "Ball, please," in his best American accent. The robot tossed him a ball. Leeth grabbed the ball out of the air and wacked it against the ground with his racket.

I took my first step in virtual reality, orienting myself on the tennis court. When I picked my foot up, the resistance went away until I set it down again. This was strange at first. My eyes told me I was moving, but my inner ear told me that I was standing still.

Leeth served the ball. I lunged and missed. "We better rally for a while," I said.

"Good idea," he said in a positive tone, but I could tell he was about to get serious.

"Ball," I called. The robot tossed me a ball. I put out my hand to catch it, and the ball steered itself into my palm. In my glove, I could feel its shape. I bounced the virtual ball off the court, the cork popping sound rendering perfectly in my ear. I tossed the ball up, serving it over to Leeth, who returned it to the left box.

Without thinking, I jogged the four paces to meet the ball, lobbing it to the back of the court. After five minutes of rallying, we were ready for a game.

Leeth served first. I missed the shot and looked up at the score. The scoreboard displayed both our last names. According to a giant Holovision screen, our game was sponsored by Rolex.

"So what brings you to Mars?" Leeth asked, his voice rendering perfectly over my headset. "You seem older than most colonists." He was right; I was thirty-two, while most colonists were in their early twenties. I guess most folks planned to do their time on Mars, and then come back to Earth, having banked considerable savings.

"I'm an engineer," I said, returning the ball.

"I'm a nurse," Leeth said. "I was working with survivors in San Diego. But SAR stopped bringing them in, so they didn't need me anymore."

"The evacuation is over," I said, missing the ball. Leeth was up forty-fifteen.

"Right," Leeth said with a somber tone, and then served the ball. "So what do you think of H3?" he asked as we continued our rally. The way he said "H" sounded like he was saying, "eye-itch."

"H3?" I repeated, thinking about triatomic hydrogen, a very unstable molecule.

"Henry Allen the third, CEO of Red Planet Corporation," Leeth said, sounding surprised I had to ask.

"Oh yeah," I said. "I hadn't really thought about him."

"Mate, that guy has been in the tabloids all year. He's been trying to lobby the world's governments to cancel the freeliver's wage and deny them access to the auto-farms. He thinks middle class people need a certain level of discomfort for the betterment of society."

"I don't read the tabloids. All I know is that he's a peculiar fellow, you know, eccentric."

A few years back when Linda Hernandez lost to Jake Bush, Henry Allen had protested the Bush Presidency by donating millions of hyperloop tickets to the homeless. It got the transients off the streets, and it stung the middle class freelivers by taking up all the reasonably priced seats.

Leeth smashed the ball into the net and jogged over to pick it up. "Anyway, H3 will be on Mars when we arrive, which should make things rather interesting. I guess he thinks he can squeeze more productivity out of the mines if he's around."

"He's not on the Mayflower is he?" I asked, pretty sure the Mayflower didn't have first class.

"Ha! Mate, you *really* don't know H3. First, he only hangs with the rich, and second, he doesn't leave for another four months."

"That doesn't make any sense," I said, returning another one of Leeth's killer serves. "It takes six months to get to Mars."

"Not for him. H3 just built himself a constant acceleration spacecraft. *Hawking* magazine calls him 'Fastest Man in the Universe,'" Leeth said, imitating a newscaster.

"So how'd you end up on this ship?" I asked.

"Well," Leeth began, "Australians are known for traveling the world. Go to any youth hostel and I guarantee you'll find at least one Aussie. But I've never been one for freeliving, you know? I gotta always be helping people, else I feel, I don't know, off. I was gonna head to South America after I finished up in California. But then I found out the Mars needed a nurse. So, I filled out the form and well… Any excuse to help people in new and exotic places."

"Well, that's as good a reason as any." I served the ball back over the net.

I got to know a lot more about Leeth during our game. He'd traveled all over Earth with the Red Cross, chasing all sorts of natural disasters. And when he wasn't wearing his scrubs, he volunteered as a lifeguard, saving amateur surfers who got in over their heads.

I lost our tennis game that day, but I was happy to have found a friend.

Later that day, a looping message played on the Mayflower's communal holovisions. The video opened with a view of Mars from space, the camera zooming in on the planet like a spacecraft on approach. It reminded me of the videos shown to American schoolchildren during the Cold War, warning them to get under their desks in the event of a nuclear blast. At first I couldn't decide if it was meant to be a kind of artistic irony, but then I considered the source. It was more likely the company had inadvertently reinvented the authoritative-hysterical style. The view of Mars was accompanied by a deep voice narrating in a flat mid-Atlantic accent:

"One global risk persists on Mars. Storms! Martian storms usually last only a few days, harmlessly covering all our domes and solar panels with dust. However, it is possible that one of these storms could last months or even years. If a multi-year planetwide storm were to occur, some of us might like to evacuate, but like the Titanic, there are simply not enough life boats."

The video then showed a row of Martian ascent vehicles and shuttles parked at the spaceport, covered in Martian soil.

A logo appeared and the narration continued: "Red Planet Mining Corporation would like to assure you that we have plenty of power and supplies to wait out almost any storm. We will continue to provide you with regular status updates on our disaster readiness."

The video panned back into space.

"We hope you enjoy your stay on Mars, and look forward to working with each of you as we build a better tomorrow."

I had known about the storm threat for as long as I had known about the colony. Geeking out on Mars trivia was a given at NASA. But the warning—as retro-silly as it had been presented—worked. I had watched the Earth receding and played tennis in zero G, but the announcer's earnest presentation brought it home to me for the first time that I was going to *Mars*. I was headed farther than far, and there was no going home for a long, long time.

Chapter 9

THE ASSIGNMENT

Three weeks into our journey to Mars, I received my job assignment. The message came via a priority SpaceNet channel. I floated freely in my room, having just gotten back from taking my morning shower. I tugged on some clothes before opening the message.

Dear Mr. Orville,

We hope you have enjoyed your journey so far. The attached files contain all the materials necessary to prepare you for living on Mars. Your assigned job will be **Director of Solar Panel Distribution**. Please follow the training schedule provided.

Yours Truly,

Red Planet Mining Corporation

The attached schedule assigned eight hours of work, Monday through Friday, for the rest of my trip, with two days off per week. I looked over the schedule. Basically, it contained a long list of video seminars and training simulations. The stuff seemed pretty standard and pretty boring. I closed the file.

The next attachment was a document called *A General Guide to Life in the Colony*. This file had a 3D interactive map of the colony that even had the address and layout of my apartment:

Stephen Building, Suite 258

42 Hawking Drive

Three O'clock Dome

Harmony Colony, Mars.

The apartment bordered a dome wall and appeared to have a view of the hills to the east. I wondered if most people's accommodations were as nice. The apartment came fully furnished. It had to be. I doubted there was an Ikea on Mars, although if we needed anything, I suppose we could simply print it. I closed that file and went on to the next.

The third file contained information on a vehicle called the "Pelican." I knew a little about the aircraft used on Mars, but the file contained 3D images of the aircraft, along with its flight characteristics.

The Pelican's spherical cockpit hung from the fuselage like a gullet. It had wingspan of a hundred and twenty feet and cruised at six hundred kilometers per hour. *Not bad*, I thought. It was powered by two engines called wasps. In large circular cowlings, teardrop shaped fans slapped Mars's thin atmosphere like a bumblebee beating its wings.

I noticed a button marked "Flight-simulator" and the corners of my mouth began to curve upward. I selected the icon with a gesture.

"Please connect motion control arms before putting on the headset," said a computerized female voice.

Our assigned rooms each came with four motion control arms. Two for your feet and two with feedback gloves that connected to your wrists, just like the tennis sim in the gym. I strapped into the restraints. For the moment, the system induced no resistance whatsoever, and I continued to float freely in my stateroom.

I donned the Oculus headgear and suddenly I was in the cockpit. I could feel the rudder pedals on my feet and the control stick in my hand.

The Pelican sat in a hangar not much bigger than the plane itself.

"Welcome," said the simulator. "This aircraft is the MF-33 Martian flyer, the Pelican, current model." The simulator talked me through the controls and how to contact the Martian Air Traffic Control.

"Pelican, this is MATC," a male voice said in a very flat tone. "You are cleared for take-off from the PDC hangar." The computer pronounced MATC, like mat-ic, which had a nice ring to it—much better than "ATC" or "Tower." I followed the computer's instructions, pushing the throttle forward. The system shook, simulating takeoff.

The Pelican rocketed out of the hangar and into the Martian sky. I leveled off at five hundred feet and got my first look at the colony.

I could see the circumferential, my new home: twelve domes encircling a larger central dome. Transparent channels connected each dome and within these channels, cars raced from one dome to the next.

In the distance, the spaceport abounded with activity. A delta-wing shuttle landed on the runway while an MAV launched into orbit. Green lights on the control tower flashed and radar dishes rotated.

Up on a nearby hill, the colony's research and development center rested inside a bio dome filled with trees. Near the dome's roof, birds soared in an artificial breeze. Outside the lush hilltop haven, a single windmill rotated, not generating power obviously. Martian winds didn't exert much force; the windmill just measured wind speed. Other weather stations were strewn about nearby.

Following the simulator's instructions, I dove into Valles Marineris, Mars's deepest canyon where autonomous mining trucks drove in and out of the mines. The vehicles looked like dump trucks without cabs, bumping along on oversized tires.

Following a set of directions on the heads up display, I banked the Pelican into a northern branch of the canyon and back to the colony. A suspension bridge above the canyon connected the spaceport to the rest of the colony. As I approached the bridge, warning sounds resonated through the cockpit.

"Caution," said the simulator, "you are not permitted to fly this aircraft under the bridge."

I pulled up on the control stick, and the Pelican shot up into the sky, clearing the bridge by a few hundred meters. I continued up, at full throttle, until the computer said, "This session is complete. Would you like to proceed to the next lesson?"

"No," I said, but then I thought of something. "Computer, can you change the location to Earth, San Francisco, and keep me in the air?"

"Location established. Please confirm request transition to free flight."

"Confirmed," I said. Mars's red sky faded to blue.

The simulation displayed San Francisco as it was before the impact. It was beautiful. I soared over the Golden Gate Bridge, towards Alcatraz. Below me, a thousand seagulls circled above the waves. I banked hard over Fisherman's Wharf, cruising down toward Market Street and the Embarcadero.

To my right, Union Square bustled with shoppers going in and out of Macy's where Marie had loved to shop. I'd let Branson play in the fountain and chase pigeons while waiting for a table at the Cheesecake Factory.

On my left, auto-cars raced toward Oakland on the Bay Bridge. Beyond that, Berkeley's Campanile rose over the historic campus. The Campanile was one of the tallest clock towers in the world. Well, when Marie taught there it was, before it was destroyed by the impact.

I flew over the Mission district and above Bernal Heights where we had rented our apartment. I banked right again and found myself over Alamo Square, where colorful Victorian houses overlooked a park.

Memories flooded back as if watching a movie in fast forward. I saw Marie and Branson, rolling down the square's grassy hill, laughing hysterically. They laughed so loud. I would stand and watch, not wanting to grass-stain my pants. I remembered an indescribable joy as my son tumbled in the freshly mowed lawn. We picnicked in that same park beside a garden decorated in children's shoes. Marie rushed up the hill, chasing after Branson as he wandered toward the tennis courts where old men grunted as they stumbled around the court on aching knees.

Something changed and my view began to cloud. Was the computer simulating fog? No. Tears welled up against the rubber in my headset. I pushed the stick down and the cries of proximity alarms filled my ears. The Pelican dove into the San Francisco hillside with a thundering crash. My view panned away from the crash site, displaying a smoldering crater. A menu popped up. "Reset simulation?" the computer asked.

"No, end program," I said.

I ripped off the headset and found myself alone in the silence of my room.

Chapter 10

PLANETFALL

The remaining five months on the Mayflower passed by surprisingly fast.

Leeth and I continued to play sports on a daily basis. In our third month we moved on from tennis and started playing hockey. By the fourth month, we had quite the league going. With twelve players plugged in for every game, the computer rarely had to use bots to fill in for shortages.

I even became an expert at my job, at least in simulation. The training programs were interesting and many involved flying. I also enjoyed driving jeeps over Martian terrain and exploring the surface in a spacesuit. I couldn't wait to do these things for real.

For most of the journey, we could see Mars from the theater, but only as a red star in the vast sky. People enjoyed floating at the windows, trying to point it out. Then, with one week left in our journey, Mars began to grow.

When the arrival countdown switched from days to hours, alerts sounded throughout the spaceship. The orbital insertion burn was set for ten a.m. Martian standard time. Most of us had downloaded the Martian time app for our watches and were now accustomed to the twenty-five-hour clock.

There was even a running joke about staying up until thirteen o'clock at night. It was like George Orwell's book *1984*, which began with the line, "It was a bright day in April, and the clocks were striking thirteen."

Everyone was excited for planetfall. We would experience gravity's pull for the first time in six months. I was quite nervous about returning to gravity. Despite our exercise routines, and the gravity-simulating running track, we'd still have difficulty walking once we reached the surface.

At nine forty-five a.m., everyone gathered in the theater. Leeth and I took the same seats as when we had first met. From our perspective, the planet occupied more than half of the windows in the theater.

Shortly after settling into our seats, the arrival countdown reached zero.

"Re-orientation thrusters firing," said the ship's computer.

We jerked to our right as the Mayflower's starboard thrusters fired. Mars rotated across our field of view. It was breathtaking. Down below, I could see the canal-like canyons that had fooled early astronomers into thinking intelligent life existed on Mars. I could also see the manmade canals. Most of these were the result of strip mining. Other canals reflected a blue-green light. *These must be the farms,* I thought. *And there is the colony!*

From space, Harmony Colony was barely visible, with the spaceport's runway being the most prominent artifact. I could just make out the circumferential: twelve domes positioned in a circle, with a thirteenth dome in the center.

The whole area surrounding the colony glistened. *The solar arrays,* I thought.

Leeth broke my trance. "Drink, mate?" he said, handing over the flask.

"How the hell do you still have any of that!"

"Told you I had a lot," Leeth said. "This is the last of it though, so you better enjoy it."

I took a swig. When I handed the flask back, the port thrusters fired to complete our reorientation. The theater faced out into space with the spaceship positioned so its two engines, each the size of school buses, pointed towards the Martian horizon. The sun beamed through a window and Leeth held up his flask to protect his eyes. I held up my hand to do the same.

"One minute until orbital insertion," the computer said. "Please ensure your seat belts are securely fastened, and check that the area in front of you is clear of any floating objects."

The ship's cleaning drone had been busy all morning. If there were any debris floating around the ship, it would fall to the rear of the spacecraft once the engines ignited. I was pretty sure none of us wanted a floating tennis shoe or stray French fry hitting us in the face.

When the countdown reached zero, the ship rumbled as deceleration pressed us into our seats. "Orbital insertion in progress," the computer said.

According to the screens, we were experiencing one G of acceleration. But after six months with no gravity, it felt like a sumo wrestler was sitting on my chest.

Another timer appeared. "Twelve minutes, eleven seconds remaining," it read.

"Twelve minutes at one Earth gravity!" Leeth yelled, sounding like crocodile Dundee, "Ridgy-didge!"

The ship continued to shake as the engines did their job. The spacecraft's structure carried the engine noise into the theater. It felt like sitting in a car with a booming subwoofer.

The Mayflower curved around the planet in reverse as the engines burnt their remaining fuel. The blinding sun glided from right to left until Mars was visible once more. To our left was Phobos, Mars's largest moon, orbiting against a background of stationary stars.

With three minutes remaining in the orbital insertion, we crossed the terminator and experienced our first Martian sunset. For ten seconds, the theater turned bright red, as incoming sunlight passed through the Martian atmosphere.

"Wow," I said.

"Beauty, but I've seen better," Leeth joked and I shook my head. We had become fast friends, but appreciating a solemn moment wasn't his strong suit.

Then, there was silence. We jerked forward in our seats as we returned to zero G.

"Orbital insertion successful," the computer stated. "Shuttle docking will occur at one p.m. Martian standard time."

"Well, that was fun," Leeth said. "Do you have time for an early lunch?"

"I think I'll go pack my things," I said, unbuckling my seatbelt.

"Alright. Just remember, this is our last taste of space chow, from now on, it's autofarm fruits, factory vegetables, and vat beef."

"That's a sad thought," I said, rolling my eyes.

I took a final look at my stateroom, my home for the past six months. The room's display showed a slideshow of Marie and Branson. A shrine to my past life. In Vegas, I had purchased the matching Washington Capitals ball cap my son used to wear. It was the one personal item that meant the most to me. I retrieved the hat from its place by the window, placed it in the bag and left the room.

There was still another hour until the Martian shuttle would arrive. I decided to head up to the galley to grab lunch.

I floated up to the galley to find Leeth still there. He motioned to a spot around the table next to a starboard window. This was Leeth's favorite place to sit. From the table he could see out the windows in the theater, as well as out the side windows. Using a Velcro strap, I fastened my saddlebags to a rail, and slid my feet into designated foot holders.

"Anxious to get down to the surface I see," Leeth said, taking a bite of a peanut butter and jelly sandwich.

"Yeah well, you know what my philosophy is," I said, waiting for Leeth to reply. He didn't. "If it needs doing, do it now."

"I like my philosophy better," Leeth said. "Eat first, lose your luggage and have it delivered to you by the airline. That way, you don't need to carry it to your hotel."

"I'm not sure this airline will deliver your stuff if you leave it on board," I said.

"Well, it's worth a shot," Leeth said.

I floated over to the food dispenser and selected mac and cheese. The auto-kitchen assembled, heated, and served the food in about thirty seconds. I grabbed a drinking bottle and filled it with coffee. Back at the table, I set the bowl and bottle down, feeling the magnets tug the items to the surface.

"Hey check it out," Leeth said, motioning with a nod to the nearest window.

"Right on time," I said. The shuttle's thrusters fired, aligning the spacecraft to the Mayflower's docking port.

The Martian shuttle was quite a bit different than the one we had taken from Earth. The Earth based shuttle had short wings designed for landing in a thick atmosphere. The Martian shuttle's wings formed a giant triangle around the entire fuselage. Landing on a Martian runway was pretty similar to Earth, but Mars required a much higher approach speed to compensate for the thin atmosphere.

From our table in the galley, we watched as the shuttle made its final approach to dock with the cruiser. The shuttle banked as it approached and I saw the docking port located on the shuttle's nose. The shuttle connected with the Mayflower head-on, as if it were giving our spaceship a kiss on the cheek.

A few minutes later the hatch opened and a woman floated in. She wore a white jumpsuit with the COTS logo printed across the chest. Her brown hair floated in a spiral. She reached for a microphone connected to the wall.

Before she could say anything, Leeth yelled. "G'day Martian!"

"Hi there!" she called. She looked no older than twenty.

"Don't mind him, he's drunk," I called. Leeth wasn't actually drunk, yet, but he did get louder with each additional shot.

The woman looked at Leeth, then smiled, and winked. Then pressing the button on the microphone said with a drawl, "Welcome to Mars orbit! I hope y'all enjoyed the flight." I looked around at the people floating nearby. They were nodding.

"I'll be your flight attendant for the descent down to the planet. Please collect all carry-on items and come aboard the shuttle at your earliest convenience. We'll depart for Mars in exactly thirty minutes."

I expected Leeth to excuse himself while he went to gather his things, but this didn't happen. "You packed *everything* in your checked bags didn't you?" I asked, giving Leeth an inquisitive look.

"Yup," he answered. "Don't you know your first bag flies for free?"

Leeth and I boarded first, procuring the seats in the front row. We watched as the rest of the passengers trickled in.

"You know mate, I think you were the oldest person onboard," Leeth said.

"Thanks," I said, "When you turn thirty-two, I'll skip the party."

"When I'm thirty-two, I'll be back on Earth and retired," Leeth said.

"Uh huh."

Once everyone was aboard, the flight attendant floated up and down the aisles. When she was confident that every seat was filled and every overhead bin secure, she fastened herself into a jump seat near the hatch across from Leeth.

"No safety briefing?" Leeth asked.

"Haha, no," the attendant replied with a warm chuckle. "If anything goes wrong, we'll crash into the surface of Mars at five thousand miles per hour."

"Oh, too right," Leeth said and leaned back in his seat, giving me a mocking look, and taking another swig from his flask.

We heard a clunk, and I looked across the aisle and out the port windows. We had detached from the Mayflower and were drifting away from the larger spacecraft.

Once we were sufficiently clear of the Mayflower, a computerized voice reverberated through the cabin. "Thirty seconds to deorbit burn," it said.

Unlike the launch from Earth, and the two orbital transfer burns on the Martian Transport, this engine firing was barely noticeable. The shuttle's nose pitched up and hissing noises sounded through the cabin.

The shuttle attendant looked bored.

"That's it?" Leeth asked.

"That's it, I guess," I said. "We're going down!"

We heard a twisting sound, like a winch pulling a heavy object. I looked out the window, and watched the spacecraft's control surfaces cycling through a check phase in preparation for our decent. Just like an airliner, there were slats, flaps, ailerons, and dive brakes. The bottoms of the wings were covered in a tan-colored heat shield.

We reached the upper regions of the Martian atmosphere and the wings began to glow.

"Leeth, hand me your flask," I said.

"It's almost empty, mate!" he protested.

"Don't worry, I'm not going to drink it!"

Leeth passed me the flask. I held the flask two feet above my lap and let it go. The flask floated down, taking thirty seconds to reach my thighs, but the result was obvious.

Gravity!

"Let me give it a go!" Leeth said. I handed back the flask and then looked out the window. The wing glowed brighter than before. Orange and red flames flickered up and over the leading edge.

Leeth held the flask over his head and dropped it down into his lap. This time, it took only ten seconds to cover the distance.

Out the window, the view of the wing was replaced by a blur of yellow and grey, as flames of ionized particles engulfed the shuttle. After another minute, the view of the wing returned, this time without the flames.

Leeth was still picking up the flask and dropping it into his lap. By now, the flask fell in less than a second. My head felt heavy and my arm wanted nothing more than to rest on the armrest.

We flew over mountains and canyons and I realized that the Martian landscape contained a wide variety of color. There were reds, oranges, yellows and browns in every conceivable hue.

Lower and lower we descended, traveling almost a third of the way around the planet as we decelerated from orbit. The ground rushed by faster and faster as we continued to lose altitude. The shuttle began to bank, conducting a series of S-turns to bleed off speed and altitude.

"One minute until landing," the computer announced as we approached the runway at one thousand miles per hour.

"You do this every day?" I asked the flight attendant.

"Yup," she said, maintaining her bored expression. She probably made this trip dozens of times each launch window.

Right before we landed, the shuttle passed over an array of solar panels and some dump trucks driving down a red dirt road. *Nothing like real estate near the airport,* I thought.

The shuttle hit the runway with a lurch and the wings pitched downward. Thrusters fired and brakes screeched. I pressed down on the armrests to keep my back against the seat. For almost a full minute, the sound of rockets, wind, and rumbling tires filled the cabin. Then there was silence.

The attendant picked a phone from the wall. "Welcome to Mars! I hope ya'll enjoyed your flight." She started clapping and several other folks began clapping, as well. Then, someone started cheering and other people joined in, escalating the din. Soon, the entire shuttle was full of hoots and hollers.

Once everyone had calmed down, the attendant continued. "Please remain in your seats until the shuttle is safely parked at the gate and the hatch has been opened. Use extra caution when exiting the shuttle, as most of you will experience trouble walking after several months in zero G. You will find walkers and wheelchairs located just inside of the terminal."

She took a deep breath and continued, "Each of you has been assigned a representative to pick you up in the arrivals area. For those of you with checked luggage, please collect your bags from the carousel in the terminal." It amazed me that after over a hundred years of air and space travel, a baggage carousel was still considered an efficient way to deliver bags.

The shuttle continued down a taxiway and across a tarmac. From the window I could see two gates. The jetways were cylindrical, which meant they were pressurized.

The shuttle came to rest at the gate. There was a hiss-pop and the hatch opened. The sound of moaning reverberated through the cabin as everyone aboard attempted to stand.

"Gahh!" Leeth moaned, "It feels like I'm wearing a lead vest!"

I tried to stand. "This *is* tough," I said.

A line of limping and sluggish individuals formed in the aisle. Leeth stood up and supported himself by resting a hand on the seat across from him. He opened the overhead bin and passed me a bag. Even at one-third Earth's gravity, the bags felt twice as heavy as they should.

Leeth and I were the first to leave the shuttle. After limping up the jetway, I looked back. It was like watching a zombie movie, dozens of people hunched over, stumbling up the ramp. One person lost their lunch.

Leeth entered the terminal first. "You've got to be kidding me!" he yelled, then laughing historically. "Look at this, mate!"

I chuckled. Right in front of us was a line of old people walkers, with tennis balls on each of the legs. Leeth went over and grabbed one.

"Don't. Just don't," I said.

"Well I say, sonny," he said, doing his best old lady impression. "Don't you look spry for a young guy?"

I let go of the railing and took my first unsupported steps. *I'll be fine.* As nauseating as the Mayflower's treadmill had been, it helped to mitigate the gravity shock.

We followed the signs to the baggage claim area and terminal exit. Leeth was the only person to use a walker and he did it just to be funny. Other people hopped onto golf carts and drove themselves to the exit, beeping the little horn as they tried to navigate around Leeth, who was limping down the center of the corridor.

In the arrivals area, several folks stood around holding up tablets with names displayed in big letters. I scanned the room and saw "Orville."

The man holding my name was a tall handsome fellow of South Asian complexion. He stood leaning against a column and looked rather bored.

"John Orville," I said, walking up to the man, reaching out my hand.

"Kevin Patel. Nice to meet you," he said with a hint of an Indian accent. "Welcome to Mars. My car is right outside."

Kevin had been born in America but moved to India at age five when his father took a job with the Indian Space Research Organization. Kevin had been fascinated by space from a young age, and went on to get his engineering degree from the Bangalore Institute of Technology. After completing the degree in only three years, he moved back to America where he was accepted to a Masters program at MIT.

I said goodbye to Leeth and we made plans to meet up as soon as we were settled in. With a saddlebag in each hand, I followed Kevin outside. "Outside" was a large glass tube with parking spots running along the terminal and two additional lanes for moving traffic. Several cars drove along the tube, some occupied, some empty.

Harmony Colony's greenish-blue bridge was visible in the distance, its roadway surrounded by a flexi-glass tube a hundred feet in diameter. Under the bridge, solar arrays glittered blue like an ocean while the arrays on the hillside glittered green like a forest. I squinted, imagining I was looking at a lush valley. Across the bridge, Harmony's skyline punctuated the landscape with its expansive twelve-dome circumferential, pierced by the larger central dome.

"You know what's great about Mars?" Kevin said.

I looked at him and shrugged.

"There's tons of parking," he answered.

I threw my bags into the trunk and climbed into the passenger's seat. A small Lego Starfighter hung from the rearview mirror. "Chocolate bar?" Kevin held up a small brick labeled "Mars."

I looked at the chocolate bar for a moment, but didn't reach for it. "It's a tradition," Kevin said. I ate the chocolate and let it melt in my mouth.

We left the airport and crossed the bridge leading to the colony. The scale of everything was breathtaking. I'd seen the colony a hundred times in the simulator but being here was different. The domes rose hundreds of feet into the air and the buildings inside took on a bluish tinge from the glass.

Looking to my left, something took me by surprise. I knew the colony's layout from the simulations on the Mayflower, but there was a new dome, one that wasn't in the sims.

"That dome, is it new?" I asked.

"That, sir, is the Alamo," Kevin answered. "A custom-built luxury dome for Mars's upper, upper, upper class; basically, the CEO, Henry Allen the third, Red Planet executives, and their families. You know about H3, right?"

"Oh yeah, I heard all about him. Eccentric, billionaire, comedic-philanthropist," I said, trying to summarize Leeth's tabloids.

"Comedic philanthropist," Kevin repeated. "That's about right. although, his work to free zoo animals ended poorly when he set an antelope loose in Beijing."

"I didn't hear about that one," I said.

"No? The antelope got into a local high school," Kevin said.

"Did anyone get hurt?" I asked.

"No, but the school was investigated for unusually high test scores."

"I don't see the correlation."

"Well, the antelope freaked out because of all the cheetahs." He paused. "Get it? Cheaters, cheetahs?"

For a moment there was silence. I looked over at Kevin, who was sporting a large grin. I broke out laughing for the first time in a long time.

PART II

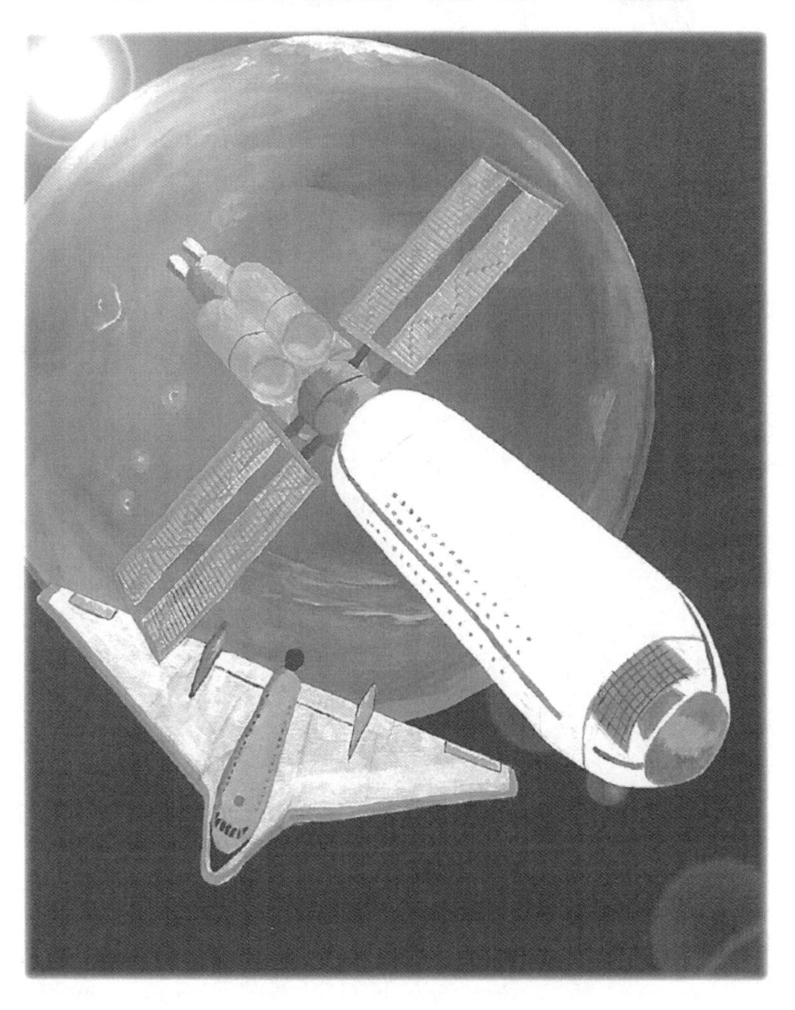

Chapter 11

LAUNCH WINDOW

I merged into the left lane of the circumferential highway, passing a slower moving autonomous delivery vehicle. It was early, and the sun had just risen above a distant hill. My electric SUV purred along from one dome to the next through the flexi-glass channels. The Martian Council, a small group of volunteers in charge of municipal laws, let us drive our vehicles manually, which was a nice perk. I'd forgotten how much fun piloting a vehicle was this close to the ground.

In the distance, a shuttle glided in on its final approach. It sailed through the wispy Martian atmosphere towards the runway at mind-numbing speed. I didn't hear it until after it landed, when the whoosh and rumble finally reached my ears. Two Earth years had passed since I landed on Mars. A new launch window had opened and shuttles were arriving daily. Three thousand new colonists were arriving, and my job was to ensure we had enough power to support them.

My team expected this shuttle. It carried engineers from the COTS-Bounty, engineers trained to help deal with Martian storms.

It was springtime on Mars, with mid-day temperatures rising to minus thirty degrees Celsius. We were also approaching perihelion, the point in Mars's orbit when it's closest to the sun. This year's storm probability was expected to be particularly high. On Earth, storms were caused by temperature and pressure differentials. On Mars, high-energy particles from the sun caused static electricity to build up in the atmosphere. The static drew the dust upwards where it was circulated by prevailing winds.

I thought of the video that had played on the Mayflower. One line stuck in my mind: If a planet-wide storm were to occur, we should evacuate, but like on the Titanic, there are simply not enough lifeboats.

Hopefully, this would not be true for much longer.

I pulled into my parking spot at the solar panel distribution center, the PDC. The sky appeared Earthly blue through the tinted dome. A cool breeze carried the scent of lilac across the boulevard. There must have been a temperature variance between the neighboring domes. I wondered if the engineers did that on purpose. If so, it was a nice touch.

I stepped inside the building and a hologram waved hello. The holographic receptionist's large eyes gave it a puppy face, despite the lack of nose and slit for a mouth. I had been told it resembled a character from *Astro Boy*, a Japanese cartoon from the 1980's.

"Hey, Linda" I said (all holo-receptionists were named Linda). Linda's eyes focused on my face, irises dilating as the computer ran a facial recognition scan.

"Good morning, John," it replied.

Twin sliding doors led into the core of our operation. I found James Rogers, the plant's foreman, directing some loader drones from a tablet computer. Jimmy was an original member of the infrastructure expansion team and had been on Mars far too long. He had spent his life working with his hands, and Mars was the last of a series of tough jobs. What I did was relatively easy, but Jimmy had been on Mars since the early days.

"How's it going, Jimmy?" I yelled above the hum of the machinery. Jimmy set down the tablet and worked a wrench on a milling machine dedicated to carving out the grid modules that could not be printed.

"Working on the holiday, too, eh? It's Landing Day you know."

Landing Day had been established to celebrate the anniversary of the arrival of the first colonists. Now a planetary holiday, it was celebrated on the Martian year, so it only happened every 668 sols.

Jimmy shook his head. "The unions would never allow this. Working on a holiday? No way, José. Stuff got done when it was done."

"Yeah, well," I said. Knowing what I did about H3, talking about a union sounded like a good way to get kicked off the planet.

"I'm going to take the Pelican. Gotta finish some survey work on the relays for the new residential sector. I want to make sure we're in tip-top shape when we turn on the power." It had been weeks since my last flight, and I really just wanted to get back in the air.

"She's all yours," Jimmy said, flipping his thumb to the hallway leading to the hangar.

I sprinted up the stairs to the pressurized chamber on the hangar deck. Pressure suits hung along one wall, and on the other, a jetway ran alongside the Martian aircraft.

I donned a pressure suit and strode down the jetway. I inspected the yellow Pelican from a picture window. A diagnostic projection on the glass indicated that the Pelican's two lightweight electric turbofan engines were in optimal working condition. A minor defect was detected on the carbon fiber wing, and added to the repair log. But there was nothing that would prevent today's flight.

I strapped in and hit the master-on. Increasing the throttle to full, I released the brake, launching the Pelican along the magnetic track and rocketing from the hangar like a bullet from a gun.

A 270-degree transparent display in the cockpit provided an x-ray view of the colony. It displayed important information like the energy output from each solar array. Most importantly, it monitored the electrolyzers and hydrogen fuel cells, the systems that kept the colony powered when the sun wasn't shining.

We didn't use much nuclear power on Mars. The main reason is that solar is cheaper per kilowatt, but besides that, United Nations Space Law frowned on launching nuclear reactors into space. In 2035, the European nations had successfully negotiated a bill banning reactor launches indefinitely. There was a loophole; if you built the nuclear reactor in deep space, the rule didn't apply. To my knowledge, there was only one reactor kicking around Mars. H3 had had it built, at great expense, for his super-fast spaceship. He kept the reactor as a backup somewhere in the Alamo dome.

I flew north, tagging several unutilized southern-facing hillsides. This told the drones to add panel infrastructure in that area. Harmony Colony was located north of the Martian equator, and these sloping hills gave us optimal coverage.

Assembly drones milled about the front lines of the construction project. The drones looked like insects. Each had six large wheels and several mechanical arms. I tapped a few commands to optimize their routes.

I was about to head back when I noticed something out of the ordinary: a new dome out by the spaceport. It was small, maybe a third the size of the domes in the colony but had several modular buildings connected to it and even had an oversized airlock.

What the hell? I said to myself. How was there construction I don't know about?

Curious, I piloted the craft toward the mysterious dome.

"MATC, this is Pelican Papa Delta Charley, you wouldn't mind if I flew over the spaceport? I'd like to do a systems check on the infrastructure."

"Roger that, Pelican, fly over approved. Residual turbulence from recent shuttle landings should be minimal," the tower replied.

"Copy that."

I flew low and slow over the canyon, parallel to Harmony's two-kilometer suspension bridge. As I got closer, I noticed a canal connecting the spaceport's main terminal to the new dome. Like most canals connecting the domes, it had a flexi-glass roof. Inside the canal, several tan trucks flowed toward the new dome.

I piloted the Pelican lower. A man at the end of the channel waved the trucks into a modular building. He wore a tan uniform and had something slung over his shoulder, which had to be a rifle of some kind. *What the hell?*

I banked lower still, passing within fifty feet of the canal. This time, I could see other people in the channel; some even looked up. These were soldiers! On their backs, they carried the first guns I'd seen since leaving Earth.

I entered the observation deck, still wearing my flight suit. The deck protruded from the south end of the six o'clock dome. Its floor-to-ceiling windows overlooked our staging area and several control consoles enabled us to access the colony's electrical systems. The observation deck was where we coordinated activities out on the surface. It was also our break room.

"Well, shit," Jimmy said after I explained what I had seen. "Someone doesn't watch the news!" he took a sip of coffee and brought up a news report on the HV.

The room's holovision showed Robert Bowden, Harmony's most trusted anchor. Actually, besides social media, he was the colony's only source for news. "Last night, the Martian Transport Constellation II, arrived in orbit. Early this morning, a shuttle carrying one hundred and fifty members of the Multinational Defense Force arrived on Mars for two years of intensive training. Please welcome our guests to our fine colony!"

Kevin came around the corner, removing his work gloves and pouring himself a cup of coffee. He wore a t-shirt with the image of a

Lego moon rover that appeared to drive forward as he walked across the room.

"You working on the holiday, too?" Jimmy asked, scowling at the animation on Kevin's shirt.

"What holiday is it?" Kevin took a sip of his coffee and made a face. He added four creamers and tried it again.

"Landing Day," I said.

"Oh yeah, ah, right. What's up?" Kevin asked, taking another sip and nodding at the coffee, satisfied with his concoction.

"I just got back from a survey flight. Did you know we now have a military base out by the spaceport?"

"Haven't you been watching the news?" Kevin responded. "I think it's kind of cool. Maybe we can go watch the war games from the Look-Off."

"Under what conditions would you ever need to fight in conditions this harsh? Hell, there's not even another colony to fight."

"We could just ask them," Kevin suggested. "There were quite a few military folks here when I arrived on the planet, mostly senior US military officers who lived with us in the circumferential domes. I asked them why they were here, and they said, 'Space is the ultimate high ground.' I guess the U.S. government found it important for them to be here."

Jimmy was shaking his head. "I've been here since the beginning, and yeah, the military comes and goes. But don't you go snooping around. You don't want any trouble."

"Trouble? What does that mean?" I said. "I'm just upset they set up a base without even asking us. Now we have to power that thing!"

"Listen," Jimmy said, pointing at me with his coffee. "The MDF is a private military force; they probably paid big money to be here. Who knows what other back room deals they have going on. Let's stop pretending the corporation has our best interests in mind."

"Listen, Jimbo," I said. "We're just workers on an oil rig in the middle of the ocean. That's it. We do three things, research, mining, and construction so we can do more research and more mining." I was getting worked up. "Do they realize what those weapons could do to a dome?"

"It's flexi-glass, John, and it can take a few hits." Kevin added.

"Uh huh," I responded. "I wouldn't want to risk it."

"It sounds like a fun experiment, though," Kevin said. "How many bullets does it take to breach a dome? You never know when that information will come in handy."

Jimmy rolled his eyes. "C'mon, hippies, it's not the first time we've had war games on Mars. When the Navy Seals were here in 2058, you could feel the concussions in the ground."

Kevin rolled his eyes. "On that note, let's go for a beer."

"At eleven in the morning?" I said.

"It's five o'clock somewhere. And you said it was a holiday," Kevin pointed out, knowing I'd cave. Jimmy just shook his head and walked away.

Chapter 12

KICKED OUT

Kevin and I piled into my SUV and headed to the central dome. When we arrived I told the vehicle to go park itself and we entered the bar. The bar sat on top of Mars's only shopping complex and overlooked the pavilion, a popular hangout for the colony's residents.

"Hey, Power Team!" someone yelled from deep within the bar. I looked through the crowd of people and saw Leeth waving an empty pitcher of beer.

Kevin tapped me on the shoulder and whispered, "Forgot to tell you, Leeth got dumped again."

"Really?" I said, but not entirely surprised. It happened enough that I didn't keep track any more. "Maranda, the COTS shuttle agent?"

Kevin nodded.

"Welcome back to the Mars Bar," Leeth said. "Where've you been? It's almost noon!"

"You okay, Leeth?" I asked. "Kevin told me about Maranda."

"They come and they go, mate."

He seemed to be taking it well.

"What are we drinking?" Kevin asked. "Next round's on me."

"Keith's for me," I answered.

"Victoria Bitter," Leeth said. Kevin nodded, turned and went over to the bar. The beer wasn't imported from Earth, they brewed it here, but they did a fair job simulating the flavors of our favorite beers. The recipe for Alexander Keith's IPA could be traced back almost three hundred years to Halifax, Nova Scotia.

I told Leeth about the new compound out by the spaceport.

"You're not the only one they surprised," Leeth said, taking the last sip from his glass. "That *Defense Force* requested use of *my* clinic."

Kevin returned with the beers. "Look over there," he said, motioning with his eyes.

We watched as four soldiers trickled into the establishment and headed for the bar. "Maybe we can ask them why they're here," Kevin suggested.

"We know why they're here Kevin," I said.

"I want to know why *they* think they're here," Kevin countered. "You know, get the inside scoop. It's not like they're training to fight Martians!"

"You mean aliens," Leeth clarified. "Technically, we're the Martians."

"You're only a Martian if you're born on Mars," I countered.

"I'm going to find out!" Kevin said, setting his beer down on the table and walking up to a soldier twice his size. Based on his lapel, he was a sergeant. "Excuse me, sir," Kevin said, his accent stronger than usual. He must have been nervous. "Excuse me, why are you here?"

"We're here for the beer, kid," the sergeant muttered. "Haven't had a decent brew in months."

Kevin came back to our table. "They're here for the beer," he reported.

"Yeah, we heard him," I said.

Leeth started to get up. "I want to talk to them."

"Oh, no, don't you go over there." I put out a hand to stop him, but Leeth shook it off and went over anyway.

Kevin looked at me. "I think Leeth's already drunk."

Leeth tapped the man on the shoulder. "Mind if I buy you guys a drink?" he asked. The sergeant shrugged.

Leeth got the bartender's attention. We watched as he poured a line of shots. "This is going to get messy," I muttered. I'd dragged Leeth from the colony's drunk tank on several occasions. Enough times that I knew Captain Daniels, the colony's chief of police.

Kevin's watch vibrated and he looked at it and frowned. Lack of real time communication with Earth was difficult for all of us. Even when Earth and Mars were at their closest, a message traveling at the speed of light took almost four minutes to make the trip.

"What's up?" I asked.

"Message from home," he replied. "My grandmother's been sick. The doctors don't think she'll make it through the year."

"Tell me about her," I said, setting my beer aside for a moment. When bad things happened on far-away Earth, there wasn't anything a colonist could do about it. People on Mars had learned to stop everything and listen when someone had a family emergency. It was considered incredibly rude if you didn't.

"I called her Dadi, which means 'Father's mother.' My dad worked for the ISRO, but Dadi got me excited about space. She's why I became an engineer. We'd watch sci-fi shows and put together Lego spaceships. You know, the ones that actually hovered on a bed of magnets?" Kevin made a flying motion with his hand.

"I never had that set, always wanted it though."

"It's tough, being on Mars. Not being there for your friends and family back home." Kevin took a sip of his beer. "I regret not seeing my sister's graduation or being there for my dad when he was in the hospital. It's times like this when a ten-minute comm delay seems like an eternity."

I just nodded at this. I'd only sent a few messages back to Earth, and I didn't care much for the replies. My mother kept asking me to come home, as if we'd suddenly become close if I did.

Leeth came back to the seat holding the soldiers' berets. "Dude, what the hell," Kevin said.

Leeth shrugged, giving Kevin a sideways smile. "They starting imitating my accent, called me a ratbag. I thought it'd be funny!" Leeth said.

"Give'em back, Leeth," I said, as the soldiers approached our table. "You're outnumbered."

Leeth got up and turned around, bumping into the stocky corporal as he did.

Kevin sighed. "Drinking brings out the worst in people," he said.

"Careful, buddy!" Leeth yelled, slurring his speech.

"Ratbag," the corporal said, shoving Leeth on the shoulder. Leeth turned and connected with an uppercut. We heard a loud "click" as teeth snapped together. For a moment, the soldier just stood there stunned.

The soldier came around, striking Leeth in the mouth. After spitting a glob of blood onto the floor, he hit back, chopping the young soldier in the neck. The corporal coughed and stepped back, his hands to his throat.

"Dude, what are you doing!" Kevin yelled.

Leeth spat again, picked up the hats and threw them at the soldiers. This time, two soldiers tackled him, taking Leeth's arms and throwing him across the room. Leeth flew across the bar, tumbling awkwardly in the low gravity and knocking into several unoccupied tables.

Leeth hit a wall and slid to the floor. Someone whistled and the bar went silent. It was the sergeant; he stood there, removing his fingers from his mouth. I ran over to Leeth, who was borderline unconscious, and pulled him up into a seated position.

"What the hell?" Kevin said, facing the sergeant. The sergeant reached over and pinched Kevin's collar, crushing the chip governing the animation on Kevin's shirt. Kevin brushed him off, and stumbled back toward Leeth and me.

The bartender stepped between us. "Just get the hell out before I call the police," he said, and then pointed at a seemingly unconscious Leeth. "And tell your friend not to come back."

I dragged Leeth to his feet and carried him out of the bar. Kevin grabbed his other arm and we helped him down the stairs to the pavilion. Several soldiers milled about, apparently enjoying the open atmosphere after being cooped up in the transport. Two squad cars pulled into the pavilion and four cops began jogging toward the bar. I guess someone called them anyway. I pulled Leeth into an alley and out of sight.

Leeth opened his left eye. His right eye was swollen shut. "Applebee's, anyone?" he asked.

Kevin gave him a dirty look. "Shut up, Leeth."

After getting Leeth to his apartment and onto his couch, I headed home for some rest. I looked out my living room window, taking in the intricacies of the Martian Landscape. Rock ledges jutted from distant ridges while the memories of ancient riverbeds etched in channels of polished stone. The sun shone on the solar arrays in the hills as drone trucks moved in and out of the mining bunkers. The view actually reminded me of Las Vegas.

I grabbed a slice of leftover pizza and a ginger ale from the fridge and sat down on a fiber-plastic couch. I just closed my eyes, happy to be home in the peace and quiet. After lunch, I planned to take a long nap before meeting Leeth and Kevin for the Landing Day festivities.

The main event was a movie projected on the roof of the central dome, a documentary of Mars's colonization. The old hands said it was really cool and something not to miss. The central dome essentially became the solar system's largest planetarium.

I'd seen the show before but not on the big screen. The documentary began sixty years ago, when most people believed a manned mission to Mars was impossible. There were some great quotes from people like Elon Musk, "Fortunately, the people who said it couldn't be done didn't impede the people doing it."

It included the footage from 2031, when the first humans landed on Mars. The mission was short by our standards, the astronauts spending only forty days on the surface. After that, it documented the mission of 2035 where astronauts and cosmonauts spent a year on the surface. Their goal was to prepare Mars for colonization by learning to live off the land. The video ended with the launch of the first construction drones in 2040, when Harmony Colony began to take shape.

I opened my eyes and took a bite of the pizza. My watch buzzed, a text from the company: *New PDC employee. Pick up at spaceport immediately.*

A new employee? Between Kevin, Jimmy and I, we had power management down to a science.

Name? I texted back, not expecting an answer from whoever was in charge. I didn't get a response. Most of our assignments didn't come from any specific person; we just got instructions from "Corporate." I had always been okay with ambiguity, but on Mars, it was a constant. As employees of Red Planet Mining, we just had to learn to roll with it.

I put my lunch back in the fridge and drove to the spaceport. I pulled up to the curb in front of the terminal and stepped out onto the sidewalk.

"You're late!" someone yelled. A tall man limped towards me. He had obviously come from space and was getting used to gravity again. The sun reflected off a vehicle behind him, and I couldn't see his face.

"Yeah, sorry, I was in the three o'clock dome. It's a long drive." I paused. *I know that voice.* I picked up my pace toward the man, fighting back tears.

"Good to see you, too, Johnny!" Avro said.

We hugged, clapping each other on the back.

I grabbed one of Avro's wheeled suitcases. "I'm speechless. Why didn't you let me know you were coming?"

"I wanted it to be a surprise."

"Well, you succeeded," I said, dropping Avro's suitcase in the SUV's front trunk.

We pulled away from the spaceport and Avro filled me in on his last two years. "I was stationed in San Diego. Eventually, the Cartel's guerrilla war stagnated and there wasn't any progress on any front, but no one was getting hurt either. To tell you the truth, it was boring."

"Were there any more survivors?" I asked. "Civilians, I mean."

"A few," Avro replied, "Literally, a few, as in three."

"What's it, like, in California?"

"Bad. It seems like everyone in the occupied territory actually wants to be there. The Cartel is actually trying to secede."

"So it's basically Somalia seventy years ago," I said.

"Basically," he replied. "So anyway, six months ago I was recruited by Red Planet. They patched into my HV with their sales pitch right as I was preparing to go on leave. I was planning to go east, maybe meet a girl, settle down and raise a family. When I got the call, I thought, 'okay, I've got time for one more adventure.' But I had one condition."

"What was that?" I asked.

"I asked to work with you," Avro said. "You were the best wingman a guy could ask for, and I'd be honored to fly with you again."

I was flattered, and I admit, the thought of Avro on the team made me very happy.

"The PDC team was only assigned one plane," I said. There were others, of course, but shipping anything to Mars was so expensive that our backup aircraft was shared between several departments.

Avro smiled. "Not anymore."

CHAPTER 13

SPECIAL REQUEST

Early the next morning, Kevin and I arrived at the PDC's observation deck, mildly hungover from the prior evening's festivities. Avro was already there, coffee in hand. He had stayed home the previous night, using the time to get settled in. I introduced him to Kevin and they shook hands.

Kevin and I stepped closer to the window and looked down onto the PDC's tarmac at a machine that looked like a bulbous spider.

Avro joined us at the window. "This is the MVA, the Martian Vertical Aircraft. It's nicknamed the Arachnid. Basically, it's a helicopter for Mars. That array of thrusters provides the lift." Avro pointed at eight arches that emanated from the top of the fuselage like the legs of a spider.

"That thing is sweet!" Kevin said. "Can I fly it?"

Avro looked at Kevin, glancing at another of his holographic t-shirts. "Sure, I'll give you a shot at the left seat. It's pretty automated, basically flies itself."

"This is really something," I said, admiring the craft. The fuselage of the Arachnid resembled a medevac helicopter with large, sliding doors on each side. "I guess the company's looking to increase our productivity. This'll sure beat driving out to the array."

"Exactly," Avro said. "With this aircraft we can get anywhere in the colony in under five minutes. The Arachnid can haul up to eighteen Martian tons of equipment; that's enough to carry a construction drone.

It can fly pressurized, or unpressurized, making EVAs much—"

"We call them GODs," Kevin interrupted.

"No, we don't," I countered.

"Going Outside Dome," Kevin clarified. "You know, a GOD."

"Anyway," Avro said. "Want to go for a test flight? Just remember, I've only trained in the simulator. This will be my first time flying the actual aircraft."

"God, yes," I said. Two years flying just the Pelican had me eager to experience a new aircraft.

Kevin looked at me, "Why can you say GOD?" he said, then turned to Avro. "And it's your first time?"

"Don't worry, Kevin," I said. "Avro can fly anything."

Our watches buzzed, summoning us to the conference room. The test flight would have to wait. We grabbed our coffees and headed in.

I sat down at a desk in the conference room followed by Jimmy, Avro and Kevin. After the morning pleasantries, we turned and faced the floor-to-ceiling display at the front of the room.

The image of a 1960s era rotary phone flashed on the screen, signaling the incoming call. Jimmy leaned forward tapped an icon in the center of the table, accepting the call.

The call came from Environmental Engineering, the newly arrived team tasked with mitigating the storms. They were headquartered in the observation dome to the northeast of the colony, sharing the dome with the Zubrin Research Station and enjoying some of Harmony Colony's best views.

"Morning, boys, great to see ya," a man on the screen adjusted the camera. He spoke with a smile and an accent I couldn't quite place. Irish, perhaps?

"Good morning," Jimmy said. He leaned back in his seat, putting his feet up on the table. "Welcome to Mars."

"I'm Jeff Watson, the new senior environmental engineer."

Watson looked fit. He must have spent five hours a day in the transport's gym. Unlike the blue jeans and white shirts most of us wore at work, Watson's clothes appeared tailored. His hair was meticulously styled, which made me wonder if Mars had a new barber.

I introduced the others, Avro last.

"Avro, like the Arrow?" Watson asked, with genuine curiosity in his voice.

"How do you know about that?" Avro asked, a big smile suddenly crossing his face.

"The Avro Arrow was one of the first fighter jets to reach Mach two. Canadians are very proud of that aircraft." That explained Watson's accent and his friendliness.

Avro continued the history lesson. "And when the Avro Arrow program was canceled, many of the engineers moved to Los Angeles to work for Lockheed Martin. My grandmother was one of them. It's where she met my grandfather."

"So why did you call us?" Jimmy said.

"We have a solution for the storms. And we need your help," Watson said. "The plan involves electrical power. And lots of it."

"We've got the electricity. How much do you need?" I said.

"Well, let me explain how we're going to do it and then we'll discuss our power needs. Can you see the presentation?" The screen faded to a map of the planet. Watson's picture moved to a small box on the top left. We nodded the affirmative. After eighty years of PowerPoint, there was still the occasional issue.

"Yes? Okay. Good, let's get started," Watson said, clearing his throat. "So: static electricity is the problem."

"Static electricity builds up during periods of increased solar activity, creating storms," Kevin said in a news anchor voice. "Pretend we're not idiots and tell us what you need."

Watson smiled, and I knew he was a politician through and through.

I said, "Don't mind Kevin. He forgot to pack polite when he left Earth."

"Not a problem," Watson said. "Let's move on."

On the screen, an animation showed a solar flare billowing through space. When the fiery cloud approached Mars, the video switched to a surface view of Mars, showing a plume of dust lifting off the ground.

"In order to fight the storms, we need to dissipate the static charge."

"Counteract the Sun's radiation?" Avro interrupted. "You're talking about completely geo-engineering the climate. How do you expect to use electricity on a dust storm when our electricity comes from solar?"

Watson smiled again and leaned forward as if he was about to say something profound. "Please, this will all make sense in a moment." A map of Mars appeared on the screen. "Our team carried with us a series of coils that will produce an opposing charge in the atmosphere. When laid out in the right pattern, the coils will completely remove the planet's ability to produce storms of any magnitude."

Watson paused, then announced, "We call it Project Bakersfield."

The next slide showed a rotating view of Mars from space. Running from north to south, along the lines of longitude, was a series of red bands making Mars look like a crater-covered basketball.

"These red bands represent the anti-storm coils. They circle the entire planet providing a defensive shield against any increase in solar radiation, eliminating the possibility of a static-induced storm."

Avro and I looked at each other, then back at the screen, which displayed another animation. The scale of what he was describing was massive.

"As you can see, the coils are distributed from these trucks. The distribution method is similar to laying deep sea cable."

An animation showed a large yellow truck towing a rotating drum. As the truck moved along the surface, it laid the coil behind it.

"We've assembled ten of these trucks, each capable of laying coil at ten kilometers per hour. We'll be laying one hundred thousand kilometers in all. With some simple math, you can see that we'll lay the entire network in only six weeks."

"Sounds like a pretty good plan," I said. "Where do we come in?"

Watson closed the presentation and his image again filled the screen.

"First, you need to connect Project Bakersfield to the grid."

"Sounds easy enough," Kevin said. "There's an extension cord in the garage."

I looked over at Avro, watching him pinch his temples.

"Moving on, we have permission from H3 to install a relay to the nuclear reactor in the Alamo, so the system can be used at night, although at an extremely reduced level of efficiency. Compared to the new solar array you're about to build, the nuclear reactor will be a drop in the bucket."

"So who gets to work with the folks in the Alamo?" I asked. "We've never had any interaction with them before."

"I will be your liaison with the Alamo," Watson answered.

"You've been to the Alamo?" Kevin asked. "Most people we meet from there don't talk about it."

"I have, actually. It's very nice," Watson said.

"That's it? It's nice?" Kevin said.

"Finally," Watson said, "the question you've all been waiting for." Watson paused. I think he was trying to size us up or just trying to determine if we were competent at all.

"How much power do you need?" I asked.

"Project Bakersfield requires five gigawatts of power."

"Five gigawatts?" Kevin shook his head.

"Okay, question time. Yes. We're talking about geoengineering the atmosphere of a planet. But we're also very good at math. You'll have capacity by the time the trucks have completed laying the cable."

"Oh, yeah? And how do you figure that?" I asked.

A grin spread across Watson's face. "Because we've got a warehouse with five gigawatts of panels just waiting to be installed."

CHAPTER 14

UNDERGROUND SECRETS

Working on deploying five gigawatts of solar panels in six weeks gave us a weird feeling. Maybe it was the fact that we were asked to do six months work in only six weeks. Something was off about Project Bakersfield and we weren't sure what.

Every morning we arrived at the PDC before sunrise. I'd spent more time in a spacesuit in the last two weeks then I did in the previous year. Kevin continued to insist that we change the spacewalking abbreviation from EVA to GOD.

The logistics of the operation went like this: a flatbed drone arrived before sunrise stocking our distribution center with panels. At the same time, our machine shop printed parts for making ad hoc repairs to the grid. If nothing went wrong, our construction drones would take the panels from the PDC and install them out on the surface. It was simple if nothing went wrong, but something always went wrong.

Two weeks into the operation we prepared for our busiest day yet. By the time I arrived at work, we had seven stuck drones, three misaligned solar arrays, and a rogue support structure.

I was in the observation deck, going over the colony's power consumption reports when I noticed a massive spike in the Alamo's usage. The Alamo had tripled its consumption overnight, dipping into the colony's reserves.

I patched in a call to their engineering department. "Hey, John

Orville here at the PDC. What's going on over there? Your power consumption is off the charts!"

"Ah, yeah, about that. We're ah… we've just built some additional reserve hydrogen tanks, we're filling them now. You're probably seeing the residual spike from the electrolyzers." Electrolyzers used electricity to split water into hydrogen and oxygen. His story was plausible but I didn't buy it. He sounded like he was lying.

"Ah okay," I said. "How much hydrogen are you making?"

"Don't know sir, but I can find out," he said.

"You do that. PDC out."

Avro and Kevin were already getting into their spacesuits for the day's activities. I joined them and began suiting up, as well. We sealed the connection rings on our spacesuits and stepped into the PDC's airlock. The airlock opened just in time to watch the sun rise over the distant hills. Unlike Earth, where sunrises shine in pinks and yellows, Martian sunrises radiate blues and grays, making for a very alien looking sky.

Kevin attached a utility rover to the underside of the Arachnid's abdomen. I made sure we had the right tools on board while Avro completed the preflight activities, including fueling the Arachnid and topping off oxygen.

With the pre-work complete, Avro strapped himself into the pilot's seat, I took the copilot's chair, and Kevin sat in the jump seat.

"MATC, comm check, over," Avro said while buckling his harness over his bulky spacesuit.

"MVA, this is MATC, we read you five by five," Mars Air Traffic Control replied. "What's your destination, over?"

"MATC, we're headed to the eastern ridge to work on some panel repairs."

"Be advised, there will be MDF training activities on the eastern plains."

"Copy, we'll try to stay out of their way."

Avro activated the Arachnid. Pyramid-shaped blue flames licked from the eight thrusters like pilot lights on a stove. Avro grasped the collective throttle control, lifting the craft into the morning sky.

The Arachnid kicked up a plume of dust and the colony sank beneath us. We headed east, into the sunrise. Avro and I pulled down the sunshades on our suits, adding more hues to the already colorful sky.

Avro landed five kilometers from the colony on the shoulder of a service highway that ran below the ridge. We hopped out of the Arachnid and went to work.

Nearby, a defective construction drone twitched. Kevin went over to it, attempting a reboot. He was the planet's lead expert in human-drone interface. After about thirty seconds, the drone sprang to life and rolled away.

Avro slid open the aircraft's door and undid the tie-downs holding our equipment in place. I disconnected the rover from the aircraft and booted up a tablet displaying the location of the misaligned panels.

With the supplies placed onto the rover, Kevin drove the vehicle up the hill while Avro and I trudged after him.

Despite the low gravity, the climb was exhausting. By the time we reached the lower array, Avro and I were both breathing heavily. This wasn't a problem, since we knew we could tap into the O2 tank on the side of the Arachnid.

With no spaces between the solar panels, the upper ridge looked like one giant sheet of glass. The panels were fifteen feet up, accessible using a ladder. We walked through the supports as if they were trees, the array covering us like a forest canopy.

Kevin took a moment to admire the view from the edge of our synthetic forest.

"Gotta love the pink sky," I said, tapping commands into the tablet and looking up at the solar panels.

"Pink sky in the morning, Martians take warning. Pink sky at night, Martians delight." Kevin rhymed, pulling a ladder from the rover.

"This is Mars, boss," Avro said, "The sky is always pink. You can't take warning and simultaneously take delight."

"Sure you can," Kevin said, leaning the ladder against a support beam and stepping on the first rung. "Hey guys, check it out!"

In the valley, several grey trucks rolled into view and a few dozen MDF troops piled out. You would have thought their dark blue spacesuits would contrast with Mars's red soil, but they didn't. The dark coloring helped them blend into the shadows created by large boulders on the plain. That gave me a bit of a chill: someone had given this a lot of thought, and if they were really training for some kind of Earth action, why would they have bothered?

In the distance, scores of airborne targeting drones buzzed over the horizon and towards the troops.

"Looks like a live fire exercise," Avro said.

"And we've got the best view in the house!" Kevin said. The drones circled and kicked up dust as the soldiers dove for cover behind large rocks and launched smoke grenades to confuse the drones.

"What's the range on their ammo?" I asked, worried not only for our safely, but for the grid.

"They're using self-destructing shells," Avro replied. "The bullets have a range, usually a half a mile, and break apart once they reach that distance."

"This is quite something," I said as we stopped our work to watch the show. The soldiers were over a mile away and at least several hundred feet below us. They fired at the drones, which fell from the sky in fiery plumes. When the soldiers had taken out that wave of drones, we watched as they carried one of their comrades on a stretcher, loading the fallen solider into a medevac drone. The medevac lifted into the sky, and zipped back towards the colony.

Next, a wave of spider-like drones poured over the ridge. This time the soldiers came out from their cover and started shooting the things to pieces. The mechanical beasts jumped around, moving quickly through the barrage of bullets. Some of the spiders made it through, leaping on top of the soldiers, and their victims convulsed as if being electrocuted. Their comrades eliminated the rest of the wave. There were more stretchers, and more medevacs.

The next wave of attackers came on two legs, looking like headless kangaroos. They flanked the soldiers, traveling in a pack, and running at cheetah-like speed. The herd ran up one ridge and down another. The MDF soldiers changed positions around the boulders, running from one rock to the next, trying to flank the attackers.

I could see several soldiers activating their comms, calling in an artillery barrage. Shells dropped down on the battlefield, taking out several of the scrawny beasts, leaving large craters in their wake.

The kangaroo drones swept west, adjusting to the platoon's new position.

"Shit!" I said. The Arachnid was at the bottom of the hill, "The Arachnid!" The drones swooped around and the herd passed over where our aircraft was parked.

We started running down the hill waving our hands. Kevin hopped into the rover and started after us.

At this point the soldiers were surrounded. They opened fire on the drones in all directions. Several of them fell but the bullets sprayed everywhere. We took cover behind the rover even though none of the projectiles made it up the hill. Instead, each bullet self-destructed in a cloud several hundred feet away. I keyed the frequency for Central

Control. “Central this is PDC, we need you to call the MDF and have them halt their training until we can evac –“

Before I could finish, a stream of high-powered bullets ripped through the Arachnid, puncturing the fuel tanks and shattering the cockpit. The bullets passed through the machine, leaving little puffs of dust in the dirt on the opposite side.

The dust settled, blown away in the breeze. The drones forced the soldiers east, leaving us alone with our pokey rover and bullet-riddled Arachnid.

I opened the map-app on my tablet and zoomed in on our location, looking for a good extraction point. If we could relay the information to the colony, they’d be able to send a rescue party.

Avro tapped his wrist and spoke. “Panel team to Central Control, do you copy?”

No answer.

“Try MATC,” I said. “Frequency 1880.”

Avro switched frequencies on his wrist panel.

“MATC, this is the panel distro team. We are stranded five kilometers to the northeast. Do you copy?”

We checked all our comm units. None of us had any signal.

“That’s funny. It looks like the frequencies are jammed,” Kevin said.

“Not all the frequencies. We can still talk to each other,” I said. “But our VOX comms are super short range.”

We turned and saw an automated mining truck barreling down the road.

Avro and I looked at each other. “Well, it beats walking,” Avro said.

I stood in front of the truck and it slowed down. Avro and Kevin climbed a few rungs up a ladder leading to the truck bed. They grabbed a handrail and clung to the truck like garbage men. I jogged around the side of the truck and hopped up to join them. The truck continued on its way.

We rounded a large rock and the road sloped down into a mining bunker.

I leaned around the side of the truck, trying to get a better look at our direction of travel.

"Looks like we're headed into a mine. They should have O2 stations and a hard line to the colony. Heck, the mines are interconnected, right? We can probably walk back to the colony without the spacesuits."

"Wouldn't that be nice," Kevin said, "walking through town in our underwear."

⚡

The light dwindled as we moved deeper underground. We turned on our spacesuit lights and were surprised that we couldn't yet see a door or airlock.

"Okay, guys. I'm getting concerned," Kevin said, checking his O2 levels. "We're a quarter mile into this bunker and haven't reached an airlock."

Avro panned his suit lights around the walls. "The entrance can't be much farther."

"There it is," I said. I illuminated a giant door with my light.

"Thank Shiva! Worst GOD ever!" Kevin said as the truck lumbered into the airlock.

The airlock's interior was polished steel and shone as if newly installed.

The hatch behind us sucked itself shut and lights came on, filling the room with an orange glow. The three of us dismounted the truck and stood as a windy whirlpool swirled around us, cleansing everything of the Martian dust.

Once the room had ample pressure, the hatch hissed open and the truck rolled out. We should have seen the darkness of a mine. Instead, we were blinded by light.

We stood in the airlock, peeking out the door, helmets clinking together as we all tried to get a better look.

One by one, we stepped out and took off our helmets. A warm sun beat down on our heads as birds chirped. High above us, a falcon circled. I tried to get a look at the nearest wall, but it was hidden behind a large oak tree.

"Well, I'll be damned," Avro said. From the look of it, the space was enclosed in a giant dome, one as big or bigger than the colony's central dome. Nestled in the trees were buildings that looked like Italian villas.

"This explains the power drain," I said. "They must have just turned it on. Whatever this place is, I'm willing to bet this caused the Alamo's power surge this morning."

"I don't see a welcoming party," Avro observed. "We might as well check it out!"

We walked across a glade and a large fountain and amphitheater came into view.

"You know," I began, "We've all heard the silly rumors of an Atlantis on Mars, but this is something else. There's probably a pretty damn good reason this place is kept secret."

"Yeah," Kevin said, "they don't want us stomping on the azaleas."

We walked down a tree-lined path and other structures came into view.

"Agreed," Avro said. "These residences seem really nice and I don't think this is part of our pension plan."

We paused as a thumping sound echoed around us. The thumping increased in volume until a black helicopter passed overhead. The chopper circled once and landed in a clearing. As it settled to the ground, four men in black fatigues jumped out, guns in hand.

We stood in our spacesuits like snowmen, each with a helmet under his arm.

"Should we run?" Kevin asked.

I pictured us wobbling like penguins in our spacesuits, trying to outrun a team of soldiers.

Resistance was futile.

Chapter 15

H3

"Get in," one man said, motioning toward the chopper with his gun. We boarded the helicopter and sat along the back wall. Avro and I sat on the outside with one leg dangling out each door. Kevin sat in the middle, his gloved hands holding his helmet firmly on his lap.

The helicopter ride gave us new perspective of this underground utopia. The habitat wasn't devoid of people, although it wasn't overflowing either. There was a couple out for a stroll holding hands, a woman jogging, and even kids riding gyro-bikes.

I pointed them out to Avro. He was as surprised as I was. The low Martian gravity interfered with proper bone growth, so there were typically no children on Mars. But there they were.

"Maybe they spend a few hours a day in a centrifuge," Avro said.

"Like a ride at the fair," Kevin added.

Just then we flew over a small amusement park, complete with a variety of spinning rides.

I pointed at one of the rides. "Well, there you have it."

"Save it!" snorted one of the men.

The helicopter landed on the front lawn of a large estate. Manicured shrubs swayed in the helicopter's draft, fighting to hold onto their roots. Our captors herded us from the helicopter, leading us to a set of stairs. At the top of the staircase was the front door of a multi-story mansion.

One of the men pressed a button by the door.

"Send them up," a voice said.

We entered a great hall. The room had high ceilings, giant chandeliers and fine art on every wall. There were several expensive looking sculptures and even a few tapestries. On the far wall, a fifteen-foot-tall wax Napoleon Bonaparte stood victorious over a sea of bodies. Four glass elevators along the back wall connected balconies on each level.

The guards ushered us across the room and shoved us into an elevator. When we got to the top, they shoved us out and directed us through a set of mahogany doors into a large room. They seemed to enjoy shoving.

The room had a domed ceiling inlaid with stained glass tigers and other beasts. The room was round and surrounded by bookshelves. A ladder riding on a brass track ran all the way around.

A large mahogany desk rested near the back of the room. On this desk, a brass reading light illuminated a leather writing pad and a pen.

Behind the desk, Henry Allen the Third, better known as H3, sat in the largest wing back chair I had ever seen.

He had flawlessly styled brown hair without a hint of a receding hairline. I knew he was in his late fifties, but thanks to expensive stem-cell treatments, he didn't look a day over forty. He wore a three-piece navy blue tailored shirt with a baby blue tie and gold cufflinks. Round glasses rested on a perfectly shaped nose. His ears, however, were small, and for some reason, I found this amusing.

H3 smirked, a closed mouth smile that gave him a look of being impressed and not impressed at the same time.

"Welcome boys! Welcome! I'm sure you know who I am, so let's skip the introductions," he said, his face returning to a smirk. "What, may I ask, is that dreadful noise?" His head twitched as he accented the final word.

"Huh? Oh, sorry!" Kevin said as we became aware of our spacesuits.

Spacesuits are effectively small spaceships, with heating units and oxygen systems. Ours even had gyroscopic stabilizers. All of these made subtle noises in the otherwise silent room.

We went to work throwing switches, powering down the suit's electronics, silencing the whirring songs of various pumps and gizmos.

"Better?" Kevin asked.

"Much better," H3 replied. "So John, Kevin and Avro, how's my power team doing? You know you are the most experienced engineers on the planet? Granted, you have little competition, but still."

"You looked us up?" I asked.

H3 smiled and nodded, tapping a tablet he held in his palm. "Few folks find themselves outside the colony. It's been easy to keep this place a secret."

"Well," Kevin said, "We found it, now you have to kill us."

H3 laughed. "Very funny, Kevin. The truth is, I need you guys. You're my power team! Literally *my* power team. You are the guys that give me the power!"

"Yeah, I did notice that your energy draw was rather heavy," I said. "Your engineers said they were filling hydrogen tanks."

"They were," H3 replied. "We just activated this place today. Sorry for not letting you know about the tanks. Better to ask forgiveness than permission, as they say. I'll be using my reactor to power this place, so you'll not have to worry about capacity for my little pet project."

H3 grinned, like a smile without the twinkle in the eye that makes it genuine. It was like he was waiting to see if we bought his story.

"This place must cost a fortune to operate." I said. We all knew the cost to fuel and operate a reactor was far greater than the cost of solar.

"Fortunes I have, and the reactor is reliable. Think of it as storm insurance. And speaking of storm insurance, I need to send you back to work. Project Bakersfield must be completed before summer."

"You mean we're not even getting fired?" Kevin asked. "Your private security detail made it seem like we stumbled on Area 51."

"You aren't getting fired," H3 said. "You think I'd send my top engineers all the way back to Earth and recruit new engineers with three weeks left before we deploy the largest atmospheric engineering project in history?"

"I guess we are quite good at our jobs," Kevin said. "The pay's okay, but the benefits make it worth it."

Avro and I looked at each other and shook our heads.

H3 paced around the office, looking solemn. "Since you're here, you might as well know why *I'm* here. As you may or may not know, Red Planet Mining's stock price took quite a hit after the impact."

"That's an understatement," Avro said. "It dropped, what, eighty percent?"

"That's about right," H3 admitted. "Fortunately, many of my friends had shorted the stock, profiting substantially from the decline."

"Insider trading?" I said. The words slipped out before I could hold my tongue. No one could have known about the Bradbury Disaster.

"No, not insider trading, John. Production was already ramping down from project Destiny. But the street didn't take our decline seriously and investors were slow to sell, many even doubled down, buying the stock on margin, and now they blame me, and my friends, for their losses."

"So that's why you're on Mars," I said.

"Precisely," H3 said. "With our wealth, my associates and I purchased several space cruisers and a few shuttles, outfitting them with the luxuries required for a new life here on Mars."

"You're talking about over half the space infrastructure in the solar system!" I said.

"Don't underestimate wealth," H3 replied. "That's the benefit of capitalism. There's nothing to stop those with cash from buying up all the assets."

Was he really lecturing us on economics?

"We used much of our wealth, however, to fund this," H3 said, panning his arm around the room. "We call it The Presidio, after that old base in San Francisco, God rest its soul. The inspiration comes from Athens in ancient Greece. We even have a Parthenon!"

"How..." I said, not sure if I was asking a question.

"We converted a mine," H3 said, matter-of-factly. "The mining operation creates giant underground caverns. We just cleaned one up."

"*Clean* is an understatement. This place is heaven on Earth," Avro said.

"Well, Heaven on Mars anyway," I added.

"Thank you," H3 said. "However, *this* heaven is only accessible to those in the Alamo."

The Alamo, it seemed, was the tip of a very large iceberg.

H3 continued to pace around the room, delighted to be sharing his accomplishment with listening ears. "The Presidio is a large underground dome. Its ceiling is half a kilometer high and its perimeter ten kilometers around. Like a planetarium, a giant projection illuminates our sky." He stopped for a moment staring out a window and up at the sky. "You arrived here a few hours late. It was quite the show when we turned it on. The software is simple, basic astronomy software really."

"Impressive," I said.

"Oh, what the hell. We've been testing it all day. Check this out." H3 opened a door onto a rooftop patio and we followed him outside.

H3 typed on his tablet, darkening the sky and ceasing the warmth from the artificial sun. Then, the first stars appeared and the Milky Way cut across the sky in time lapse, right before a glorious sunrise. It was so bright I had to look away but I could feel its warmth on my face.

"The colonists think they are seeing mining equipment going down into the mines, but it's actually wealth, rare treasures from Earth's most priceless collections. Those statues on the grounds," H3 was gloating now, "they're originals, straight from Italy. We've even been buying up Picassos. Most estates have at least one."

We were speechless. This was a truly amazing accomplishment.

"Here's the deal," H3 said with a stern look. "You are going back to work. You are going to finish Project Bakersfield, and you're not going tell anyone about this place."

"Why the secrecy?" I asked.

"This place is a great experiment, free from the radiation and cramped quarters of the surface. But not everyone can live here and I don't want to attract attention. That's why."

"Who runs this place?" Kevin said. "Like, support staff and stuff."

"The drones, Kevin. It takes very few workers to run a society these days, and that's really what's so wonderful about it. But I'll never allow freelivers here; you've got to earn it."

"If all the work is done by drones, what are people like us supposed to do?"

"You seem like a smart kid, Kevin. There's always work for the working men. And right now, you have a job and I want you to keep doing it."

"That's going to be difficult," Avro said.

H3 looked confused and I could tell he was hiding a hint of anger.

"It was the MDF soldiers. They ah, sort of, shot up our Arachnid," I said.

H3 seemed to relax at this and then chuckled. "I'll tell you what, guys. I'll give you a new one."

He handed me his tablet, a confidentiality agreement displayed on the screen. I passed the tablet to Avro. He rolled his eyes and pressed his finger down on the device.

⚡

H3's private security escorted us back into the helicopter and flew us to the far side of the Presidio. It was an engineering marvel as impressive as the colony. As we flew further from H3's mansion, we could see at least a hundred estates poking out from above the trees.

"Hey, where did these trees come from?" I asked. The trees were tall. They obviously didn't come on the Martian transports and couldn't have been grown there from seedlings.

"3D printed," the man said, "like everything else in this shithole."

"What climbed up your ass and died?" Kevin said. "At least you get to live here."

"We don't live here," another guard grunted.

The helicopter landed on a pad near the wall of the complex.

We stepped down from the helicopter and entered a hyper-tube car. The car was the size of two buses parked side by side. Its roof was a display, extending the "sky" of the Presidio. Couches and chairs filled the interior and it looked like an upscale lounge.

Like regular folks riding the metro, the three of us sat on a couch, facing forward, helmets on our laps. Holovisions popped up in front of us as we sat down. My HV showed a video of a honey badger, Kevin's an aerial view of Seattle, and Avro's a Japanese village. Looking directly at the display immersed us in these locations. Kevin was the first to put his hands together in a silent clap, issuing the universal command to shut off the system. Avro and I did the same.

Kevin seemed happy to have been on this little adventure and was eager to summarize. "Okay, so our aircraft was destroyed by a freak kangaroo drone accident. We crawled across the surface of Mars, stumbled into some sort of freakish mirage and met the king of Mars. The king, though angry, freed us, and sent us home in an oversized pontoon boat."

The tube-car came to a stop in what looked like the lobby of a Ritz Carlton. Passersby looked in to see three gentlemen in spacesuits. A group of women in cocktail dresses stuck their noses up and walked away, and some people pointed, tapping others on the shoulder.

"The circumferential channel is right out those doors," the guard said.

"Can you at least summon us a car?" Kevin asked. "I forgot my wallet."

"No."

We didn't wear pants under our spacesuits, so taking them off wasn't an option. To top it off, *one* of us had urinated in the suit's diapers.

We walked out of the station and looked around, standing in a pavilion larger than the one in the central dome. You could now count us among the few individuals who had seen the Alamo with their own eyes. It wasn't like the rest of the colony. The interior looked more like a shopping mall than anything else. Unlike the domes in the circumferential, with buildings and roads, the Alamo was a solitary structure.

"That explains why the Alamo isn't transparent," Avro said, looking around in every direction.

"Those look like condos," I commented, pointing at the structure's exterior. "I bet those places have killer views!" Multiple levels of elevated walkways led to the condos with escalators situated at various intervals. People in business suits walked from place to place, holding tablets in one hand and lattes in the other.

"These people look like boring office workers!" Kevin observed. I nodded my agreement, although they also looked rich.

A stylish woman in her early forties walked up to us. She looked friendly until she opened her mouth. "Get out," she said, "you don't belong here."

"Well, a happy Monday to you too!" Kevin said.

"There's the exit," she said, pointing to a security checkpoint. "Use it."

Kevin glared at her and then checked her out just to piss her off.

The next morning, Kevin, Avro and I arrived at the PDC at around the same time. We filed onto the observation deck and found Jimmy eating breakfast.

"Watch this," Kevin said, looking at Avro and me. "Hey, Jimmy!"

"What," Jim said, rolling his eyes.

"So our plane exploded, and we found a giant underground lair filled with Greek buildings and fine art."

Jimmy didn't look up from his bacon and eggs. Kevin often said ridiculous things and today was no different.

I shook my head, gave Kevin a dirty look and poured myself a coffee.

"What?" Kevin said. "I'm not the one who signed a confidentiality agreement."

Avro sat down, stirring hot water into dried porridge while Kevin ate a chocolate bar.

We finished our breakfast in awkward silence.

Jimmy looked up after he finished his eggs. "There's a note on the window. I'm not sure how it got there," he said.

I walked over to the observation deck's window and picked the paper off the glass.

Dear Power Team,

Sorry about your plane. Here's a new one.

Kind Regards,

3

I tossed the note and looked out the window. On the tarmac rested a brand new Arachnid.

"This is about you not coming back last night, isn't it?" Jimmy asked.

"It's a long story," I said.

"It's bloody expensive to print and assemble an Arachnid. You must have friends in high places."

"You have no idea."

Chapter 16

AMELIA

That night we met at a Mexican place called El Planeta Rojo. Mariachi music played tastefully in the background, and a dozen sombreros adorned the walls. We sat down in a booth made of poorly printed wood and Avro ordered a round of Coronas.

"Leeth, you look exhausted." I said. "What's going on?"

"It's these training exercises. The MDF has a medical field unit, but they're bringing me the patients needing rehab. I've got two soldiers in comas."

We told him about the war game we had watched and how the MDF shot up the Arachnid.

"How'd you get back?" Leeth looked at us, skeptically.

"It's a long story, but we got to see the Alamo, that was cool," I said, not going into much detail. Kevin didn't get it, I didn't think, and Avro hadn't said it, but the confidentiality agreement was serious business. We were stuck on Mars. The company could fire us if we opened our mouths, and then what?

Leeth rubbed his forehead. "These military training exercises are ridiculous. They're making a mess out of the landscape, people are getting hurt, and it's an unnecessary strain on the colony's resources."

"I know the feeling," I said.

"I feel used, you know," he said, leaning back. "And they've got this gal, this woman, they have her locked in a padded room at the clinic.

They asked me for meds to 'mellow her out.' I just don't know how I feel about that. Actually, I know exactly how I feel about that. I'm pissed off. That's how I feel about it."

"They're holding someone against their will?" Avro asked.

"Did she commit a crime?" I asked.

"They wouldn't say," Leeth said.

"If you think she's innocent, we should at least alert the Council and call the media." Avro said. "I know this isn't Earth, but if you do something wrong, you get your day in court."

"Yeah," Leeth said, "exactly." Leeth had recently lost his driving privileges after disabling his auto-car's autopilot and treating the circumferential highway like the Indianapolis 500. And still, he had been treated fairly, I thought. His sentence – a hundred hours of community service – seemed fair. Hell, I though they should have given him more.

I looked up at the holovisions that surrounded the room. Most of them showed soccer games, but one showed the news. I nodded, directing everyone's gaze to the display. Robert Bowden stood near the spaceport while several MDF trucks rolled by in the background. I pointed at the holovision, spreading my fingers to increase the volume.

"After three days of intense training exercises, the Multinational Defense Force returns to base for some much needed time off. Things seem to be getting awfully intense in the training regimen. Earlier today, residents caught this on video near airlock five."

The video showed two MDF soldiers hauling a woman by the arms. "Let me go! Let me go, dammit!" she swore. They hauled her out of an airlock and into the back of a troop truck and closed the door.

"That's her!" Leeth said.

"According to the MDF, this woman was panicking and acting erratically on the training field, putting the lives of her comrades in danger. Confusion remains on how to handle civilian versus military law on Mars, but let us know how you feel by posting @MarsTalk." A series of social media posts streamed across the page. Some people posted "inhumane," and others just said, "Deserter, throw her in the brig!" One said, "MDF go home!"

"This is ridiculous!" I said. "It's a training exercise."

"Agreed," Avro said. "This is strange. But her incarceration is obviously public knowledge."

"Why don't we just break her out?" Leeth said. "I need a solider with me to access the patients. But besides the cameras in the rooms themselves, that's it for security."

"Handing her over to the Council should give her some sort of immunity," I said. "At least until they figure out if her charges are legit, you know, innocent until proven guilty?"

"How do you know we wouldn't be breaking some law?" Kevin asked. "What if the MDF comes after us?"

"I'm not worried about the MDF," Avro said. "The Martian council hasn't granted them any special authority. I think the worst that could happen, if we let her out, is that the Council will hear her case and simply give her back to the MDF, but the point is, she needs some sort of trial."

"Every time we open her cell, I want to strangle the guards." Leeth was seething.

"Do not do that," Avro said. "Your bar fight was one thing, but assaulting someone in the hospital will get your thrown off the planet."

"I'm guessing the locks are electromagnetic?" Kevin asked.

"Yeah, I think so," Leeth said.

"Let us deal with the lock," I said. "We just need to think of some reason to mess with the building's power."

"There's a reason security seems light," Avro said, "They don't need it. Every solider has one of these." Avro held up his arm and pointed to a scar on his wrist. "It's a tracking devise."

"Leeth, I'll tell you what," I said. "If she's still in there tomorrow night, we'll come up with a plan to get her out. In the meantime, you should file a report with the Martian council. Her story was in the news, so I'm sure they're being inundated with similar requests. But at least try to get her released using official channels first."

Leeth nodded and took the last sip of his beer.

The next day we went back to work as usual, but the woman in Leeth's clinic occupied all our thoughts. The Martian Council had been set up for a reason, to provide law, order and good governance. Until now, they seemed to have been doing a pretty good job. Mars had a functioning police force and a simple judiciary court. We even voted on who would represent us. They didn't have much bargaining power with the corporation, but that had never been an issue.

According to SpaceNET, hundreds of people had called the Council to ask for Leeth's patient's release. The response was worrying: "Currently, Multinational Defense Force personnel under MDF command are outside our jurisdiction. However, we will be reviewing the case and will make recommendations to MFD leadership during the Council meeting next Friday."

It was the middle of the day and I was flying over the arrays, completing a survey flight over some recent drone construction. Avro and Kevin had just completed an EVA and were heading home in the Arachnid.

"Hey, Johnny, is it getting hazy out here, or is it just me?" Avro said over a private channel.

I squinted at the horizon; the pink haze seemed to be taking on a grey hue like the sky right before a thunderstorm.

My radio crackled on our primary channel. "Call it in boys, a storm is brewing," Jimmy said from the dispatch station. "It's coming in fast, you better get back here."

I shook my head. "Why couldn't it have held off two more weeks!" I yelled into my headset. We were on schedule but the coil crews had thousands of miles of cabling left to go.

Avro switched to the primary channel. The gain on the high frequency band gave his voice a sharpened tone. "Make sure to tell the crews in the coil trucks. They'll need to stop and set up camp."

I met up with the Arachnid several miles south of the colony. We formed up like geese heading to Canada in the summer.

The thin air around us darkened as Martian dust rose in swirling columns, as if sucked by millions of imaginary vacuums. Both aircraft were self-contained and didn't require air intake like planes back on Earth, but we'd be flying blind if too much dust caked on the sensors.

"Johnny, Avro here, set your landing procedure and trust your autopilot. Don't try to fly your approach manually."

A red carpet spread out below us as the dunes, rocks, and hills below faded away.

"I can't see the colony, this is crazy!" I shouted.

We skimmed over a rising tide like swirling pot of tomato soup. I felt my stomach lurch up into my throat as a downdraft punched my aircraft. I pulled up on the controls to compensate.

"Okay, setting the autopilot now," I radioed.

The Pelican dropped into the storm, maintaining several hundred kilometers per hour. The plane would maintain that velocity all the way to the hangar.

My view turned bright pink, dark red, and then grey as I descended deeper into the cloud. Dust caked on the windshield and I prayed the sensors could see better than I did.

To my left, I could still distinguish Avro and Kevin in the MVA. They were fifty meters off my port. Avro's retrorockets fired, bringing the Arachnid into a hover, followed by a rapid descent.

The horizon line on my HUD twisted left and right as the Pelican plotted its approach vector. Turbulence pummeled my body left and right in my chair. The HUD's vertical approach vector lines passed like streetlights seen from a speeding car.

The magnetic decelerators captured the skid plate on the bottom of the Pelican, pushing me forward against my harness. Jets in the hangar blasted the plane with compressed air, offsetting the torque and cleaning the dust off the vehicle. The result was exhilarating. A three-second, five-G deceleration brought the Pelican from three hundred kilometers per hour to zero, all within a couple hundred feet. When the aircraft came to a complete stop, the hangar door closed.

Unstrapping my harness, I climbed through the jetway and ran down the stairs, meeting Avro and Kevin at the airlock.

They were covered in dust. A storm couldn't blow away the Arachnid. Martian air pressure was too low, but they had tied it down anyway, it was standard practice.

In the airlock, a current of wind circled around them, the entire cylinder turning red as the compression fans revved up to full power.

With the dust clear and the airlock pressurized, Avro and Kevin stepped out, releasing the seals on their helmets.

"Well, that was fun," Kevin said. "I'm going to go throw up now."

Chapter 17

THE PLAN

As the storm entered its second day, dust-covered domes left the entire colony in darkness, which was intermittently penetrated by the occasional lightning strike. When the discharge missed the colony's lighting rods, the lightning drew patterns in the sand along the dome wall all the way to the ground.

With Project Bakersfield temporarily on hold, Avro, Kevin and I took the evening off while Jimmy held down the fort at the PDC. He'd been through a dozen storms, and for him it was business as usual. In my apartment, Leeth joined Kevin, Avro and me for a game of Martian Monopoly.

A *NewsFlash* briefing played in the background. Robert Bowden spoke in front of a large screen, describing the colony's energy management system, something we were intimately familiar with. "The colony holds its energy reserves in hydrogen," Bowden said, pointing to a simulation of several large underground tanks situated around the colony. "Combining the hydrogen with our oxygen supply provides heat and electricity. With careful rationing, this reserve can last well over a year.

"Rationing will begin at fifteen kilowatt hours per day. We recommend limiting hot food and long showers. Streetlights will be turned off, and commercial offices will remain closed until the storm has ended. Central Control asks that any quota exceptions be filed accordingly." This was nothing we didn't already know. I turned off the holovision.

We sat around my living room's coffee table. Martian Monopoly was a game we found somewhat ironic. Kevin liked to claim that his piece was H3, and that as CEO, he had won before anyone rolled the dice.

"This sitting around sucks," Leeth said. "That woman started screaming last night, a reaction to the meds or something. I think someone told her about the storm and she just freaked. Screamed all through my shift and pounded on the padded door."

"What was she screaming about?" I asked.

"No idea, couldn't hear the words through the padding. But I found out her name from the MDF medic: Amelia Shepherd. She *was* a lieutenant. The medic seemed just as upset as me for keeping her, but as he said 'orders are orders'. We need to get her out of there. I can't watch them treat her like that."

"That would give us something useful to do," Avro said. "If this guy," pointing at Kevin, "makes me binge watch another episode of his stupid *Firefly* show, I'll lose it!"

"What?" replied Kevin. "It's a classic! How were you not raised on Whedon? It's like you were raised in a cave."

Avro handed me some cash, purchasing Broadway, I sorted the colored bills into the bin.

I looked at Leeth, who couldn't care less about the game. "If we help break her out, I think we need to play dumb. You know, plausible deniability."

"The hospital has an electricity quota," Kevin said. "What if people suddenly decide to recharge their cars in the hospital's underground parking garage? That'll trigger an alert we'll have to address."

"That's true," I said, "and we'll have an excuse to mess with the building's circuit breakers. I can temporarily ground any system the MDF has installed, that should release any electromagnetic locks."

"What's the hospital's quota?" Avro asked. "I'm guessing it's around fifty kilowatt hours?"

"Maybe fifty, in total," I answered, "but they'll use half of that during the day."

"A dozen cars should exceed that in fifteen or twenty minutes," Avro said

Leeth sighed, "I still don't know where you're getting the cars."

Kevin tapped the game board. "John, what are you waiting for? It's your turn."

"Hold on a second, I'm concentrating," I said. "We need a reason for people to be driving," I replied. We all paused, deep in thought.

"What if they actually need to go to the hospital?" Kevin said, a grin slowly spreading across his face. He held up his drink and winked.

I looked around, now both Avro and Kevin were beaming. Avro looked over at Kevin, "You have a still hidden in the machine shop right? Moonshine?"

"I do, and yes," Kevin said, sounding extremely proud of himself.

"Where is this going?" I asked, very confused. "I have no idea where this is going."

"Kevin's going to spike the punch," Avro said, leading me on, making me ask the questions.

I rolled my eyes. "Where is he going to spike the punch?"

Kevin answered, "At the greatest party since 2069."

The next day, Kevin printed several hundred flyers. Each read, "Greatest Storm Party since 2069" as well as other important details such as "Free Drinks." I recommended circulating an email and posting on

social media but Kevin insisted on poly-paper flyers, stating, "It's not junk mail if it's on paper!"

This wasn't Kevin's first party and he had all the contacts. First he called Magnus Haze, Mars's premier trance rock band. They accepted the gig, and their sound guy agreed to procure the space and file the quota exemption on Kevin's behalf.

The band set up in an empty warehouse in the two o'clock dome. The interior had more than enough room for the band, as well as a DJ podium and a makeshift bar. The garage had formerly held Project Bakersfield's coil trucks, currently stranded out on the surface. The two o'clock dome had no residential apartments, so the colony's police wouldn't bother to kick them out. They might have even joined in. Mars's cops were as bored as everyone else.

Avro found a couple of guys vaping in an alley near the pavilion. They agreed to pass out the fliers and bartend for free drinks. To give them extra credibility, we let them say the party was their idea.

That evening, Kevin arrived at the garage, dragging a large empty keg behind the bar. He wrote "Phobos Moonshine" in sharpie on the keg, mixed in some tang and tap water, then added two liters of actual moonshine to the mix. He'd start them off light and harden it up as the night went on.

At ten p.m. a twenty-minute long keyboard solo rocked the two o'clock dome. People poured in from every dome in the circumferential. Many people walked, but some drove, leaving the cars to park themselves along nearby streets.

Kevin milled around as guests trickled past the bouncers. He lit the garage using LED Christmas lights. The lights flashed on and off, providing minimal light, which was ideal for a party. Kevin wore white pants and a traditional Indian collared shirt. His sports jacket shimmered, changing colors from silver to metallic blue and red.

A blonde and a brunette floated past him on Meissner heels. They looked overdressed for a party in a garage. Kevin grabbed two drinks from the bar and headed over to the women.

"Hey," he said to the brunette, handing her a drink. She took the drink and checked him out.

"Nice jacket," she said.

"Thanks, nice shoes. I heard from someone at Central that everyone's quotas are being cut to one kilowatt hour."

"What! That's ridiculous!" the brunette said, clumsily tipping her cup, splashing alcohol onto the floor.

"Can you do me a favor?" He handed her an envelope. "Can you give this to the DJ? I think you're taller than me. I'll get you another drink."

The woman looked at Kevin, took the note, and smiled. She twisted a knob on her belt and her shoes gave her an extra five inches of height. She bounced her way over to the DJ and got his attention. They chatted for a moment and she passed him the note.

Magnus Haze's drummer completed a raging solo and the crowd went wild. Then he stood up and tossed his drumsticks into the crowd. The band took a break, letting the DJ take over as the musicians went to the bar.

After the first mix, the DJ made an announcement. "Word in the dome! Quotas are being cut, so you better party like its 2069!" he mixed the announcement with a pulsing drum beat. "Charge those cars tonight! I say again, charge those cars tonight!" The DJ turned up the volume and hundreds of people took to the dance floor.

With the seed planted, it was time to get people to the hospital. Kevin walked up to the bar and handed the bartender a wad of bills and then winked.

The bartender nodded, reaching for the jugs Kevin had planted under the bar and poured the clear liquid into the keg.

At midnight, Leeth's clinic received its first visitor. Thirty minutes later, it received its fiftieth. All fifty parking spots in the parking structure were filled and a parade of empty auto-cars circled the nearby streets waiting to park. Inside the garage, orange charging cords glowed in the dark. The vehicles were sucking the building's quota dry.

At the PDC, I received the call I'd been expecting. On my phone was Director Jackson Carver from Central Control. He must have been awfully surprised to see a quota violation at one in the morning.

"John? John Orville? Yes, sorry to wake you, this is Jackson." He talked in typically southern fashion, slow and relaxed. This was the first time I'd actually seen him without his sunglasses. We usually talked during the day when he was in the control tower on top of the central dome. He looked tired, and if it weren't for his dark complexion, I'm sure there'd be bags under his eyes. "We've received word from the hospital that they've flagged a quota violation. I'll need you to clear that."

"Oh, hi, Jackson, I hear they've got a run on the clinic's parking garage, I'm going to go down to the substation and disconnect the garage's power. Those people can charge their cars at home."

"Damn right they can. Why are they charging at the hospital anyway?"

"I have no idea."

I drove to the hospital's substation located on the outside of the building. Using a universal key, I opened the panel. I saw the fuse marked "parking garage" and ignored it.

I got Jackson back on the line.

"Ah yeah, hey, Jackson? John here again. I'm having trouble with the breaker, feedback or something. I talked to one of the doctors. There are no surgeries going on. Mind if I cut the power to the clinic? That should free up the breakers."

"That's fine, but be quick about it. This is a hospital you're talking about."

⸙

In her padded cell, Amelia heard a buzz indicating the arrival of a food tray.

"What the hell?" she said. The meal arrived at least five hours late and her stomach rumbled. A dim red light illuminated the tray. Amelia immediately realized the entree was missing. *Oh God, they're trying to starve me!* she thought.

She picked up a muffin, throwing it at the wall. She punched the padded food dispenser, momentarily too pissed off to eat.

Looking back at the tray, she decided what nasty food to eat first. She reached for a coreless apple, inspecting the bruises. Then she saw the note. Confused, she picked it up, and held it under the food dispenser's red indicator light.

"Go to the bathroom at the end of the hall and wait," the note read.

"What the hell?" This time it was a real question instead of a rhetorical one. "How the heck am I supposed to..." she paused, something was happening.

The lights went out. Not that it was ever particularly light in the padded room, but it was never completely dark. Amelia assumed the power outage and note were related. She pushed on the door. It opened with a creak.

Amelia looked down the hall. In one direction she could see light from the outside. She ran over to the window and noticed a line of cars driving toward the hospital, then down into the garage. To her left, a stairwell descended into the darkness. On her right was a bathroom, a men's bathroom.

Well, she thought, *I did get a note under my muffin.* She pushed open the bathroom door. Inside, it was pitch black.

"Shit!" she said aloud, but just then, the clinic's power came back on. Amelia looked in the mirror, studying her face. Her breath fogged up the glass, and she wiped it clear with her sleeve, glancing at the scar on her left wrist.

Leeth opened the door. "Hey," he said, "you get my note?"

Amelia stared at him. She was here, wasn't she?

"Doctor thinks I'm with a patient. Here, take this."

Leeth handed Amelia a cylindrical metallic bracelet and a neoprene wrist brace.

"It's to cover up your RFID tag."

"I know what it is," Amelia said, placing the bracelet over her wrist. "You shouldn't have helped me."

Leeth shrugged. "I had to put a stop to your screaming somehow. Use the door at the bottom of the far stairwell. It leads to the dome's wall-alley. There's a change of clothes in a tree a block to the north. Head north, through the channel into the three o'clock dome, and someone will meet you there."

Amelia looked at Leeth, turned, and walked out of the restroom. She flew down the stairs, finding the door at the bottom. Looking both ways and finding the alley empty, she followed the curved path behind several other structures. On her right she saw her reflection in the dome wall. Her bright orange scrubs almost glowed in the dark. When the hospital curved out of sight, Amelia stopped at a twelve-foot-tall tree.

Placed between the branches like a bird's nest, she saw a pouch the size of a purse. She jumped up and pulled it down. The parcel contained a pair of sweatpants, a baseball cap and a collared shirt.

She looked around, her eyes fully adjusted to the dark. The alley was empty, which was not a surprise. Mars didn't have transients. Well, not yet anyway. Most people were at home in bed.

Amelia changed into the clothes and tucked her brown hair up into the ball cap.

Something bulged from the left breast pocket of the shirt. Reaching in, she retrieved a pair of eyeglasses. She looked at them, and noticed a holographic projection of open eyes in the lenses. The eye color in the novelty glasses was bright blue, not her eye color. They must have supposed this would add to her disguise.

Amelia stepped out onto the street. Several people were leaving the hospital and heading in different directions. A dozen people headed toward the channel leading to the three o'clock dome.

Amelia eyed the people moving in the direction she intended to go. It was quite a scene; people had bandages over their eyes, while others stumbled in threes, holding each other up.

These people are drunk! she observed, wondering what the hell was going on.

Amelia joined the gaggle as they walked down the street. She figured she might as well blend in, doubting they'd notice her novelty glasses in the dark. The group moved slower than she would have liked. Walking down the street felt great after being imprisoned in the hospital.

When they passed through the channel, Amelia looked back in the direction she had come. The street teemed with people from what must have been a raging party. In the distance, she could see the clinic with its emergency sign illuminated. In front of the hospital a police car flashed its lights, illuminating the dome in a vibrant light show.

An MDF truck zoomed past, stopping in the channel behind her. Several soldiers got out, and started milling through the bodies. Someone must have reported her missing. Each soldier held up a facial recognition detector, which they panned around the crowd.

Amelia kept her head down until she came out of the channel and into the adjacent dome. She looked around, not sure what to do next.

"Psst!" A voice said, "Amelia, over here!" It was male and had a slight Latino accent.

The voice came from the door of a nearby apartment building. Amelia couldn't see who was talking, but the door was propped open, so she walked over and stepped inside.

"How did you know that was me? It's dark out here," she whispered.

"Look at your hat," the voice instructed.

Amelia looked at the hat. "What the… nice. Really nice."

The hat she wore was illuminated by a glow-in-the-dark Batman symbol.

"I'm not sure how I didn't notice that," Amelia said.

"It lit up when you put it on. Follow me. We need to get to another building." It was dark in the hall and Amelia couldn't see the person's face, but she could tell he was tall and fit.

Amelia followed the shadowy figure though the building and into the alley that ran along the dome wall. He seemed to know where he was going. They continued walking past several buildings until coming to a stop.

"This is it," the man said. "Go to apartment 228. The door is open. You can sleep on the couch and there's food in the fridge."

"You're leaving?"

"We all need an alibi," the man said. "Mine is that I'm home in bed. And I don't live here."

"All right then," Amelia said. "Apartment 228?"

"That's right. I'll see you soon." He briefly placed a hand on her shoulder and then disappeared into the dark.

Chapter 18

A NEW ROOMMATE

I arrived home that morning to find Amelia sleeping on the sofa. She found the sheets and pillows we had laid out for her but she looked uncomfortable. Her bare feet hung over the arm of the couch. A half-eaten box of Oreos and a milk-stained glass rested on the coffee table. On the kitchen counter sat an empty box of vanilla ice cream. I smiled at this. I guess if I were in her situation, I'd want ice cream too.

At nine hundred square feet, my apartment had one of the larger floor plans in the colony, even if it was only a one-bedroom suite. The living room's picture window faced the outside of the dome. The area directly outside was a staging area and made my apartment a great place to watch the drones exchanging supplies and whatever else drones did. But during a storm, there was nothing to see. It was eight in the morning and the window looked like a black hole, as if the colony rested at the bottom of the ocean.

When I opened the fridge, letting its light trickle into the room, she woke up.

"Wah?" said a tired voice from the living room, "Who's there?"

So much for sneaking back to bed. I turned on the kitchen's LED.

"John Orville. How are you, Amelia?"

"Glad to be out of that stupid cell," she replied groggily.

"I bet," I said, pouring myself a glass of OJ. "Want some orange juice?"

"Sure," she replied, moving into a seated position. "So why'd you do it? Why risk yourselves breaking me out?"

"Risking ourselves?" I said, "You have the law on your side here. From what we could tell from the news, they had no reason to hold you. You should go to the Council today. They'll at least give you some sort of immunity—"

"No!" Amelia yelled, then calmed down. "We can't let anyone know where I am."

"Why? What's the big deal?" I asked.

"I'll tell you, but wait until your friends are here. The guy from the hospital—"

"Leeth," I said. "And the other guy was Avro. They'll be here this afternoon. Oh, and Kevin too. He's the one who threw the party, our distraction."

"And that's everyone who knows about you helping me?"

"That's it. If anyone asks, we didn't help you. You got out on your own."

"Smart," Amelia said.

"So why'd they send you to the hospital and not the brig?" I asked.

"A brig couldn't drug someone. In the clinic, they prescribed me drugs for the criminally insane, drugs that would mess me up. Even if I did speak up, no one would believe me."

"Did the drugs work?" I asked.

"Fortunately for me, your friend the nurse is terribly unreliable," Amelia said with a smile.

I smiled. "I don't think that's why. Leeth was worried about you. He didn't believe that what the MDF was doing was right and probably refused to give you the drugs."

"Oh, I ah, didn't realize that."

"Well, that's Leeth for you," I said. "Anyway, I'm exhausted. I'm going to turn in for a few hours. Maybe tonight I'll sleep on the couch and you can have the bed."

"Thanks," Amelia said. "Thanks for busting me out, I mean. We can talk about the sleeping situation later."

I showed Amelia where the extra toothbrushes were and lent her a pair of socks. Then I went to bed.

*

Four hours later, a beam of sunlight hit me on the head. I rolled over, pulling the pillow over my face. *Wait a minute, the storm is over!*

I got up and faced my bedroom window. Like the living room, a floor-to-ceiling window faced the dome wall. Sweeper drones purred back and forth across the dome's glass, sweeping the dust onto the ground.

With the storm over, we'd all need to get back to work. I called the PDC and Jimmy answered via Skype.

"John, good to see you," Jimmy said. "Nice of you to dress up."

I was just wearing my boxers. "Thanks for letting me sleep in," I said.

"Since you volunteered for that shift last night, I figured you'd need your rest. Anyway, the Pelican is ready to go but Avro's MVA is half buried. I've got some guys from Central digging it out now. There's a sand dune blocking our equipment garage. I've called for extra drones to clear the sand but there's a delay. Apparently, all the cleaning drones are occupied at the spaceport."

"What can I do to help?"

"Nothing I can think of, but you probably won't be going out on the surface until tomorrow. I've got everything under control until then."

"Will do, Jimmy," I said. "I'll see you tomorrow then."

I hit the red "End" button on the screen, and looked up at the mirror that hung over the dresser. Looking closely at my reflection, I noticed a few grey hairs amongst the brown. I thought of Marie, wondering if she had had any grey hair. She'd never let me know if she did. I'm sure she'd dye her hair, intent on looking young forever.

Putting on my pants and a shirt, I headed to the kitchen for some coffee, which I could now make without worrying about a quota.

Shortly after I was showered and dressed, Avro, Kevin and Leeth showed up at my door. Kevin carried a canvas bag that looked like something from an army surplus store.

"I hear you had an eventful evening last night," Avro said, giving a slight bow, and shaking Amelia's hand with both of his.

"I know that voice!" Amelia said, "You're the one from the alley!"

"You got me," Avro said.

Amelia looked at Kevin. "Nice shirt." Kevin's shirt showed an active battle between two large drones with laser guns for arms.

"If it's too distracting, I'll shut it off."

"No, it's fine."

"These are for you," Kevin said, handing the bag over to Amelia. She set the bag on the kitchen table and began pulling out items of clothing.

"Not bad," Amelia said, holding up a blouse. "Where'd you get these?"

"Did John tell you about our party?" Kevin asked.

"He did," Amelia replied.

"Well, the warehouse had a fire suppression vat or some such thing. I don't really know. Anyway, there was a pool." Kevin paused, smiling. "So at about midnight, twenty guests decided to do a little skinny dipping."

Amelia dropped the shirt she was holding.

There was an awkward silence, until Kevin spoke again, "Anyway, I thought the clothes might come in handy. I used Smart-Bleach when I washed them."

"Ah, thanks," Amelia said.

"Is anyone hungry?" I asked. My guests nodded. Avro and Kevin exchanged small talk with Amelia while I made an afternoon snack of Cheerios and chocolate almond milk.

Amelia asked what we did for fun since I didn't have a VR unit in the apartment. Kevin mentioned that we spend most of our time hanging out at Applebee's, which was true since Leeth had been kicked out of the bar. Amelia laughed, while Avro turned a bright shade of red.

We all sat around the kitchen table as Amelia told her story.

"The Multinational Defense Force is not here just for training. Only the officers know this, but we're here to protect the Alamo."

For a moment we just stared at her.

"Protect them from what?" I asked. "That doesn't make sense. There's no reason they need protection. The Alamo is just a gated community. They live there because they can afford to. No one's going to protest that."

"Agreed," Amelia said. "Not yet. But they're planning something, something that could upset the colonists. We're here to make sure nothing interferes with their plans."

"What plans?" I asked. "You must know something."

"I don't know any specifics. Maybe they're closing the mines, or firing a large portion of the workforce. I really have no idea."

Avro looked concerned. "Tell us why they arrested you."

"I'll get to that," Amelia began, "I'm an officer. There are only a small number of us. Ten actually, including me. Only we know we're here to protect the Alamo. The other one hundred forty NCOs think we're on a training mission. The officers have been developing and training for several contingencies."

"What contingencies?" Avro said, and we all leaned closer.

"Protests, for example. It doesn't sound serious, but protests can turn violent and the corporation needs to worry about that sort of stuff. Then, there's equipment malfunction. A hydrogen explosion in the fuel cell system could lead to food and air shortages. You would expect there to be considerable civil unrest. There's your run-of-the-mill space disasters, meteor impact, transport accident," Amelia counted on her fingers. "Solar flare, subterranean magnetic shift—"

"Okay, okay," I interrupted, "but why the secrecy?"

"Because they don't want people freaking out. The colony has police, why move in the National Guard if there's no trouble?"

Kevin looked grim. "Some people are already freaking out about you guys, but most of us are sort of used to it. Military training on Mars isn't new. But if you're here to enforce anything, people should be pissed. Heck, I'm pissed. And there's not a damn thing we can do about it."

"We can go to the media and talk to the Council," I said.

"We could," Avro replied, "but why would they believe us? We're going against their official story."

"What if Amelia goes on the news or in front of the Council and tells her story?" Kevin suggested.

"It'll never happen," Amelia said. "They've branded me as a criminal, a coward and insane. If I try to go public, they'll take me out. These guys mean business and I haven't even gotten to the juicy part."

"You mean your arrest," Kevin said.

"Yeah, that," Amelia said. "Like I said, we've been building contingency plans to protect the Alamo."

"That makes sense," Avro said, "especially if you're hired to protect people."

"Yeah, but get this. If there's a protest and people fight to get into the Alamo, we have orders to shoot. They really don't want outsiders in the Alamo."

"Holy shit, really?" Avro said.

"Really. I know. Sucks, right? But that's not what I got in shit for," Amelia answered, "Listen. Most of our contingencies are designed to stabilize a situation. But there's one contingency that's different." Amelia paused to take a breath. "It's the category five storm contingency. Does everyone know about storm categories?"

"Yeah," Avro said. "This storm was cat-two. The categories are based on wind speed and storm duration. In really bad storms, you get lighting. They take that into consideration, too. In a cat-five, the wind speeds are two, two fifty, something like that, and the storm is strong enough to sustain itself indefinitely."

"Exactly, if there's cat-five a storm, and all the energy reserves are drained—"

I cut her off. "If there's a storm, we ration. The colony can survive a year, or more, on reserves."

"I understand that," Amelia said. "But listen, if somehow, the colony starts running out of energy, people will die."

"Of course, they would," Kevin said. "Without the electricity powering the CO2 scrubbers, everyone would suffocate in a matter of days, or freeze from lack of heat. Not sure which would come first."

"Yes, but listen, if it comes to that, the MDF has one job. Reduce population. Specifically, we're going to start blowing up domes!"

"You've got to be fucking kidding me," Avro said. "Blowing up the domes?"

Amelia said, "They justified it like this: The lives of the many outweigh the lives of the few. Star Trek shit, right? But the way I see it, the lives of the rich outweigh the lives of everyone."

"It's a good thing we'll have Project Bakersfield then," I said.

"You better hope it works, too," Amelia said. "That's the worst of the contingencies but it's also why they canned me."

"What about you running from the training area and going crazy?" Kevin said. "One report said you were shooting shit up like a crazy person. Putting other soldiers in danger and stuff."

"They made it up." Amelia said. "They had to charge me with something. I protested their contingency, said I'd go public, and then next thing you know, they've hauled me into a transport, dumped me on the field without a comm. After a few minutes stumbling around, trying to get away from the battle drones, the NCOs arrested me. They obviously had orders to do so."

"Shit," Avro said, sympathetically. "Wait, how would they blow up the domes. That's crazy. You mean they really planned this all out?"

She said, "Yes, well, the plan is to take a vehicle into the storm and breach the dome with explosives. Again, only myself and the other nine officers know this. They'll tell the rest of the soldiers the dome collapsed in the storm."

"That's ridiculous. These domes are strong, really strong!" I said.

"Yeah, but think about it. If a dome collapsed with no other explanation, you would have to assume it was the storm," Amelia countered. "Maybe lightning hit a hydrogen tank, I don't know."

"Yeah, I guess so," I agreed. "That's the rational way to think about it, but people aren't rational."

"How do you convince the MDF, an organization with peaceful roots, to kill innocent people?" Avro asked.

"We don't *convince* them to do anything," Amelia replied. "Desperate times call for desperate measures. The officers do the dirty work and the soldiers come in later to clean up the mess."

"So what do we do now?" I said. "The people have a right to know what's going on, and if I had any say, I'd have the Council order the military to turn themselves in. Have the police collect their weapons."

"I doubt they'd give in so easily," Amelia said. "The Alamo's not going to let them."

"What if we call Earth? Tell the folks back home what's going on. See if they can exercise some political pressure."

"Listen," Amelia said. "Believe me, you don't want them finding out you're trying to stop them. You'll end up like me, on the run."

"So what do we do?" I asked. "If there's anyone who can stop this, it's us, the engineers. We control the electricity and that gives us a lot of power, literally. We also have access to vehicles, aircraft and spacesuits."

"We need time to think of a plan," Avro said. "This is huge. In the meantime, we finish Project Bakersfield. At least that will prevent the worst of your contingencies. Amelia, do you have any suggestions?"

"Honestly, no," Amelia said. "I don't know what to do. But I know this: you guys are really something. Leeth too. I mean shit, you seem like true friends."

Amelia wouldn't let me sleep on the couch, insisting it was okay to share the bed. She noticed this made me uncomfortable and constructed a wall down the middle of the bed with a sheet duct-taped to the ceiling. The gesture meant a lot to me. It also turned my room into a fort and this made me smile. It reminded me of Branson and the couch cushion forts we'd built.

On the second night, Amelia wanted to talk about something. We sat down on the edge of the bed.

"I noticed you're wearing a wedding ring," she said.

"You did, huh?"

"Yeah, I did. Where is your family? Are they back on Earth?" she asked, pointing at the photos sitting on a shelf.

"I don't know where they are. We were in California during the impact. I was in Los Angeles, they were in San Francisco."

"I'm sorry," Amelia looked into my eyes. I looked back into hers, noticing for the first time they weren't quite blue, but more of a steel gray.

"Until I know for sure, I'm not giving up hope. In my heart, they're still alive."

"What if you never find out?" Amelia asked.

"Then I can't say I didn't try."

"What do you mean?"

"Avro and I spent a year together on the Search and Rescue team. I swear we searched every inch of California."

"You must have saved hundreds of lives! You are a hero. Avro is a hero," Amelia argued, trying to find some solace.

"We saved thousands of lives. But that didn't take away my anger."

"It wasn't your fault," Amelia said.

"I was an engineer at NASA. I was in the control room when everything went down!"

"It wasn't your fault! That was an accident, plain and simple. Shit happens, John, and once it does, there's nothing you or anyone else can do about it."

Amelia was right. It wasn't my fault. Deep down, I accepted this. Right then, I put my hands up to my eyes and cried. Amelia leaned over and held me. Her hair smelled like my shampoo, and for a moment, just for a moment, I felt at home.

After three days stuck in my apartment, Amelia was going stir crazy. I guess being a homemaker wasn't for her.

We watched the media coverage of her escape on the news, which basically consisted of several low ranking soldiers wandering around the central dome and looking confused. The Martian Council made a statement that they wouldn't help track down Amelia unless formal charges were filed. Amelia assured us that they were looking for her but was confident the red tape provided a much needed distraction.

Amelia insisted on going out, so we came up with several locations that didn't have security cameras. The research bio dome was the most relaxing place on Mars and would provide the greatest amount of freedom for Amelia. The bio dome rose a few hundred feet above the rest of the colony, granting a clear view of the entire circumferential. We just needed a plan to get her there without being caught.

We decided we could use Avro's Electro-Davidson. Except for the whine of the electric pistons, it was a relatively discreet way to travel. The bike had a fifteen-kilowatt battery, producing over two hundred horsepower. Most importantly, the helmet visors were tinted, allowing the rider, or riders, a level of anonymity.

Letting Amelia ride the motorcycle made me nervous. If she crashed, she'd be discovered and would end up back in the hospital. But Amelia told us to "grow a pair," grabbing the helmet the moment she heard about the idea. So down in the parking structure, Avro taught Amelia how to ride.

As an added precaution, Amelia dyed her hair red and shortened it to about six inches. Using hair gel, she molded a cowlick in the front and sculpted the remaining hair behind her ears. To complete her new look, she popped the lenses out of the novelty glasses and wore those as well.

With her transformation complete, she looked like a pop star, a far cry from the military officer she actually was.

Amelia even started talking about turning herself in. She reasoned that once Project Bakersfield eliminated the storm threat, her secrets were a lot less dangerous. Her plan was to meet in secret with a psychiatrist, admit to being insane, and convince the shrink she was no longer a threat to herself or others. Then, she'd turn herself in to the Martian Council and ask for a fair trial.

At worst she should be placed on the next cruiser back to Earth with a discharge from her unit. At least that's how we reasoned it anyway.

Three weeks later, on a Wednesday, our drones screwed in the last solar panel and Project Bakersfield was complete and ready for testing. The cable-laying trucks had finished laying the anti-storm coils, and the cabling crews headed back to the colony after their long expedition around the planet.

The following Saturday, the Martian Council held a party or sorts, celebrating the end of the storms. It was nothing like Kevin's party, basically just sandwiches and alcohol-free tang, but it was nice to be recognized. The celebration was held in the central pavilion, and a few hundred people gathered as members of the Council made long speeches, thanking the various people involved.

I stood with Avro and Kevin near the podium and looked around at the crowd. In attendance were several young men and women from the mining operation, who tended to dress casually. Then there were the engineers, standing around with their sleeves rolled up (Kevin being the only exception). The folks from Central Control all wore matching golf shirts. A few of the colony's police officers stood nearby, looking bored like police typically do.

But I noticed something strange. In every speech, they were thanking the gracious benefactors from the Alamo. People looked around and clapped every time this was brought up, but curiously, none of the folks from the Alamo, including H3, were in attendance.

The speeches were followed by a ribbon cutting to declare the project complete. It was here where we met Jeff Watson from Environmental Engineering and Director Jackson from Central. We drank champagne and shook hands but it was pretty low key.

After the ceremony, Leeth joined Kevin, Avro and me in the bio dome with a case of Martian IPA. We stood at the Look-Off, a secluded section of the park with a great view. Behind us, birds chirped in the trees, and several joggers passed by on the trail that snaked around the research complex.

"What a view," Avro said, nodding in appreciation as we stood facing the circumferential, admiring the storm coils emanating from the colony.

"Yup," I said, taking a sip of the cold beer.

"Yup," Leeth added.

"Yup," Kevin repeated.

"Yup," said a female voice, from behind us.

"Ack, woman!" Kevin said, "Where the hell did you come from!"

"I was over there, on that bench reading a book."

"Glad you could make it," Avro said, putting his arm around her.

"Well, now that you're all here, I'd like to propose a toast," Leeth said, pulling out his flask.

"Is that Kevin's moonshine?" I asked, pointing at the flask.

"Sure is," Kevin replied, pulling out a flask of his own.

"Classy," remarked Amelia.

"To the end of the storms," Kevin said, raising his flask and taking a sip.

"To the end of the storms!" we all repeated and passed the flasks around.

That evening I found out why no one from the Alamo was at the ceremony. Kevin sent me a text telling me to check *NewsFlash*. I accessed SpaceNet from my holovision and brought up the report.

Robert Bowden stood in a pressurized mining canal while autonomous trucks rumbled by. He waited for them to pass before starting.

"Red Planet Mining Corporation has issued a statement regarding the future of the mining activities here on Mars. As many of you know, recent advances in drone tech have enabled greater automation in the mines, and several new drone models arrived during the recent launch window. The company reports that productivity gains from these devices have been outstanding, and the need for human oversight in the mines is rapidly declining."

Bowden continued, "For this reason, staffing in the mines is set to decline immediately. One thousand people will not be showing up to work tomorrow, and a month from now, another thousand employees will be off the job.

Amelia was right, I thought.

"Red Planet Mining has carefully considered the situation and assures its departing employees that they will receive a living wage until the launch window opens next year. However, due to the extreme cost of spaceflight, the company will allow non-working colonists to remain on Mars. These citizens will be given a small salary in exchange for not returning to Earth."

The report ended and I switched off the holovision. For the first time ever, Mars was going to have freelivers.

Chapter 19

BAKERSFIELD ACTIVE

The next morning, Kevin and I went back to work while Avro took the day off to spend some quality time with Amelia. Jimmy had taken the night shift and was sleeping in a bunk on the ground floor of the PDC.

Despite our long hours, Amelia and Avro had grown close in the past weeks. I guess she got tired of our bed fort because she even moved into Avro's apartment. Their relationship reminded me of a high school romance, but instead of hiding from her father, she was hiding from everyone.

Kevin stood as he worked the data screens that stretched along the windows. His station was command-and-control for the construction drones. I sat at Jimmy's station, where he functioned as a dispatcher, helping coordinate the teams on the surface.

Out the large windows, we could see two of the ten storm coils running outward from the colony and over the horizon.

"So when does the system go online?" I asked. We hadn't heard from Watson since the ceremony and since our role in Project Bakersfield was complete. Keeping us in the loop wasn't a priority.

"Not sure," Kevin said. "The integration team still has some testing to do. The system is preventative, so it doesn't matter if it's active all the time. The probability of a storm happening on any given day is less than one percent."

I stared out the window, studying Project Bakersfield's anti-storm coils. The coils reminded me of oil pipelines running through the desert, embedded into the soil so that vehicles could pass over them. Up until today, the silvery coils were inert. Today, something was different. The coils pulsed with colorful electric distortions that traveled along the coils outward toward the horizon.

"What was that?" I asked.

"Oh, that? They're testing the coils in bursts. Look closer."

I squinted. Sunlight reflecting off distant solar arrays made it difficult to see. I put my aviators on and saw static electricity like St. Elmo's fire running in blue flames over the coils.

"I thought you needed oxygen for St. Elmo's fire," I said. I shuddered a little. Sailors had often regarded St. Elmo's fire as a bad omen.

"You do," Kevin answered. "There's oxygen in the soil. When the coil creates an electro-magnetic field, the dust surrounding the coil becomes charged and O2 is released."

THRUMP. The sound came from outside and a layer of dust jumped up into the air. THRUMP. The dust settled back onto the ground.

"That was weird," I said, standing up and leaning against the window.

"That *was,* indeed, weird," Kevin said, looking at the readings on his display. I glanced over to what Kevin was looking at. His primary display showed a map and the location of all our drones. He pulled in a camera feed from a drone's point of view.

The dust jumped again. "I have a bad feeling about this," I said.

"What's wrong?" Kevin asked. "That's probably just the system cycling through the abatement sequence."

"That dust lifted off the ground! Don't you see what this means?" I said.

"No."

"If a negative charge prevents a storm, what happens if the coils produce a positive charge?"

"I don't want to think about it," Kevin looked up from his display. "Most likely we are experiencing a real storm somewhere on Mars and this is the system doing its job."

"Get Avro on the line, I want another opinion. Where is he anyway?"

"He's with Amelia," Kevin answered. "I assume they're up at Make-Out Point."

"The Look-Off?"

"Yeah, the Look-Off," Kevin said.

"You know, someday you're gonna have to stop talking like you're fourteen."

"But not today," he said.

Our phones chimed. Avro was calling us. I unclipped my phone from my wrist and transferred the call to the display window.

"Hey, guys," came the voice from the screen. "Have you seen this?" Avro pointed at the view. From Avro's and Amelia's vantage point, a cloud was rising from beyond a hill.

"Yeah, we're seeing the same thing," I said. "Looks like a storm, so why hasn't the system neutralized it?"

"I have no idea," Avro said. "But I'm worried we did a lot of work for nothing."

"Kevin, get Central Control on the line," I ordered. "And Avro, don't go anywhere."

"On it," Kevin replied and punched in the commands to bring Central Control up on the adjacent screen.

"Central, this is PDC," I said.

It was bright in the central control tower and Jackson wore leather blinders on his sunglasses. "Jackson here," he said.

"Jackson, what's going on out there?"

"We are experiencing a storm," the director replied without any hint of concern. "As you can see, Project Bakersfield is working to counteract." He paused as if everything was okay.

"Are you sure the coils are resonating at the correct polarity? If I had to guess, the coils appear to be emitting the wrong charge."

"That's unlikely," Jackson stated confidently. "The system was designed to emit a negative—"

"What is it?"

"You're right," Jackson said, turning in his chair, and double-checking his displays. "The coils are emitting a positively charged electromagnetic field."

"Well, shut it down, dammit!" I yelled.

"We can't. Control of Project Bakersfield was transferred to the engineering team inside the Alamo," Jackson admitted.

"What? Why? Because we connected H3's nuclear reactor as a backup?"

"Yup. Apparently, H3 doesn't want anyone else to have access to the nuclear portion of the grid."

"So we have no control over the coil," I said. "Can we disconnect it from the grid?"

"No, we can't. The power is routed through the main bus, where the solar grid meets the nuclear one. This occurs inside the Alamo."

Kevin grabbed our camera and centered it on his face, "Are you seeing what we're seeing?" Kevin asked.

Jackson gave him a dirty look, then reached up and pushed his camera so it showed another part of the control room. Like an air traffic control tower, the control room sat on top of the central dome. The tower's two other controllers stood along the room's windows, watching as dust clouds churned in the distance. "Does that answer your question?" he asked.

Again, the dust outside our window rose several meters into the air before snapping back down onto the ground.

"Yeah, that about sums it up," I said, looking at the situation from multiple angles.

The dust rose once more, except this time, it stayed up. Debris pelted our window as pressure variances formed around the colony. Jackson's control tower went dark as a red cloud covered central dome. A storm was in full force.

Jackson reoriented his camera back towards his station. He took off his sunglasses, setting them on his console. "John, I'm signing off. We'll be back in touch as soon as we figure this out." He hung up before we could reply.

"My God," I swore. *It all made sense now.* I turned, facing Avro's picture on the screen, "The system we just built?"

"What about it?" Avro said.

"I know why it didn't prevent the storm."

"Why?" Amelia leaned into view, a nervous look on her face.

"Because Project Bakersfield is *causing* the storm," I said.

"Someone sure screwed this up," Kevin said.

"No, Kevin, not a screw up," I said. "I'm willing to bet that Project Bakersfield was *designed* to cause storms!"

An alarm went off on our panel. I looked at a map of the colony. Several more alarms wailed, and I tried to concentrate on which ones were demanding my attention.

The fuel cells were working overtime, creating electricity from hydrogen and oxygen at an incredible rate. They were tapping into the colony's reserves!

"Oh shit shit shit!" I yelled. "Kevin, the hydrogen! Our tanks! They're already half empty! Shut them down, shut off those fuel cells!"

Kevin's fingers flew across the controls.

"That power's going to the Alamo!" I yelled.

I got on the line with the Alamo's engineering team. "What the shit," I yelled into the terminal. "Shut down all power transfers from the circumferential!"

A video feed of an Alamo engineer's face appeared on the screen. He looked frantic. "We're locked out. Can you shut it down on your end?"

"What the hell? No! You're empting our reserves! Can't you see what we're seeing?"

"Affirmative PDC, we're working on it."

I listened to the hustle and bustle in the Alamo's control center. In the background, I heard people speaking. "I don't know, I don't know, Can't... no, it's not responding."

I looked at Kevin "I don't think they're in control either."

More voices from the other side. "Got it, auxiliary systems coming online, reset override complete, cutting the power—"

The line went dead. I looked at my screen. The Colony's energy reserve stabilized at twenty percent. Ten months of the colony's energy reserves were gone. Just plain gone. I tried to call the Alamo back. Nothing. Communications had been cut off.

Kevin faced the window, staring out at our darkening view. Then, in a slow voice, he whispered, "Oh, shit."

"What is it?"

"Look at the wind speeds," Kevin said, pointing to the meteorological display. "The storm," he paused. "It's category five."

Chapter 20

JUST WORK THE PROBLEM

We could tell the storm was bad from the noise. The sand in the wind beat harmonies against the observation deck's glass. It was like driving a car through a hailstorm.

I flipped on the news. Robert Bowden stood in the bio dome, just outside the meteorological center. In the background, a dust-caked dome wall took on a deep, red hue.

"Well, this is the second storm this month to hit Harmony Colony. According to the meteorological center, we haven't had two storms this close together since 2063. We're also having trouble with our deep space transmitters, so don't expect to be contacting Earth any time soon."

He doesn't know about the power drain, I thought. And how could he? Only the engineering teams would see that data, and we weren't exactly issuing press releases. I turned the volume down but kept the news on in the background.

"Kevin, we need to make sure no more reserves get stolen," I said.

"There's a substation near each fuel cell in each dome. Right now, all the fuel cells feed into the grid. If we disconnect each fuel cell from the grid, each dome will be on its own."

My watch buzzed. It was Avro. He was on his bike with Amelia on the back.

"John, we just passed the entrance to the Alamo. It looks like the MDF has set up a checkpoint. According to Amelia, they're executing their contingencies as planned."

"Shit," I said. "Got any good news?"

"Well, the Alamo's residents are still coming and going, which means they won't seal off the Alamo completely, not unless they have to."

"Meet me in the parking lot. Right now I'll need your help disconnecting the fuel cells to protect our reserves."

"What about Amelia?" Avro said.

"She'll be fine in the PDC. We'll tell Jimmy she's your girlfriend."

An hour later, we had finished isolating the power in all thirteen circumferential domes. Kevin recalled one of our construction drones, waking it from weather-induced hibernation. He programmed it to sweep the area around our PDC, cleaning up any drifts before they got too high. We didn't want to be stuck without our equipment like after the last storm.

At five p.m. the Meteorological Center held a conference call. We gathered in the observation lounge as the call came in. We decided not the share the military's cat-five contingency with Central Control. Sharing this knowledge could get us in serious trouble, especially if there was a mole. We all suspected that there were folks outside of the Alamo who were in on the conspiracy.

Jackson appeared on the screen to our left, with the Meteorological Center on our right. The video feeds displayed on the observation deck's windows.

"Status updates everyone," said a man on the right. I didn't recognize him.

Apparently, Avro didn't either. "Who are you? And where the hell is Watson?"

"Alan Gordon, chief climatologist on Project Bakersfield. We can't find Watson. I assume he's in the Alamo."

"Traitor," Kevin barked, and for the moment I agreed. When the lead person from a rouge project disappears, you tend to get suspicious.

"What are you talking about?" Gordon said. "Watson just happened to be over there when they cut off communications."

"Isn't it a bit suspicious?" I said. "Project Bakersfield was Watson's baby. It creates a storm and now Watson is nowhere to be found."

"I can vouch for Watson," Director Jackson said from the left screen. "Watson led a carbon capture project after the Fresno impact, cleaning up the air around California. He even testified before Congress to get the funds."

It was strange looking into the Central Control tower and having it completely dark. Jackson's sunglasses rested on the console beside him and there were dents in his nose where the glasses usually sat.

"I know Watson too. He's always acted in good faith," Gordon added.

"How could someone acting in good faith allow this to happen?" I inquired.

Gordon cleared his throat. "Theoretically, if you can prevent a storm, you can create one. In 2045, there were plans to deploy a hurricane prevention system in the Atlantic. The concept was simple. We'd pump warm water from the surface into deeper water. Since warm water is fuel for hurricanes, pumping it down would prevent the storms."

"Why haven't I heard of this?" Avro asked.

"Because if warm water was purposefully cycled back to the surface, it could mix with warm water from incoming currents. This would double the available fuel and create a super storm. For this reason, the Atlantic Storm Prevention System was canceled."

What Gordon said made sense, forcing me to wonder what it would take to deceive a man like Watson. Watson seemed highly intelligent, intelligent enough to oversee a large-scale endeavor like Project Bakersfield anyway. Could he have been bribed or extorted?

"You asked for updates from us, but what have you got?" I asked Gordon.

"We can confirm that the storm was generated using Project Bakersfield. But there's more. It looks like this storm is being *sustained* by a weak, but consistent, positive charge in the anti-storm grid.

"Sustained," Kevin said. "From where? They already used most of our power reserves to create the storm. Project Bakersfield isn't getting its power from anywhere but the Alamo."

"From H3's reactor," I said.

"Sounds like it," Avro said.

I did some simple math in my head; Project Bakersfield's massive solar grid was over twenty times more powerful than the nuclear reactor. I guessed that after the storm was up and running, it didn't take much to sustain it.

"Are you sure we can't cut the power?" Jackson asked.

Avro brought up a map of the colony's power grid and shared it with the people on the call. A series of green lines appeared on the map. "These green lines are underground power cables running from the solar arrays to the colony."

Avro keyed in a command and replaced the green lines with red ones. "These red lines represent Project Bakersfield's power supply. As you can see, the Alamo is the only point where project Bakersfield connects to the colony. To cut the power, we need to get inside the Alamo and physically disconnect the nuclear reactor from the grid."

"What about severing the anti-storm cabling?" Jackson inquired, this time directing the question at Gordon, whose team had laid the coils.

"You mean outside, on a GOD?" Kevin interrupted.

"He means an EVA," I clarified.

"We can't," Gordon said. "The cables are protected by carbon nanotube mesh. That mesh will stop any cutting tool. You can't even blow up the cable with high explosives. The mesh is imbedded with a protective layer of energy-dispersing resin."

"Jackson," I said, "can you give us an update on the MDF's activities?"

"Sure," Jackson replied. "They've beefed up security around the entrance to the Alamo. But besides riding the army trucks through the channels, back and forth across the bridge, they don't seem to be doing much else. I've talked to the police about this. They're pretty pissed about it. If it were up to me, I'd lock them in their base."

"Have you communicated with them?" Avro asked.

Jackson sighed. "We've tried, but since the storm began, they haven't been answering our calls. Anyway, let's agree on a power quota. We need to begin rationing immediately. I recommend starting the quota at five kilowatt hours per colonist."

"Five is fine by me," I said. That was the most aggressive quota we'd ever had, but with most of our reserves gone, Jackson was wise to be aggressive. We'd need to save as much energy as we could to keep the colonists alive.

"One more thing," Jackson said. "No talking to the media. We don't need a panic. If anyone has any more ideas on how to solve this mess, you let me know."

"You got it," I said, disconnecting the call, relieved that we could now go on to other things.

Later that evening, Kevin, Avro and Amelia met at my apartment to work the problem. Working the problem was a term used by NASA when something went wrong. *Explosion on Apollo 13? Just work the problem! Fire on the 2045 expedition to the asteroid Ceres? Just work the problem!*

Kevin plugged his car into my apartment's circuit, lending us the power to microwave a couple pizzas. He figured we'd be doing some serious thinking, so we'd *need* pizza.

The four of us sat around my round table. A single LED bulb hung over us, lighting the table but leaving the room in darkness.

"Whatever we do, we need to avoid being caught by the MDF," Avro said. "That's a priority. We can't save the colony from a prison cell."

"I think we should leak the conspiracy to the media." Kevin said. "The people have a right to know."

I countered, "If we announce that the Alamo is causing the storm, they'll deny it and blame us for building a shitty system. We don't need the public bashing down our doors."

"We can't let them learn that we know that they plan to blow the domes." Amelia said, "If we're going to stop them, we'll need the element of surprise. And they'll take me out if I go public. You can count on it. The Alamo would welcome a rebellion. It would give them another excuse to take people out."

"Okay then, forget the media. What if we get Central Control to mobilize the police?" Avro recommended. "You know, storm the castle."

"They could but the MDF soldiers have guns. The police don't," Amelia said. "Our most pressing issue is that the MDF is going to start blowing up domes. We've got to focus on that problem first."

"Agreed," I said.

Avro nodded, "There are fourteen domes excluding the Alamo and the spaceport. How do we figure out which dome they're gonna blow?"

"Let's call that problem number one," I said, standing up and heading over the room's holovision wall screen. I used the screen as a whiteboard. At NASA we were trained to map out our problems visually. This seemed like an opportunity to put that training to use.

"I've got problem two," Amelia said. "If they attempt to blow a dome, how do we evacuate the population?"

I wrote, '2 - Evacuate population'.

"What if they blow more than one dome at once?" Kevin asked.

"Prevent multiple attacks," I said and added that to our list.

Amelia addressed Kevin's question directly. "The Alamo wants to blame the disaster on the storm. Blowing one dome at a time is the only way to do this."

"Don't the domes have an autorepair system?" Avro asked, looking at Kevin.

"Yeah, for sure. Imagine a dome breached by a meteor." Kevin smashed one hand into the table, simulating the impact. "One drone seals the hole from the inside, while another flies in from outside and welds on a patch. Because this system works so well, there's no evacuation for small breaches."

"Trust me," Amelia said. "They're gonna have to make a freaking big hole. Can't we just pull the alarm?"

"The domes don't have pull alarms. Only a real emergency will trigger an evacuation." Avro said.

"I think we're onto something," Kevin said. "During a storm, even a small hole will trigger an evacuation."

"Why is that?" Amelia asked.

"Because the outside drone can't do its job," Kevin answered. "If we know which dome they plan to blow, we can trigger the evacuation by making a small hole in one of the domes. That way, we'll at least ensure the safety of the population."

"How long does it take to evacuate a dome?" Avro asked.

Kevin thought about this for a moment. "During the last exercise, it took only five minutes. That seems fast, until you realize that no colonist is over five hundred yards from a pressure channel. Most people can run this in under two minutes. If you're going to lose air pressure, you run for your life."

"Amelia, can you tell us exactly *how* they plan on blowing the dome," I said.

"Plastic explosives," Amelia said. "Four MDF officers will go into the storm and drive to the target domes. They'll lay several explosive devices along the base of the dome and fall back to the canyon, detonating the explosives with a short-range transmitter."

"That seems pretty low tech," Avro commented.

Amelia shrugged, "It's effective. That's what they're going for. They also want it to seem like an accident."

"So to sum up," Kevin said, "We make a small hole in the dome, triggering the evacuation, while the soldiers are on their way back to the canyon."

"That's not enough time," Amelia said. "The saboteurs will learn about the evacuation and think their explosives pre-detonated."

"Sounds like a personal problem," Kevin quipped.

"What would you do if you thought your explosives had pre-detonated?" I asked.

"You hit the big red button just to make sure," Avro said.

"Exactly," I said. "And if they hit the button, the real bomb goes off, and our evacuation plan is for nothing."

"Not exactly," Amelia said. "Not if *we* blow the dome."

Chapter 21

TRAINING

"Okay, you're crazy," Kevin said, pointing at Amelia. I'm sure Avro and I thought the same thing, but for the moment, we just sat there stunned.

"Listen," Amelia said. "We evacuate the colonists into the channels, and then trigger their bomb. We won't get caught and the confusion will buy us time."

"I can't even fathom the concept," I said in a loud voice. I pushed my chair away from the table and stood up. "How the hell could we even think of pulling it off?" I almost walked out of the room but instead paced around, allowing my brain to process Amelia's idea. Was she part of this all? A mole planted to make sure the plan got carried out? She couldn't be! No conspiracy was that sophisticated.

I studied her face, trying to read her. She was either crazy or brilliant. Probably both. I sat back down. We knew we couldn't fight the MDF by traditional means, but this was insane.

Amelia continued. "The bombs use a simple fuse, stuck in some C4, with a battery and a radio transmitter. I can hack that."

"Whatever you say, bomb expert," Kevin said. He wasn't completely on board with the idea either. He looked frustrated and got up to leave, but Avro held his arm, pulling him back down into his chair.

"Listen, we just unplug the explosives from the transmitter and plug it into ours. We wait until the dome is evacuated, then blow it up. If we're lucky, we'll take out a few MFD officers while we're at it."

"So you're telling us we need to go outside? Into the storm?" Avro asked. We all assumed this, Avro just wanted to hear her say it.

Amelia answered, "Yes. There's no way around that."

"Amelia, this brings up a whole new set of problems," I said. "How will we know when the soldiers leave the base and how do we find them out in the storm? I bet you can't see ten feet out there."

"Well, the second problem is easy," Avro said. "There is a way to see through the storm."

"Yeah, flashlights," Kevin said. We all glared at Kevin and I imagined trekking across Mars holding a Maglite.

"There is a modification for the spacesuit visors," Avro continued. "It's a mix of night vision and personal radar. This allows the suits to see through the dust. But the software isn't preinstalled in the spacesuits. I'll need to download the software package enabling that feature."

"I can tell you exactly when the MDF soldiers leave their base," Kevin announced, casually taking a bite of pizza.

"At least you're good for something," Amelia muttered.

Kevin rolled his eyes at Amelia. "Thanks for your vote of confidence, Mrs. Peacekeeper. The entire colony, including the Alamo and the spaceport, is a single pressurized vessel. Unless any of the barriers are up, which they're not. At least not yet anyway. Does everyone know how an airlock works?"

"Of course," Amelia said. "You get inside, the air is pumped out, the hatch opens, and you go outside."

"And where does the air go?" Kevin asked.

"Back into the dome," I answered.

Kevin snapped his fingers, "Thus raising the air pressure in the colony!"

"So we just watch for an increase in air pressure?" I asked. "It's really that simple?"

"It's really that simple," Kevin said. "The base's airlock is big so the change in air pressure will be significant. Ten millibars at least. The weather sensor on your wristwatches will sense it without issue. In fact, I'll set up the alert right now. You'll know exactly when the MDF uses the airlock."

"Alright, let's talk strategy," Amelia said and got up from the table and walked over to the holovision. "John, can you bring up a map of the colony?"

Avro, Kevin and I got up and walked over to the living area and sat on the couch. I grabbed my tablet and tossed a map onto the HV.

The thirteen-dome circumferential was centered on the map like the Japanese flag. Using the tablet, I told the software to highlight the exterior surface roads. One road ran east-west from the spaceport to the circumferential, going down into the canyon and up the other side.

"Okay," I said, walking over to the HV. "From the time the saboteurs exit their airlock, it's a fifteen minutes to drive to the circumferential using this route here." I ran my finger along the road. "Is that about right, Amelia?"

"That's the route," Amelia confirmed. "They'll blow one of the closest domes first, probably the eight or nine o'clock dome. These are also the domes where the unemployed miners live. This means that after we get Kevin's alert, we'll have only a few minutes to get suited up, exit our own airlock, and get to the bombsite."

"I guess we're sleeping in the PDC then," Avro said.

Amelia nodded, "Yup." She stood, joining me at the holovision. I noticed for the first time she was almost a head shorter than me. When we weren't standing side by side, her confidence added several inches. "After they plant the bombs, they'll drive back down the same road and take cover in the canyon. They won't hit the detonator until they're behind the canyon wall. We'll get to work as soon as they leave the bombs unattended."

"What's the visibility of the MDF's suits? Is there any chance they'll see us?" I asked.

"During a storm, everyone will have about two hundred meters visibility," Avro said. "Which means we'll need to be stationed here." Avro got up and pointed to a bluff about a hundred meters to the south of the service road. "From there, we'll be able to spot the MDF's jeep as they crest the canyon."

"From that point on it's simple," Amelia said. "We watch them plant the bomb, then switch the detonator from theirs to ours."

"Simple?" I said, skeptically.

"Well, conceptually," Amelia admitted. "Avro, John, you'll join me out in the storm. I'll need you to watch my back as I prep the detonators. Kevin, you'll need to stay behind to trip the alarm."

"And by trip the alarm, you mean punch a hole in whichever dome they are planning on blowing up?" Kevin asked.

"Exactly. Now, I need each of you to meet me at the PDC warehouse tomorrow morning at 0700."

"That's four hours from now," Kevin complained.

"Get some sleep. You'll need it," Amelia ordered.

"Need it for what?" I asked.

"Training," replied Amelia.

With all the solar panels installed out on the surface, our warehouse was empty. I told Jimmy I'd take the morning shift. He said he wasn't planning on coming in at all, which was fine with us. We spoke to Leeth and let him know we were up to something. He was on call and would stay near the clinic.

Amelia had already spent an hour setting up when Avro, Kevin and I arrived. The only light in the gymnasium-sized room was a single LED, hanging from an extension cord. Amelia stood under the light beside a table. A blue bedsheet on the table hid several random items. Behind her, two of our team's spacesuits hung from metal stands. Protective sacks covered the helmets making the suits look like marshmallow men headed to the gallows.

Kevin looked groggy. "Why couldn't we have at least slept in until eleven?" he asked.

Avro looked at Kevin and rolled his eyes. "A dome could explode at any moment and you want to sleep?"

"All right, Amelia," I said. "Whatcha got for us?"

We gathered around Amelia, "Good morning, gentlemen. Hope you're ready. It's going to be a busy morning." Amelia pulled the cloth from the table.

"Holy shit!" Avro said, drawing out each word.

"Well, someone certainly knows how to use a 3D printer," Kevin said.

An array of crossbows, arrows and a pickaxe rested on the table. I recognized other items from our supply closet, such as radios and cables.

"Where the *heck* did you get the files to print these weapons?" I asked. "What would happen if the Alamo or the MDF monitored our SpaceNET use?"

"Don't worry, Johnny. I can call you Johnny, right?" Amelia sounded even more confident than normal. "I disconnected your computers from the network."

"Then how did you get the crossbows?" Avro asked.

"I designed them myself. While you characters were having a confab with the puppet government and the weather man, I've been planning for war." Amelia pointed at a distant light switch. The room's computer recognized the gesture and illuminated the lights around the perimeter walls. I stepped back in pure shock as my eyes took in what surrounded us. We were surrounded by an entire Armada of targets. Humanoid figures stood on the warehouse floor, plastic drones hung on the walls. Some of them even moved.

"Did you put a target on a Roomba?" Kevin asked, watching the cleaning drone purr along the floor.

"Yup," Amelia answered.

"Nice use of vacuum-formed plastic!" Avro commented.

"Thank you!"

Amelia picked up a fiber-plastic crossbow, raising the stock to her shoulder. The split-limb bowstave was huge, nothing like the small crossbows I'd seen in movies. She aimed at an angry looking target thirty feet down range.

Fwap! A six-inch barb hit the first target right in the head. In the blink of an eye, Amelia pulled a long lever on the bottom of the crossbow. The device went "Cha-Chink" as another bolt clicked into place.

Fwap! Cha-Chink!

Fwap! Cha-Chink!

Fwap! Cha-Chink!

Fwap! Cha-Chink!

Fwap! Cha-Chink!

Six targets now stood with small arrows protruding from their heads. Two of the targets tipped backward and fell to the floor.

"Daaaaammmmn," Kevin exclaimed, impressed.

"Each cartridge holds six bolts. Reload like this," Amelia said, pulling a spent cartridge out from under the bow, picking up another clip off the table and slapping it in place.

"Seems easy enough," Avro said.

"It is easy," Amelia said. "But you're not wearing a space suit."

"Oh," Avro replied. "Right. Question. Why do the targets look like Kevin?" I inspected the targets. At first glance they looked like lifeless mannequins but soon realized they did look like Kevin.

"I took the template from the personnel files," Amelia stated with a smug smile on her face.

Kevin shot her a disgusted look while Avro and I laughed.

"Avro, Johnny, get suited up and let's do a radio check," Amelia instructed. "Kevin, put on this headset. I've altered the radios in the suits to use cell phone frequencies, which I've digitally encoded for secure transmissions. We don't want any MDF soldiers listening in."

"Remind us again where we found you?" Kevin said.

"Funny, Kevin," responded Amelia. "Now take this pickaxe and start practicing your swing. You'll need to hit this." Amelia held up a metal cylinder. "It's called a breacher. Stick it to the glass, hit it with the axe, and a small charge will force a slug into the glass." I figured she got the "charge" from our flares. That was the only source of gunpowder in the PDC I could think of.

Amelia prepped the bows while Avro and I suited up. We practiced loading, firing and reloading with the helmets off. Once we got the hang of the weapons, we practiced with our helmets on.

The plan was to start with the weapons loaded when we went into the storm. Hopefully, even in the worst-case scenario, we wouldn't need to reload. If we did, we'd have to grab the spare clips from a satchel over our shoulders.

After fifteen minutes of practice, we were hitting all of our targets at twenty-five yards, without issue. Avro, who had military training, could even hit the moving targets. Thanks to my aim, we would need another Roomba.

After the weapons training, we practiced getting into our spacesuits, grabbing our supplies, and entering the airlock. Of course, we knew how to do this but the process usually took minutes. We had to reduce this to mere seconds in order to intercept the MDF soldiers headed for the dome.

We broke for lunch at eleven, exhausted from the training. Kevin seemed to be the most worn out, even though he spent most of his time leaning on his pickaxe. In the observation deck, Avro stood at the kitchenette making peanut butter and jelly sandwiches. Amelia sat at a control station drinking a Coke, her feet up on a console and a distant look on her face.

"What are you thinking?" Avro asked, coming over and sitting beside Amelia.

"About killing my comrades," Amelia said. "These were people I trained with, people I bonded with. But now they're on the wrong side, and I really don't see any other options." She pulled her feet off the console and faced Avro.

"Whatever happens, I'm here for you. All the way." He paused. "Give me your hand." Avro held out his hand and Amelia put her left hand in his.

In Avro's right hand, he lifted up a sharpie and on the wrist-guard used to block the signal from her military transmitter he wrote: *We're all in this together.*

And below that he wrote his call sign. *Avro.*

Amelia smiled and a single tear streamed down her face. Avro looked at me and handed me the Sharpie. I sat down at the table, leaned over and wrote, *John*.

Passing the pen to Kevin, he smiled, and wrote, *Kevin*, and drew a starfighter beside his name.

Amelia took her arm back and stared at the words. She hated wearing the awkwardly printed device and couldn't even itch under the metal for fear of a signal getting out. But now, the thing became her most valuable possession in the whole world.

Kevin turned to the console and logged onto SpaceNET, accessing a recent briefing from *NewsFlash*. We needed to understand what the public knew. Did the colonists know that Project Bakersfield had caused the storm?

Bowden's face appeared on the screen. He stood on the steps to the Central Control building. "Project Bakersfield was an abject failure. According to Central's top man, Director Jackson Carver, the Alamo's engineering team controlled the Anti-Storm System at the time the storm hit. The Alamo used over eighty percent of the colony's reserve power before shutting it down.

"I asked Director Carver if the Alamo had permission to use the colony's reserve, here was his response."

The video switched to Jackson. "Two words: Hell. No."

Bowden continued, "Central control, along with the colony's engineering departments, will be conducting a thorough investigation of this incident." The feed ended.

"Why is Jackson covering for the Alamo?" I asked.

"Perhaps he's stalling or he doesn't want the colonists freaking out," Avro answered.

"The colonists should be freaking out," I said. "We've got only a few weeks left of reserve."

"They can freak out all they want," Amelia said. "But they're not going to actually do anything about it. Not yet, anyway. Most of these people have been through a storm but none lasting over a few days. They're not ready for a fight. But when the dome blows, everything will change."

Chapter 22

BREACH

At eight p.m. that evening, our alarms sang. As Kevin predicted, the MDF's depressurizing airlock spiked the atmospheric pressure in the colony. Kevin set the song "Staying Alive" as the alert's tone. We were resting on cots near the airlock when the alerts sounded.

"Get up, Kevin," Avro yelled, poking him in the ribs. "We'll radio you as soon as we know which dome you need to bust. And call Leeth. Tell him to prepare to receive casualties."

"Aye aye, Captain," Kevin said. He leapt from the cot and bolted to his car. He would wait for our call on the western side of the circumferential.

"This is it, team. Good luck," Amelia said, pulling the bulky spacesuit up over her shoulders. "Zip me up, Avro?"

Avro helped Amelia zip the large zipper up her front. We had modified Kevin's spacesuit to fit Amelia. Earlier that day, she spent an hour scrubbing a chocolate stain out of the inside of the helmet. We also found it amusing seeing the name "Patel" embroidered on the front and back of her unit. The name patch was a hologram with fictional space fighter planes circling the letters.

I snapped my helmet into place and keyed several commands into my arm display, activating the suit and turning on the radios. Just like we had trained, I picked up a crossbow and followed Avro and Amelia into the airlock.

"Radio check," Amelia said as she tapped her finger against her helmet.

"Avro here, I read you five by five over," Avro said as he pushed the button to activate the airlock.

"John here, five by five," I said over the sound of air rushing from the room.

"Kevin?" Amelia called. Kevin was supposed to be wearing his earpiece.

After a pause, Kevin's voice rang through our spacesuit's internal speakers. "I'm here. Would you guys hurry up already?"

"Activate visual overlay," Avro instructed. We hit a command on our wrist controls as the helmet cameras fed visual information to our visors. The airlock door opened and a rush of filthy Martian atmosphere swept in.

We stepped out into the storm, leaning slightly forward against the winds. Mars's atmosphere is thin, almost a vacuum, so the two hundred-knot winds were just an inconvenience. The dust was the issue. Fortunately, the drone Kevin had programmed to keep our staging area free of drifts had done its job.

Avro unlatched the garage door and opened it. Our visors illuminated the interior of the garage as we piled into the jeep. The vehicle had no roof, just like the Jeeps from World War II, except this jeep's seats accommodated the backpacks attached to each spacesuit. Avro tossed his weapon in the rear and hopped into the driver's seat. Amelia held a satchel of radio equipment in her lap and sat shotgun. I occupied the seat behind Amelia, setting my weapon beside Avro's.

"Don't forget to buckle your seatbelts," I said.

"Roger that… Dad," Amelia said, bucking herself in. Avro did the same. They probably didn't need the reminder.

"Let's do this," Avro said as he hit the accelerator. The jeep burst from the garage and into the storm.

Visibility was worse than I expected, but Avro knew where he was going. In our visors, the blustering dust looked like a raging snowstorm. We drove south, reaching the edge of the area swept clean by Kevin's drone. The jeep launched over several sand dunes. Avro yanked the steering column to the right, turning west toward the canyon. Martian dirt spewed from the wheels before being swept away in the violent winds.

We followed a service road that ran between the solar arrays. Our path curved up as we approached the ridge that overlooked the road from the spaceport. Behind our jeep, rushing winds filled our tracks with dust.

Avro slammed on the brakes. The jeep skidded to a stop, each wheel pushing up a pile of loose dirt. The vehicle came to rest behind a green electrical box, like the kind you find in neighborhoods with underground power. The box was large enough to hide the jeep from anyone approaching the colony.

We piled out, sneaking around the metallic structure. I looked back towards the circumferential and could barely see the nearest dome through the storm.

"Okay," Avro said pointing into the abyss. "There's the service road. We'll take cover behind that bluff." Avro motioned us toward a rock outcropping that would provide us a clear line of sight to the road and the colony but would hide our spacesuits from view.

"Roger that," I said.

"Copy," Amelia said.

We arrived at the bluff as an MFD jeep crested the canyon. The jeep's two front tires left the ground for a second as it transitioned to level terrain. We lay prone with only the tops of our helmets peeking over the bluff. Avro propped up his crossbow like a sniper rifle.

"There they are," Amelia said. "It looks like we've got four bogeys.

Hang tight, Kevin. We'll have a target dome for you in sixty seconds."

The MDF vehicle worked its way towards the colony, stopping at the nine o'clock dome. The soldiers got out and pulled their equipment from the truck bed.

"Okay, Kevin, go to the nine o'clock dome. Get in position and wait for my signal," Amelia instructed.

"Copy that," Kevin replied. "Heading to the nine o'clock dome now." It occurred to me that we were sending Kevin into the doomed dome. If we screwed this up, we'd never see him again.

"All right guys," Amelia said. "Let's hold here until we move in. No need to change positions and risk being spotted."

We watched as the soldiers placed a dozen explosive charges along the perimeter of the dome. Each charge was the size of a lunchbox, just as Amelia had described.

"See that guy who stayed behind?" Amelia said. "He's arming the detonator. As soon as they leave, we'll run over and pull the plug. Avro, you've got the best aim. Stay here and cover us."

The remaining soldier finished his work and trudged back to the jeep. Before getting in, he looked at the others, nodding. Had they contemplated the morality of what they were doing? They had obviously bought into the idea that they were killing the colonists for the greater good, but I'm guessing that didn't make the job any easier. The officer climbed into the jeep and they headed back toward the canyon.

"Okay, moving in," Amelia announced. "Kevin, trigger the alarm and get those people out of there!"

Kevin waited in a quiet alley on the western side of the dome. He parked the car and retrieved the pickaxe from the passenger's seat. He approached the glass and fastened the breacher. "This is it," he said and swung the pickaxe at his target. The breacher made a brittle crack like a single round fired from a pistol.

Kevin's hands ached from the reverberation. A small chip formed in the wall and a few tiny shards of flexi-glass fell to the ground. It didn't work.

Amelia's voice shouted over the radio, "Any time now, Kevin!"

We trudged down the ridge to bomb's trigger mechanism. Amelia yanked the bomb containing the MDF's transmitter out of the circuit.

"Here, take this," she said.

"What?" I yelled. "I thought you were going to disarm it!"

"This just became our decoy. Take it fifty paces from the dome and join Avro in the bluff. I'll meet you there. Run!"

I realized what she was doing. When the soldiers hit the trigger, the bomb would detonate harmlessly, buying us some time. If they hit the trigger too early, I'd never know.

"Kevin, about that evacuation," Amelia radioed.

"Just a minute!" Kevin said. She heard the pick hitting the glass.

"Shit," Kevin said, looking around to see if anyone had spotted him.

"I heard that," Amelia said "What's going on? Why aren't people evacuating?"

"Your stupid breacher was a dud. Any advice would be extremely helpful!"

I dropped the decoy fifty paces to the northwest and sprinted back up the ridge to join Avro in the bluff.

"Work the problem, Kevin," Avro said.

Amelia finished her work and hurried back to our position. The three of us lay down in a row. Then it happened: the MDF soldiers hit their trigger and the decoy bomb detonated with a high-pitched crack. A plume of Martian grit sprayed into the air and we felt the concussion in the ground. In a split second, the plume dissipated in the wind as if it had never existed.

From our position on the buff, we could see the MDF jeep parked beyond the crest of the canyon. One of the men got out to inspect the blast. "Kevin, hurry up before they realize the dome is still intact!" I said in a loud whisper.

The man walked up to the edge of the canyon, giving him line of sight to the dome. Through the darkness, dust and wind, the colony had to be at the limits of his visor's visual range. I watched as he trudged forward, leaning slightly into the low-pressure wind. When he noticed that the dome was still intact, we watched him hitting a trigger mechanism. He turned toward the MDF jeep and shrugged.

Kevin took one more swing with all his strength. The pickaxe buried itself into the flexi-glass. He yanked on the handle, trying to get it loose. It didn't move.

"Ah, I have a problem," he yelled.

"Just shut up and figure it out!" I said, watching as the soldier climbed back into the jeep with his friends.

Kevin looked at the axe then looked at his car, muttering, "Dammit, I like that car!"

He sat in the driver's seat and reached for the dash, hitting two buttons: one to disengage the autopilot and another to deactivate the collision avoidance system. He threw the car into reverse, backing several feet into the alley. He shifted into drive and hit the accelerator, reaching fifteen kilometers per hour. He wanted to embed the axe, not bust out into the storm.

The car smashed into the dome wall, the front end crumpling as the axe embedded itself into the bumper. The airbags inflated, slapping Kevin's face with fabric and peppering him with white powder.

Nearby, alarms raged and Kevin covered his ears. Two repair drones released from their caches and buzzed toward the small hole. People rushed into the streets in a panic, like airline passengers when the masks deploy.

Emergency power kicked on and all the streetlights illuminated, lighting the ill-fated dome for the last time.

Kevin contemplated his personal situation. What would happen if Central Control found out he had intentionally busted the dome? He worried that the blame would rest on him. This was Kevin's lucky day. The pickaxe had punctured the car's battery pack, creating a spark. The battery pack began to burn.

Kevin yanked the small Lego Starfighter hanging from his rearview mirror and fled the vehicle. Flames poured from the wheel wells and around the axe. He glanced back at his car, but within seconds, the flames were so bright he could hardly look at them. Drones arrived to patch the hole but were overwhelmed by the heat. They fell to the ground, robotic arms flailing about.

"Success! I'm getting the hell out of here!" Kevin yelled into his radio.

"Roger that," Amelia said. "Let us know when it's clear."

Avro and I trained our weapons on the MDF jeep as it crested the canyon wall and made its way back towards the dome.

"Kevin, get those people out of there!" I said. "If those soldiers make it back to the bomb we'll be screwed!"

Kevin ran onto the boulevard and towards the nearest tunnel. "The dome's gonna blow!" he yelled as loud as he could. The people heard him and accelerated their sprint to the exits. Volunteer wardens in orange vests stood in the channels, encouraging people to "Move! Move! Move!"

The soldiers reached the dome wall and parked the jeep. The four of them left the vehicle and walked towards Amelia's improvised trigger.

Avro looked over at me. "Are you ready for a firefight?" he asked.

"Hell no," I responded, but cocked my crossbow just in case. The MDF wore their rifles on the thigh of their spacesuits. If it came to shooting, we'd better not miss.

Kevin reached the channel and watched as the last of the people ran through.

"All clear!" said one of the wardens.

"All clear!" the other wardens repeated. "Seal off the dome!" The two wardens ran into the tunnel as the barrier rose behind them.

"Almost there," Kevin said. "Almost there," he said again. "Barriers closed!"

"Roger that," Amelia said. "Let the show begin."

The MDF soldiers were beginning to realize that someone had tampered with their bomb. We could tell by their body language they were chattering in obvious confusion.

Amelia flipped open the cover of the trigger mechanism, hitting the red button within. One of the soldiers turned and looked right at us. A cold chill ran down my spine as I realized we'd been seen. There was a pause. For a moment nothing happened. Then, the soldier vaporized along with his three companions. A flash of orange-red light resonated through the storm as Avro, Amelia and I huddled behind the bluff.

The charges detonated in sequence along the dome's foundation, each sounding like a thunder crack. The western edge of the dome lifted up off its foundation, exposing the structures within to the near vacuum of the Martian atmosphere.

The channels, usually filled with multiple lanes of traffic, were packed with survivors. The windows in the pressure barrier attracted a crowd, Kevin included, as people watched the events inside the affected dome.

"Oh fuck," sounded on repeat as the crowd witnessed the destruction on the other side of the glass. The structures inside the dome exploded. The atmospheric pressure in the buildings released into the walls and the buildings tore from their foundations. Trees were stripped of their leaves and snapped in half by a rush of air. Parked cars rolled westward over the spot where multi-story buildings had stood seconds before. Debris spilled out onto the Martian surface. Vehicles, trees and household items littered the landscape.

The pressure inside the dome dropped by ninety-nine percent and the storm rushed in. The Martian wind filled the dome with red dust. A few streets lights remained intact, providing a dim glow in the now defunct habitat.

I looked over at Avro and Amelia and realized I couldn't see them. My ears ached from the concussion. A moment later, a hand pressed against my visor and I could see again. Amelia wiped the dirt from the glass covering my face, and I realized we were buried in dust and debris.

"Well," Avro spoke as if we'd just taken a stroll in the park. "That was dramatic. Let's go home."

𐑍

We stepped out of the airlock to find Kevin standing there, a goofy grin on this face. "You certainly know how to mess up a neighborhood," he declared.

"Why are you out of breath?" I asked, setting my helmet on a shelf.

"I ran here," he replied, taking a weapon from Avro so he could concentrate on removing his suit.

"What happened to your car?" Avro asked.

Kevin just smiled.

"You used your car to crack the dome," Amelia said. Kevin nodded the affirmative. "Kevin, you are brilliant!"

Kevin smiled at Amelia, saying, "That's the nicest thing you've ever said."

"Well, it's not every day you save thousands of lives," Amelia said. "Avro, would you?" Amelia motioned to her spacesuit's zipper.

We gathered in the observation lounge and Avro made hot chocolate. I wanted something stronger, whiskey perhaps, having been mildly traumatized by what we had just witnessed.

"So what's next for the colony?" I asked, "And what's next for us? We didn't really think past today."

"Well," began Amelia, "those guys we blew up? They were four of the nine remaining officers who knew about the contingencies. The remaining five will think twice about blowing another dome any time soon."

"We still have a problem," I said. "H3 could probably find more conspirators and that storm will eventually kill us."

"You mean instead of blowing us up, they'll starve us out," Avro said.

"Exactly."

"There's only one thing to do," Amelia said with a mischievous tone. "It's time to storm the Alamo."

Chapter 23

REVOLUTION!

The three of us looked at Amelia as if she had three heads. Didn't we talk about this? There was no way we could storm the Alamo! What chance did we have against an army?

But Amelia had that look in her eye again so we listened. "The colonists are freaking out. We can use this to our advantage. Now is the time to get inside!" Amelia said, pressing her index finger into the table. The four of us sat at the table in the observation lounge, each cupping a hot beverage, which seemed appropriate after being out in a storm.

Amelia sat back in her chair. "Why do the colonists think the dome blew up?" she asked. The question was rhetorical.

"I don't know. Why did the dome blow up?" Kevin answered, sarcastically repeating the rhetorical question. "We're sure as hell not going to admit to it!"

"No, we're not," I said. "If anyone asks, we tell them the storm did it."

"The storm did it?" Kevin was astonished at the absurdity of the lie.

"Yup, the storm did it," Amelia said with a smile. "If it's not safe in the domes, where should people go?"

Kevin wasn't getting it. Kevin was one of the smartest people on the planet but sometimes he was a bit slow. "For the love of Ganesha, please tell me what you are talking about!"

"The Presidio, Kevin," I said. "H3's underground paradise! We tell people about the underground dome, tell them it's the only safe place, and convince them to get into the Alamo."

Avro looked as if he really liked this idea. "This should keep the MDF soldiers distracted long enough for us to sneak inside, detach the nuclear reactor, and reclaim Project Bakersfield!"

If our theory was correct, the reactor provided just barely enough energy to sustain the storm. Shutting it down, or even disconnecting it, should allow the storm to dissipate naturally.

"You make it sound easy," Amelia said. "And we might not get another chance. But we'll need help."

"It's time to involve the cops isn't it?" I said.

Amelia nodded. She knew she couldn't stay hidden forever. It was time to play her final card. "We need an army. A thousand colonists, no matter how angry, just aren't going to cut it."

My phone buzzed. It was a text from Leeth: *You guys okay? There's rioting in the pavilion.* I read the text aloud.

"Well, there's our angry mob," Amelia said.

"How do we get people to riot in the Alamo instead of the pavilion?" I asked. My mind filtered through several ideas about starting rumors or trying to reason with the crowd. None of these ideas seemed plausible.

Fortunately, Avro had the answer. "We show them the underground dome," he said. "We show them the Presidio!"

"Avro, we have no evidence that the Presidio even exists," I said.

"Yes, we do," Avro said, smiling.

"Wait, we do?" Amelia said.

"After we opened the airlock and entered the underground dome, I turned on my suit's data recorder. It was on the whole time."

"I am so attracted to you right now." She kissed him and then ran out of the room.

"Where are you going?" Avro asked.

"To make more weapons!" Amelia called from down the hall.

Kevin looked at Avro. "That is some woman you got there, bro."

Avro just nodded. "I'm calling Jackson," he said, reaching for his phone.

"Why not just call him from here?" I said, tapping the console.

"If the MDF monitors our channels, we're about to say things we won't want them to hear.

The phone rang twice before Jackson's face appeared on the screen. "Jackson, it's Avro. I've got John Orville and Kevin Patel here." Avro set his phone down on the table, letting the device project Jackson's image onto the table.

"What's going on?" Jackson shouted. "There's a dome blown to bits. The colonists are rioting outside my door and you're calling my cell?"

"Jackson," I said, getting his attention. "We have an idea and need your help. If the MDF is monitoring official communications, we don't want them to hear this."

"MDF bastards," Jackson muttered. "I'm listening."

"We both know we need to take back Project Bakersfield and at least disconnect the reactor. We need to get inside the Alamo."

Jackson seemed desperate. "And you think you have a solution?"

I nodded and Jackson leaned back from the camera. "What do you need me to do?" he asked.

"We need to borrow your mob," Avro said.

"Ha!" Jackson said. "You can have 'em but why not herd cats while you're at it. They're angry. They blame us for the storm. Heck, they think it's the end of the world!"

"Perfect. The angrier the better," I said. "We'll also need to borrow the cops, we'll need them to clear the way, prevent any soldiers from stopping the mob from getting to the Alamo and protect them once they're there."

"Our officers against a military unit? Are you nuts? All they've got are stunners!"

"Send them here," Avro said. "We have some presents for them."

"How the hell did you get guns?" Jackson yelled, pressing the camera so close to his face we could only see his eyes.

"We don't have guns," I said. "Well, not exactly. And we'll need Robert Bowden and his news crew. They'll want to hear this. We have a way to save everyone from the storm, and from exploding domes." I took a breath. "Kevin will send you the details."

Jackson thought about this for a moment. "If you can get these people out of here, I'll give you whatever you need."

We firmed up the plan with Jackson and by the time we were done, he was confident the plan was sound. The colony had over a hundred police officers, and with thousands of rioting colonists, we believed we stood a fighting chance.

After the call, Avro turned to face me. "Are you sure you're ready for this?"

"I'm sure. We better call Leeth and have him set up a medical station in the twelve o'clock dome."

From this point on, we were no longer fighting a few conspirators. We were starting a war.

Kevin put a data-package together for *NewsFlash*. There were five large holovision screens in the pavilion. Our goal was to get our story on those screens. I ran down to open the warehouse. The officers would arrive in a matter of minutes.

Avro joined Amelia in the machine shop. He had his own plans for the mob.

"Amelia, how much fiber-plastic does it take to stop a bullet?" he asked.

She turned to a terminal and entered a series of commands. "Force equals mass times acceleration, dude," she replied. "You're making shields for the colonists."

"Yup," Avro said.

"Way ahead of you." Amelia swiped her hand across the display, transferring a schematic over to Avro.

"Thirty-five millimeters. You are an amazing woman!"

Avro told the computers to print spears and shields until the machines ran out of filament. He then backed a panel truck up to the shop's door and loaded the improvised weapons as the industrial printers spat them out.

From the parking lot, I marshaled the first six squad cars into the warehouse.

A dozen officers got out, including Captain Daniels.

"Good to see you, Captain," I said. The officers stood around me in a semi-circle.

"Central briefed us on the plan. You really think you can turn off the storm?" Daniels asked.

"We hope so. The sooner we take back control of Project Bakersfield, the better," I said.

Amelia stepped out of the shop, holding an armful of newly printed weapons.

The captain recognized her, "What the hell! You're that insane woman they've been looking for."

"I assure you, Captain, I'm lucid," Amelia said. "I'm an MDF officer.

They drugged me when I wouldn't go along with their plans."

"What plans?" demanded the captain.

Amelia paused for a second. "Their plans to blow up the domes."

"No shit," Daniels said. He took a moment to process this. He put the pieces together in his mind. "Oh shit!" he said again. "That dome, that dome was destroyed intentionally?"

"It was," I said.

"And now you're helping us?" Daniels asked, looking at Amelia.

"That's why I'm here," she said. Captain Daniels and Amelia sized each other up. The captain appeared hesitant to accept help from a fugitive.

I stepped in. "If it weren't for Amelia, all of those people in the nine o'clock dome would be dead."

"What do you mean?"

"Captain, we knew they were coming, so we set off the alarms," I said. I explained how Kevin set up the pressure alerts.

"Why wait to involve us?" The captain said. "It would have been nice if you'd kept us in the loop."

"Two reasons. First, we didn't know who we could trust. We still don't. And second, we couldn't put Amelia at risk. The MDF means business and she's confident if she went public, they'd take her out."

Amelia passed the captain a crossbow and he turned it over in his hands. "What do you need us to do?" he asked.

"The goal is to get our engineers into the Alamo and take over their engineering control center. To do this, we need the mob in the Alamo to distract the MDF."

"What if they start shooting?" said one of the officers.

Avro stepped forward. He wore his SAR jacket, giving him the look of a badass military commander. "Then we're at war," he said

"First things first," I said. "You'll need to park squad cars over the Alamo's pressure barrier. We need that open long enough to get the colonists in."

"Where will you be?" Captain Daniels asked.

"We'll be hiding inside the mob," I answered.

"One more question before I talk to the rest of my boys," he said. "How the hell are you going to convince the mob to storm the Alamo?"

"With this," Avro said, holding up his phone and showing the officer the video of the underground dome and telling them where it was.

The captain took the phone and studied the images, "Holy shit, boys!" the captain said to his fellow officers. "You gotta see this!"

After seeing the underground complex, the officers agreed to help coax the mob into the Alamo. With an artificially generated storm and a clear agenda to eliminate the colonists, the officers had all the evidence they needed.

Captain Daniels requested more of Amelia's weapons, and we assured him the printers were creating them by the dozens. We were doing everything we could to even the fight.

Kevin, Avro, Amelia and I took the panel truck to the pavilion and pulled up next to the protesters. There were over a thousand people there, screaming at central control.

I slid my phone from my watch and called Jackson. Jackson sat in the Central Control tower, two hundred feet above the pavilion.

"Jackson, do you have the media?" I yelled, loud enough to hear myself over the crowd outside the car.

"I have Mr. Bowden right here," Jackson said, pointing the camera at Bowden.

"That's some footage your friend got," Bowden said, leaning into view. "I can't believe that place is for real!"

"A pleasure to have you on our side, Robert," I said.

"We're good to go here, just got word, the squad cars are in position," Avro said. "Release the footage when you're ready."

A moment later, the LED displays around the pavilion lit up.

"Breaking News!" the displays read. "Alamo hiding massive underground paradise. Could this be the only safe place on Mars?"

The crowd went silent, some staring at the holovisions, others watching on their phones or staring into space, watching the video on smart lenses.

The video transitioned to an interview between Jackson and Mr. Bowden.

"So, Jackson," Bowden began, "where did you get this footage?"

"From one of the colony's engineers," Jackson answered. "Apparently, he stumbled across a back door while out on a GOD."

Kevin smiled and elbowed me in the ribs. "It's catching on," he said.

The camera focused on Bowden's face, his eyes probing Jackson. "So what do you suggest we do?"

Jackson looked directly at the camera. "Get to the Alamo and get to that underground colony! The Alamo is guarded. You may face resistance. We have people in the pavilion passing out shields and our police force will provide cover. Be careful, but get down there, and make it fast, before other domes collapse!"

The colonists in the pavilion looked confused, but Kevin jumped out of the SUV, opened the trunk and yelled. "Shields and spears. Get 'em while they're hot!"

Colonists grabbed the makeshift weapons and began running in the direction of the Alamo. The four of us ran to the very center of the mob.

It was like running with the bulls. People swarmed around us, pushing and shoving, trying to reach the northern channel leading to the Alamo.

We arrived in minutes to find two police cars parked over the Alamo's forty-foot wide pressure barrier. The police officers were arguing with the guards at the Alamo's security checkpoint.

The guards noticed the crowd and one of them yelled, "Shit! Shit! Shit!" as he realized the mob was coming right at him. The guard picked up his radio and yelled. "Fuck the cops! We need this barrier up now!" Within the Alamo, several MDF soldiers took up position.

When the guard put down the radio, the barrier began to close. The barrier was a double door with one section rising from the ground and another dropping down from above. The lower barrier connected with the police cruisers first, lifting them off the ground until the descending barrier connected with the roofs, crushing the police cars like soda cans.

When our mob arrived at the barrier, a three-foot space remained, held open by the crushed police cruisers. Colonists poured over the barrier, running aimlessly inside the Alamo. Kevin and I climbed over the barrier, followed by Avro, who turned back to give Amelia a hand, but she just shook her head, hopping over, as if doing parkour. Captain Daniels took position behind one of the squad cars. I gave him a quick salute as I hit the surface on the other side.

Somewhere inside the Alamo, an order was given. The two guards at the gate reached for their weapons, but before they could fire, two police officers rose up from behind a squad car, firing a bolt into each guard. A dozen other cop cars pulled up to the barriers, and the officers poured out, following the rioting colonists into the Alamo. Two officers ran over to the guard station, grabbing the fallen guards' weapons. They began pouring fire into the Alamo.

All around us, bullets impacted Avro's fiber-plastic shields, but even so, several men and women fell to the ground. A dozen cops took up position and began covering fire. Bolts and bullets rained into the Alamo, hindering the MDF's resistance. The police picked off a dozen MDF soldiers in the Alamo's pavilion. Colonists poured over the bodies, picking up weapons and carrying them with them.

Twenty more MDF soldiers took defensive positions near the entrance, exchanging fire with the police taking cover behind the barrier. The colonists fought back, tossing spears at the soldiers. We outnumbered the MDF twenty to one.

Behind us, MDF reinforcements approached from the spaceport, flanking the cops. The officers climbed over the barrier, taking positions inside the Alamo as soldiers pushed a wave of colonists back into the channels.

Inside the Alamo, MDF soldiers pulled their fallen comrades into cover.

I looked toward the tram station leading to the Presidio. It was still open! Why didn't they close off the Presidio when they saw the broadcast? Then I realized what they were doing. "They're evacuating the Alamo's population into the Presidio!" I yelled.

Amelia looked confused, "Why the hell wouldn't they stay in their condos?"

We watched as the last of the Alamo's wealthy residents scurried into the Presidio's tram station like mice chased by a cat.

Something had changed. It was too quiet. On the balconies above, several soldiers began taking up positions. "Get Captain Daniels on the line. Have his officers clear the way to the tram station."

"Roger that," Avro said, reaching for his phone.

"Kevin, get these people to the Presidio. We'll focus on getting to engineering."

"What's the hurry? Don't we need the distraction?" Kevin replied, running alongside us.

"Look at the soldiers, Kevin! Look what they're wearing!" I pointed up to the nearest balcony. Several soldiers ran between the pillars and it was clear they were wearing spacesuits.

"Oh my God," Amelia said, noticing the same thing. "There're going to decompress the Alamo!"

"Oh shit!" Kevin yelled, turning to the mob. "Get into that station!" he yelled as loudly as he could. "That's the Presidio!"

Like a flock of birds, a swarm of people sprinted after Kevin as he ran towards the tube car station. The colony's police officers had cleared the way and several MDF soldiers lay on the ground. But before the mob reached the entrance to the station, a large steel barrier began sliding shut from the left and right.

"They're shutting the doors!" someone yelled. I looked around. It wasn't just the tram station being sealed off. It was everywhere!

"Quick, get something to brace it with!" Kevin yelled, standing at the entrance.

"Use this!" a man said, carrying one of Avro's 3D printed shields. People flew into the structure as Kevin held the shield in place. The mechanical doors whined in protest at the interruption.

"Hurry!" Kevin said. "Anyone left outside will suffocate!"

Hundreds of people poured through the barrier into the station, many of them holding MDF assault rifles salvaged from fallen soldiers. Bullets ricocheted off the walls all around the opening, and the officer to Kevin's right fell to the ground. Kevin slipped through the barrier, taking cover with another officer, who paused to reload a captured rifle.

In the pavilion, a dozen officers ran towards the Presidio's tram station, stopping occasionally to fire at the MDF soldiers.

Kevin stood inside the tram station, pointing people toward to the tracks. The tram had already left, but Kevin was sure it was a clear shot all the way to the underground dome.

Outside the barrier, MDF soldiers approached the tram station with guns raised. Kevin ripped down the shield and the barrier shut with a bang.

Meanwhile, Avro, Amelia and I made it deep inside the Alamo. "What now?" I yelled.

"We've got to find engineering. Look for a service door," Avro said, rushing along one of the walls. Amelia followed us, holding a rifle in each hand.

We turned a corner into an alley where two MDF soldiers kept watch over a set of doors. Before they could raise their guns, Amelia took them out in quick succession. The guards dropped to the floor in pain.

"It's locked!" Avro said, trying the doors.

The two soldiers lay moaning on the ground. "What's in there?" I demanded of the soldiers.

"I have no idea," said the one of the men. "We're just doing our job."

"Did you feel that?" I said, holding my ear and sensing a lack of pressure.

"Not good," Avro said. He ran back towards the main section and peered around the corner. Several MDF soldiers battled with the few colonists and police officers that were still standing. In the distance, the Alamo's barrier had closed, the crushed squad cars having been pulled inside.

Amelia looked around, considering our options. "We need to get into a pressure vessel before the air gets too thin."

We ran down the hallways checking doors but found every one locked. My ears popped again and I tried to breath. Nausea set in and my heart rate elevated until I could feel my pulse in my neck. We were back facing the main atrium, but this time, all the MDF soldiers had their helmets on. We watched as several colonists slouched to the ground.

"Well," Avro hissed, his breathing strained. "You can't say we didn't—" He passed out.

I looked over at Amelia, her eyes and mouth wide open. Then it got very, very quiet.

Chapter 24

WE MEET AGAIN

I awoke to a young woman pulling a needle from my arm. "Adrenaline," she said. "Just enough to wake you."

Avro and Amelia slouched in comfortable looking chairs, their eyes half open. The woman moved on to Avro and Amelia, waking them in turn.

I looked around the room, my eyes barely coming into focus. We appeared to be inside a glass dome no bigger than a large dining room. We were still in the Alamo. I soon realized that we were up high. I sat near the room's glass wall and looked down. Below us were the various elevated walkways that wreathed the Alamo's interior.

A desk sat in the middle of the room, identical to the one in H3's office in the Presidio.

"H fucking 3," Avro muttered as he tried to stand up. A guard pushed him back into his seat.

Henry Allen the Third came out from behind the desk and paced back and forth. He glowered at us from behind his thick-rimmed glasses.

"So, kids," he said, "we meet again." He walked towards the window and stared. He watched the soldiers dragging bodies from the battle that had raged below. "I see you've made a friend. Welcome, Amelia. You've been quite the prick in my little finger."

"You can end this," I said.

"Oh, can I? And why would I do that?" said H3, looking at his own reflection in the glass and straightening the cuffs on his navy blue blazer.

"John, he can't exactly run outside yelling 'Stop.' He doesn't seem to be wearing a spacesuit," Avro said.

"Your friend is right, John," H3 said, turning toward us. "I can't stop this. This is bigger than me. Do you see the soldiers out there? They're just trying to keep the peace, tapering the civil unrest *you* caused."

"That we caused?" Amelia said, considering getting up, but instead eyed the large guards standing beside her. "This shit is your doing. The storm. The dome. All of it!"

"Yes, well, if all had gone to plan, it would have been nothing but a tragic accident."

"You mean murder," I said without thinking.

"Oh, I think that's a bit harsh," H3 replied. "You see, we're in the very middle of a revolution, a revolution where these 'tragic accidents' work for the betterment of society."

"That makes no fucking sense," Amelia said.

"Oh, it makes total fucking sense!" H3 replied. "You see, in the beginning there was the agricultural revolution, when humanity began its journey toward a modern society. Then, there was the industrial revolution, and humanity finally began to see its full potential. All of the sudden, multitudes of people went from peasants to productive members of the first advanced society and they were happy!

"Then we entered the digital age and 3D printers catered to all our material needs and *unhappiness* increased. The first middle class freelivers began sucking on society's teat, living out their lives, contributing nothing and being absolutely miserable. Now, we're firmly in the drone age, an age where miserable freelivers become even more useless."

H3's perspective wasn't unique. We'd all heard it many times before. On Earth, freeliving was easy. Drones grew and delivered food to everyone at almost no cost. If you needed it, the municipality would even print you a house. We all knew this freeliving didn't bring happiness but at least it prevented some unhappiness.

"That doesn't mean you kill them," I said

"What happens after a natural disaster? Don't answer. I'll tell you: The freeliving people die and we rebuild. We rebuild without those miserable people sucking away the rest of our happiness. You see, if you delete the unhappy freelivers, overall happiness increases."

"But *you* caused the storm!" I yelled, throwing my hands in the air. The conversation was ridiculous, listening to someone justify murder.

"A technicality," H3 paused. He walked back to his desk and sat on it, his posture relaxed. "You think this is only happening on Mars? You think I'm the only revolutionary?"

There was silence. *Oh my god*, I thought of the impact of the CTS-Bradbury.

"You are not getting away with this!" Amelia said.

"Let me continue!" H3 said, looking angrily at Amelia, but letting his demeanor return to his usual calm state. "Please. I hope you are enjoying yourselves as much as I am. It is hard to keep secrets all bundled up. I'm a rare breed. The one guy in power who actually has secrets."

"Ha!" Amelia said. "You used us. You used the MDF soldiers to do your dirty work!"

"Dirty work? Call it constructive adversity."

Amelia gave H3 a skeptical look. "Constructive adversity?"

"Of course! That's what this is all about!" H3 said.

H3 began to preach, as if his words were going down in history. "I dream of a Mars that is the envy of every human in the solar system. That's not going to happen with half the population sitting on their asses. It can only happen if we clean up. Get rid of the potential freelivers, and bring in the artists, the scholars, the cultured, and the elite."

"That sound like a pretty swell vision," Avro said. "But how about the musicians, the fashion designers, and the Olympians. Mount Olympus would make a great ski hill." Avro was egging him on. I wondered if he was trying to use this to our advantage. In the movies, the villain kills the gofers first, leaving the hero for last. Deep down the villain admires and even empathizes with the heroes and gives them a chance to die with honor.

"A ski lift you say?" H3 said, "We should install a chair lift."

"So what do you want from us?" I said, hoping to end this conversation so we could get onto, well, whatever was next. If H3 wanted us dead, he would have done it already. If he wanted us silenced, he would have held us captive. It was obvious he wanted something.

"I want a few things," H3 began. "But first, as a consolation, I've decided not to give young Amelia here back to her friends in the MDF. That is, as long as you agree to play nice."

Amelia was speechless.

"Second, I see you've made friends with the media. I want you to come up with a story that clears my name, and calms the people until this storm is over."

Amelia scrunched up her face, "Why the hell would we do that?"

"The ninth dome's sabotage was a conspiracy. Let's keep it a secret, shall we? I think that's to both our advantages."

Did he know we blew up the dome? He was right though. It was to our advantage not to let people find out what actually happened, at least until we'd taken back control of the colony. Avro, Amelia and I looked at each other. "We'll think about it," Avro said.

H3 stood up, his tone and posture conveying trustworthiness. "And finally," he said, pausing, "and most importantly," he hesitated again, almost humbling himself. For some reason, he wasn't coming out with it. He strode around the room, not talking.

"What do you want H3?" Avro said, breaking the silence.

"I need you to stop the storm."

Chapter 25

POWER DRAIN

"What the hell?" I shouted, "You can't stop this thing?"

H3 shrugged. "We drained most of Harmony Colony's hydrogen reserves creating the storm and figured the comparatively low wattage of the nuclear reactor could sustain it until we'd accomplished our mission."

"Killing the colonists," I said.

"Increasing net happiness," H3 responded. "Five hours ago, our engineers disconnected the reactor. And yet, the storm still rages. Call it a slight miscalculation."

We sat, staring at H3, dumbfounded. If the storm wasn't being sustained by human intervention, the storm was sustaining itself. We had created a monster, a storm that could rage for months or even years.

"Can't you just reverse the polarity?" My voice was frantic. "Or use the coils the way they were designed?" I felt like a failure on multiple accounts. Not only was our plan to disconnect the reactor in vain but people got killed along the way. "You need to fix this. Try something! Try anything!"

"At least plug the nuclear reactor back in!" Avro added. "With the correct polarity."

"I thought you were engineers," H3 replied. "That little reactor isn't powerful enough to kill a global storm! Now the fuel cells, and the colony's remaining energy reserve, that's where you come in."

There was silence as we considered what he had just said. The colony's reserve was its lifeline. Without hydrogen and oxygen flowing through the fuel cells to generate electricity, there was no way scrub CO2. That same fuel was used in the furnaces. Without these, the colony's internal temperature would drop to subzero in a matter of hours.

Avro said it out loud, just to be sure we were hearing him correctly, "You're suggesting we power the anti-storm coils with our remaining reserve, knowing that if it fails, everyone in the colony dies."

"You diabolical son of a bitch!" Amelia said. "You'll still have a nuclear reactor."

"You're right. I'll be fine," H3 said. "But think of it this way. You can do nothing, and let everyone die, or you can try this, and they might have a chance."

He turned to the nearest guard. "Take them away."

We struggled as the guards dragged us out of H3's office. The guards manhandled us without trouble. We were still weak from being unconscious. They wrestled our arms behind our backs and led us down a cylindrical hallway.

We all thought the same thing. Was H3's idea to kill the storm just another part of the conspiracy? Was he trying to get us to kill the colonists?

The guard who held me whispered in my ear. "There's someone you need to meet," he said.

"What?" I said. The guard didn't say another word, but I relaxed and gave Avro and Amelia a look that said: *Just go with it.*

The guards shoved us into an elevator, freeing our arms once the doors closed. The elevator descended deep into the Alamo. Transparent walls allowed us to see the dome's internal structure. The design was brilliant, with pressure vessels within pressure vessels.

The steel doors opened into the Alamo's version of Central Control. The room teemed with activity. There were engineers at stations using gestures to control large colorful displays.

In the center of the room, a familiar face directed everything.

"Watson," Avro yelled. "You bastard. You orchestrated this chaos!"

Watson stopped what he was doing and walked over. "Follow me," he said to us. "We're all in this together, trust me." Watson looked grim. We didn't trust him but his demeanor breached the tension and we relaxed. "Corporals, you can leave us now," he said to the guards.

We followed Watson across the busy room and into a hallway of bleached cinderblocks.

"Where are we going?" I asked.

"You'll see," he said.

"We have questions," I said.

"Ask me anything. I'll be honest," Watson responded.

"Is H3 telling the truth? Have you lost control of the storm?" I said.

"H3 is telling the truth," Watson said. "We disconnected the reactor from the coils hours ago. We expected to see a measured decrease in the storm's energy but we didn't."

Avro grabbed Watson's arm, spinning him around. "You helped create the storm! How can we trust you?"

"I *unknowingly* helped create the storm," Watson explained. Avro let go of his arm. "As you know, Central Control transferred control of Project Bakersfield to the Alamo because of the nuclear reactor. But the coils were hardwired into the grid with the wrong polarity. There was nothing I could do."

"So who hardwired it?" Avro asked, as we continued down the hallway.

"We think it was an engineering officer from the MDF force. We've only recently been allowed back into the reactor room now that things aren't going to plan."

The hallway was dimly lit but there was a light at the end. The light illuminated a silver door, large enough to drive a truck through. Watson pressed a key card on a panel located on the wall and the large door swung open. The nuclear reactor rested on the other side.

The reactor looked like an electrical transformer. At three and a half feet high, it barely rose above my navel. A crane ran along the ceiling for loading the nuclear fuel and several cables connected the reactor to transformers on the walls.

I studied the device. The thick cables extruded from ports like snakes. The ports were labeled in handwritten sharpie. One said "Presidio Main." Another said "Alamo Backup," and another "Backup CO2 scrub."

The device had one empty port. It read: "Storm." I found the simplicity amusing.

Watson pointed to the empty outlet. A coil of thick wire lay on the floor beside it. "As you can see, we've disconnected the reactor from the Anti-Storm system."

"You mean storm generator!" Amelia corrected.

"Yes, well, the storm isn't getting any more energy from us," Watson said.

I continued to study the reactor. "That thing is mobile!" I observed, noticing a dolly beneath the reactor.

"It is," Watson concurred. "This is the only one. If we need power elsewhere, we move the reactor. It saves us the trouble of running transmission lines."

"So why bring us here?" I said. "What's the point of all this?"

"After the hydrogen for the fuel cells runs out, this is all we've got. This reactor could sustain the population of the Alamo. But with hundreds of colonists in the Presidio, this power source won't last that long."

"You mean the colonists in the Presidio are okay?" I asked.

"They're fine. There are too many of them for the MDF soldiers to relocate by force. Apparently, they've put up a substantial resistance."

"Well, that's a relief," I said, thinking of Kevin.

"The point is," Watson continued, "if this storm continues, people will die, including the people in the Alamo. It's in everyone's best interests to stop this storm at any cost."

"By 'any cost' you mean using the colony's fuel cells in a last ditch attempt to use Project Bakersfield the way it was designed? Those fuel cells are the only thing keeping us from suffocating, freezing, and starving."

"I realize that," Watson said. "But we've got to work with the cards we're dealt."

"And if that doesn't work?" Avro asked.

Watson leaned in and whispered, "If that doesn't work, meet me back here. I have a plan that nobody, I mean nobody, but you and I will understand."

"And what's that?" Amelia asked, annoyed that she wasn't included in Watson's list of people who would understand.

"If you drain the fuel cells and the storm still rages, a lot of folks are going to want to kill you," Watson said.

"What's your point?" Amelia inquired.

"With what I have in mind, they'll want to kill me, too." Watson handed me a plastic key fob.

"What's this?" I said, looking at the card. It was white, and the only thing written on it was a serial number, RPM-A-0000012-78.

"That," he paused, "is the key to the Alamo. It opens all service entrances, even the ones on the outside of the dome."

⚡

Watson led us out of the Alamo. The guards opened a small hatch in the barrier to let us pass. As we walked down the street in the twelve o'clock dome, we noticed Leeth's medical tent standing in a parking lot. I looked inside but no one was there. I turned on my phone's flashlight, panning it around the room. The place was a mess. Gauze and bandages littered the floor. There were eight cots set up, all of them stained with blood.

I sent Leeth a text message: *Everything all right buddy?*

Ten seconds later, Leeth texted back: *Screw you.* Followed by: *you're lucky no one was killed.*

"Leeth's fine," I said.

It was quiet in the colony as we walked back to the PDC.

⚡

We slept in shifts as we kept in touch with Watson, who was working from the other end. Avro and I went to each dome's substations and reconnected the fuel cells to the grid.

By noon the next day, everything was set up and we were ready to go. We met in the Central Control tower to push the button that would send the colony's remaining power streaming through the coils in a last ditch attempt to quell the storm.

"What the hell!" I whispered to Jackson as a *NewsFlash* camera crew set up equipment in the already cramped room.

"John, if you're right and this works, you'll be a hero. If it doesn't work, everyone here is going to die. The public has a right to know what's going on."

"If it doesn't work, they'll kill us!" I whispered.

Avro worked at a computer terminal while the rest of us stood by, supervising. Amelia joined us in the tower, no longer hiding after H3 had let us go.

I saw Robert Bowden coming up the stairs that led to the control room, followed by his personal cameraman. They were filming.

"Mr. Orville, is it true you've been inside the Alamo?" Bowden asked, kicking off an impromptu interview.

I turned and looked at Amelia. She nodded, letting me know that everything would be okay. "Yes, we've been in the Alamo," I said.

"Weren't you arrested? Why did they let you leave?"

"Once they found out we were on the storm taskforce, they invited us to their engineering control room. They're trying to fight the storm, just like us."

"There were rumors going around that the Alamo was causing the storm? What has changed?"

"Nothing has changed," I lied, and then said truthfully, "we theorized that the Alamo was sustaining the storm with their nuclear reactor but this is not the case."

"And what happened to the mob that stormed the Alamo? Are they safe? We heard there was quite a firefight."

"Most of the protestors made it to the Presidio. I assume they are still there and holding out."

"You assume?" Bowden questioned. "And didn't they try to suffocate you?"

"That was crowd-control. Harsh but effective." It disgusted me that I was defending the MDF's methods but right now we needed sanity.

Avro looked up from the displays. "Polarity confirmation received, we're ready to activate the system."

"Translation, please," Bowen said pointing the camera at Avro.

"Seriously?" Avro said, looking at Jackson.

Jackson shrugged and Avro continued, "When the storm began, the polarity of the Anti-Storm system, Project Bakersfield, was, ah," Avro paused, "the polarity was off. It was a miscalculation."

"But it's fixed now?" Bowden asked.

"We think so," Avro answered.

"You think so? That's not convincing. How much of our power reserves are you using on this little experiment?"

"All of it," Avro answered honestly. I wished he hadn't.

The news camera panned around the room. Bowden's face was expressionless. He moved closer to Avro as if to stop him, but Jackson held out his arm, holding him back.

"It's time," Jackson said. "Hit it."

Robert Bowden looked terrified. "Are you sure you want to push that button?" he yelled. "You just told us that if you activate this system, we lose all our reserve power."

"Yup," Avro said.

"That means no more lights, at all," Bowden said.

"You'll have the batteries in your cell phones and cars," I said. The camera turned back to face me.

"We'll have no more air!" Bowden yelled.

"Oh, we'll have plenty of air," I said, throwing tact out the window. "To clarify, it's the carbon dioxide that will kill you. We need power to run the CO_2 scrubbers."

I expected Bowden to ask about the plants that produced much the colony's oxygen. But he didn't. Plants need sunlight for photosynthesis so during a storm the trees and other plants don't absorb CO_2 or produce O_2.

"That means we'll have no more heat!" This was Bowden's last argument. It was too late to turn back now.

"This is going to work," I said, pointing at the camera, hoping to end the questioning.

"Activating storm abatement coils now," Avro said. The room went quiet and we could hear the sound of the wind against the roof above our heads. A map of the planet showed Project Bakersfield's basketball pattern turning from red to green.

"System active, power at two hundred percent," Avro read off the display, "reserve power at ninety-five percent."

"Meteorological Center reporting," Jackson said, "Winds at two hundred knots." He paused. "Winds at one hundred ninety knots and declining."

"It's working!" yelled Bowden. We listened to the wind. After a minute, the sound was noticeably let intense.

"Reserve power down to sixty percent," Avro read.

Sixty percent! The colony's hydrogen was rushing through the fuel cells like fuel out the nozzle of a rocket. We were draining power faster than I thought possible.

"Meteorological Center reporting," Jackson said. "Winds at one hundred fifty knots and declining."

Bowden faced the camera. "It's a race against time here in Central Control. Will we run out of power before dissipating the storm? Only time will tell."

Earlier that day we had reviewed the power requirements of our improvised system. We decided that operating the system at twice the level required to prevent a storm was the best starting point. As the winds died down, we planned to reduce the power input. Avro made that decision and reduced the power.

"Reducing system consumption to one hundred percent," he read, as he worked the digital controls on his display.

"Winds at one hundred ten knots and declining," Jackson reported.

Bowden whispered to the camera. "Less than a minute to go. Are we in for a sunny day or a dark and slow death?"

I'm not sure how Bowden decided that there was only one minute left. Maybe a countdown made for good HV footage. I looked over the displays, doing some mental calculations of my own. The situation reminded me of a seventh grade math problem where you had to calculate how long it would take to drain a swimming pool.

"System at one hundred percent, reserve at thirty percent," Avro read off the display.

"Winds holding at eighty knots," Jackson reported, reading a display that showed wind speed graphed over time.

"Jackson, if we kill the power now what do you think will happen?" I asked.

"According to the meteorology folks, if we don't bring those winds all the way down, they could go right back up," he replied.

"Reserve down to seventeen percent. What's the wind speed?" Avro asked, sounding frantic.

"Winds are holding steady," Jackson reported.

"Avro, boost the system strength to two hundred percent," Amelia suggested. "It's all or nothing!"

"No!" Bowden yelled. Avro ignored Bowden's protest, agreeing with Amelia. One hundred percent was enough to prevent a storm but apparently not enough to dissipate one.

Avro slid his fingers along the console. "System back at two hundred percent, reserve power at fifteen percent, fourteen, ten, five percent, three percent, one percent." The room went more silent than ever. "Reserve power depleted."

Our world darkened. Terror swept over me as I realized that our fears had been realized. Did we just do H3's dirty work? Perhaps we'd never find out.

The holovisions in the pavilion flickered and turned off. Lights around the room dimmed as battery-powered emergency LEDs flicked on. The displays remained illuminated. Central Control must have had limited battery backup.

"Jackson," Avro said. "Wind speed, please."

Jackson read from his display. "Winds at sixty knots," he paused, "and climbing."

"Well, there you have it," Bowden said into the camera, "an epic failure."

"I'm filming you," said the cameraman, "but we're not transmitting."

Chapter 26

THE REACTOR

Chaos erupted in the Central Control tower. Jackson got on the radio with the metrological center, yelling at them about their inability to predict the weather. Avro muttered to himself about how our calculations could have been so off. I was just trying to hold off Bowden, who was overwhelming me with questions I couldn't answer.

"Well, shit," Amelia yelled, loud enough to silence everyone. "You guys are just bursting with issues."

"Have a tissue," Avro replied, trying to break the tension. The Central Control tower usually held only two or three people and you could walk across the room in under four paces. With six people up there, we were practically on top of each other. The room had warmed with the additional bodies, but without power, it would be freezing up here in a matter of minutes.

"Let's work the problem," I said, a bead of sweat trickling down my face. "Bowden, will you to go down to the pavilion and report the news in person. Half the colony is going to show up on our doorstep, and we need to distract them so we can get out of here."

"The hell I am," Bowden said. "People are looking for someone to blame, and I say that's you!" he pressed his finger into my chest and moved in so close I could smell that he was sweating too.

"Listen, there's something we didn't tell you," I said to everyone in the room. "One of the engineers in the Alamo has another plan to stop the storm, and he's confident it will work." I didn't tell them it was Watson, and if they had asked, I would have lied. There was no way they'd trust Watson given the current situation.

"Well, what is it?" Bowden asked, stepping back and throwing up his hands.

"Thanks for keeping us in the loop," Jackson said, obviously angry, but he appeared ready to listen.

"We don't know," I said. "But the engineers in the Alamo have resources that we don't."

"You don't know?" Bowden exclaimed. "Everyone has only a few sols left before we freeze and suffocate, and you want us to help you, even though you have no idea what you're doing?"

Avro stood up from his chair and answered Bowden's question, "Yes."

"Why?" Bowden barked. "You're asking me to confront a group of people who think they're about to die and tell them what? That you're going to try one more thing?"

"It will give them hope," Amelia said with a shrug.

"Bullshit. You want to get to the Alamo because you think it will increase your chances of survival."

"They're no better off in the Alamo," I said.

"It's true," Avro said. "The Alamo's nuclear reactor can keep a few hundred people alive at most. But the Alamo is supporting thousands of people now."

"Is that true?" Jackson said, looking at me. "Is the Alamo doomed as well?"

"It is," I confirmed. "In a few sols both the Alamo and the circumferential will need to reduce the population to a level the systems can sustain."

I didn't really think about this reality until just now, but as the CO2 levels rose, we'd need to either cut some people off, or let everyone die at once.

"Barbaric," Bowden said.

Avro grabbed Bowden by the shoulder. "There's a saying in Navy Search and Rescue: 'So that others may live.' In a week, people might volunteer to die so that others might live to wait out the storm. That doesn't make them barbaric. It makes them heroes."

"I never thought about it like that," Bowden said.

"What do you say, Bowden? Will you help us?" Avro asked, putting a hand on Bowden's shoulder.

"I'll talk to the people," Bowden conceded.

"Thanks," I said, and Bowden motioned to the cameraman to follow him down the stairs. We waited until he left the room.

"So what's the plan?" Jackson said, "I can only help if you keep me in the loop."

"I recommend you join us at the PDC. With the temperature dropping up here, you'll need to evacuate anyway."

"Whatever you need," Jackson said. "But why the PDC?"

"We need to take a jeep into the storm and access the Alamo from the outside. We can't let anyone know what we're up to," I said.

"Wait, you have a key to the Alamo?" Jackson asked.

"Yes, Jackson," Avro confirmed. "We have a key to the Alamo."

We set Jackson up at Jimmy's dispatch station in the observation deck. Jimmy was nowhere to be found. He had probably joined the protesters in the pavilion. As a union man, he was never one to walk away from a picket line.

Everything we had at our disposal had a limited life. Whatever charge was left in an item's batteries was all we had to work with. Our jeep had a few hundred kilometers of range and both aircraft were fully fueled and charged. Most of electronic doors would work for another week but the airlocks needed to be operated manually. The spacesuits were fully charged and would last about eight hours each.

Avro, Amelia and I suited up and piled into the airlock. We checked our comms, but besides that, none of us spoke. We had no idea what Watson had in mind and it wasn't worth speculating.

The winds whipped at our spacesuits as before and we were constantly brushing dust off our visors and sensors. Kevin's drone had stopped sweeping our staging area but we still managed to get the garage open.

I drove this time and Amelia rode shotgun. Avro sat in the back. We drove past the remains of the nine o'clock dome, observing the debris strewn about the vicinity. We then reached the service door on the southwest edge of the Alamo.

Avro hopped out and used Watson's key on the terminal beside the Alamo's service airlock. The hatch opened.

I pulled the jeep into the Alamo and activated the airlock. The airlock worked as designed, pressurizing the chamber while blowing the dust off of us and the jeep with a tornado of forced air. The airlock had power. Someone knew we were coming.

The interior hatch hissed open, revealing the inside of the Alamo. We recognized the long white hallway that led to the nuclear reactor.

In the distance, someone in the corridor rushed toward us. It was Watson. We got out of the Jeep, took off our helmets and nodded our hellos.

"Thanks for coming. I'm sorry it came to this."

"It was close," Avro said. "We almost had it."

"Are you sure draining the reserves wasn't part of H3's plan all along?" I asked. "Somehow I feel like we're being played."

"You and me both," Watson said. "But I assure you, this next idea is all me."

Watson paced around the vehicle, looking into the jeep's bed. "Thanks for bringing the jeep. We'll need it. Back it up to the steel door. I have a package ready for you."

"You're kidding," Amelia said, knowing exactly what the 'package' was. Watson probably wanted us to steal the nuclear reactor and plug it into the central dome. This would save more lives in the circumferential by letting the folks in the Alamo die. I thought of Kevin and the other colonists in the Presidio. Could we just let them perish?

It reminded me of the trolley dilemma from a philosophy class I had taken. There are five people riding a trolley. The trolley is about to crash, killing all five people, except that you could throw a switch leading the trolley down a safer route. However, the safe route has an innocent person tied to the tracks. The person at the switch is forced to choose: let five people die, or deliberately take a life. Except in our case, there were thousands more people tied to the tracks.

Before our minds filled with the philosophical implications, Avro spoke up. "What the hell are we supposed to do?" he asked bluntly.

Watson looked at each of us in turn. "What happens when you drop soap in water with pepper floating on the surface?"

"Pepper shoots to the side of the bowl," Avro answered, glaring at Watson. "Anyone who passed the fourth grade knows that."

Watson nodded. "Think of the nuclear material as the soap and the dust storm as the pepper."

We immediately understood Watson's plan. But he was taking the dilemma to a whole new level.

"Do you have a plan to go along with this?" Amelia blurted, as we all climbed back into the jeep.

"I do," Watson replied, sitting in the back beside Amelia. "But you may not like it very much."

"This ought to be interesting," Avro said. I tapped the accelerator, driving the jeep further into the Alamo. I turned the jeep around where two hallways intersected and began backing down the hall, guided by the jeep's reverse camera.

"What's the plan, Watson?" I asked.

Watson's plan was crazier that I could have possibly imagined. "We need to get the nuclear reactor into an MAV. Once the vehicle reaches the upper atmosphere, we blow it up."

"You're kidding," I said, hitting the breaks, but I noticed Avro perk up. He sat in the front passenger's seat, looking back at Watson who sat behind me.

"I'm serious," Watson said. "The fallout will kill the storm. No doubt about it. The original design of Project Bakersfield involved the use of dirty nuclear weapons. The effective range is only three hundred miles, but that's enough to get the solar panels back on line. From there, we'll run Project Bakersfield the way it was designed."

I backed up through the steel door, stopping five feet from the reactor.

"That's brilliant," Avro said as we got out of the jeep. "But how are you going to blow up the MAV?"

"With these," Watson said, reaching for a duffel bag and tossing it to Amelia, "I swiped them from the soldiers."

Amelia looked into the bag. "Breaching charges," she said, looking impressed.

Watson's plan used the last substantial source of electrical power on the planet. As soon as we disconnected the reactor, everyone in the Alamo would be after us. Avro looked at me and nodded, convinced the plan was sound.

"I brought you these as well," Watson said, reaching behind the reactor.

"Holy shit," Amelia said with a smile. "Where'd you get these?" Watson handed Amelia and Avro each an MDF high-powered assault rifle.

"Scavenged them after the riot. Thought they might come in handy."

"Thanks," Avro said, setting his new rifle in the jeep.

The four of us gathered around the reactor, preparing to transfer it to the jeep. We kept the reactor plugged in while Watson used the room's crane to lift it off the dolly. With the nuclear reactor in the air, Avro and I guided it toward the jeep. The reactor fit snuggly into the bed.

We disconnected the crane and stepped back. The power supplies hung over the tailgate like umbilical cords. Those cables were the Alamo's life line, after all.

"What now?" I asked. "Just unplug it and hope for the best?"

"Give me sixty seconds to get back to the control room," Watson said. "Once I'm there, I'll open the service doors leading to the Alamo's pavilion. There will be soldiers there but without the reactor it'll be dark. Keep your headlights off as long as you can. Once you're there, I'll open the barrier to the rest of the colony."

"Are you sure you'll have enough power for that?" Avro asked, knowing that the barriers had limited battery backup.

"I can re-route the Alamo's battery reserves. It's not much but I can control the barrier doors. The spaceport will have its own battery backup as well. Not enough for life support, but enough to launch a single MAV."

"Okay," Avro said, "let's do this."

Watson nodded, turned, and jogged down the hall.

"John, Amelia. Are you ready?" Avro said, his hands gripping the large power cords protruding from the reactor.

"Ready," Amelia said.

"Ready," I said.

As Avro pulled the last remaining power cord from the reactor, the room went completely dark. Avro climbed back into the vehicle.

"Buckle up," I said, hitting the accelerator.

The jeep sprinted out of the reactor room and down the hall. We took an immediate left toward the Alamo's pavilion and waited for the pressure doors to open.

"Anytime now, Watson," Amelia muttered, as I switched off the headlights.

The door to the Alamo's pavilion opened to mass confusion. MDF soldiers and Alamo security ran in all directions, guided by flashlights mounted to their guns.

I tapped the accelerator, letting the jeep creep into the large room. We hadn't been spotted. I drove further into the square toward the barrier to the rest of the colony. Behind us, several people ran down the hallway from where we had come. It would only be a matter of minutes before they realized the nuclear reactor was missing.

In the distance, we saw the barrier to the colony opening. The guards at the checkpoint started screaming at each other. They probably suspected another mob.

Someone yelled, "The barrier is opening! Prepare for an ambush!"

From all around, soldiers started running toward the exit. Some even hopped into trucks. The soldiers seemed confused to find no one on the other side. A few vehicles and soldiers ventured into the channel to investigate.

A dozen soldiers stood between the exit and us, panning their lights across the room, looking for anything out of the ordinary. We could stay hiding for only a few more seconds. "Screw it!" I hissed, turning on the headlights and hitting the accelerator.

"What the hell are you doing?" Amelia yelled.

"Getting out of here!" I replied.

I increased our speed as we approached the door and MDF troops started diving out of the way.

"Stop that jeep!" someone yelled. Soldiers scrambled for their guns but it was too late. Our jeep crossed the barrier, entering the channel that connected the Alamo with the circumferential. I merged right, heading toward the ramp that led to the bridge.

The jeep's high beams illuminated the channel in a xenon glow. Support beams flew past as I accelerated, giving the illusion that we were traveling at impossible speeds. We approached the end of the channel and I could see the bridge's cylindrical glass tube up ahead. Something was off about the bridge. It was moving!

"Oh shit," I said, staring at the highway ahead of us.

The bridge swung and twisted like a dock in a hurricane.

I looked over at Avro. He looked like he was enjoying himself. "Who's looking for adventure!" he cried. It wasn't a question.

"Ugh!" Amelia moaned.

I pressed the accelerator to the floor and topped one hundred fifty kilometers per hour. We hit the bridge with the roadway level but rode up a curving track as the deck lifted up and to the left.

Glancing in my rear view mirror, I saw several pairs of headlights. Soldiers hung out the passenger side windows, guns in hand. I doubted they'd shoot us from behind. If they damaged the reactor, their pursuit would be in vain.

"How many are there?" I asked.

"By the looks of it?" Amelia leaned out the window, looking toward our pursuers. "All of them."

The first MDF truck left the channel and entered the bridge at high speed. As it did, that section of deck whipped up and to the right, flipping the truck. It rolled against the glass.

"Ah, guys? I don't think I can stay on the road," I said as the road under us wobbled to a forty-degree angle.

"We're going to tip!" Amelia screamed.

"No, we're not," I yelled, pulling the jeep to the right. I drove onto the shoulder, putting one wheel on the sidewall until the structure formed a V shape beneath the vehicle.

"Oh no, you're not!" Amelia yelled at me, as the wobbling bridge forced me to pull further to the right.

"Oh yes," I said, driving onto the tube shaped wall. It was like traveling through a twisty straw.

We drove along the transparent flexi-glass that held in the air. Lit by our headlights, dust-drenched winds poured a red current beneath us. I looked back again. There were three vehicles in pursuit.

The bridge slid down its previous trajectory. As the angle decreased, I steered the vehicle back onto the deck.

The roadway under the jeep rose to our right. I piloted the vehicle to the left and grudgingly back up onto the glass. I gauged our progress by observing the bridge's structural girders. *Halfway there!*

The three trucks followed us along the wall. Amelia climbed out of her seat and into the truck bed with the reactor.

"What the hell are you doing?" Avro yelled.

"This!" Amelia pointed the gun at the flexi-glass wall behind our jeep and unloaded an entire clip into the glass. Shards of flexi-glass sprayed into the air as the bullets ate away at the improvised roadway.

Seconds later, the first pursuing truck drove over the place where Amelia had fired. The glass gave way under the weight of the truck, and the truck wedged itself into the hole. The second truck slammed into the back of it, driving the first through the glass. The first truck disappeared into the maw, plunging to the canyon floor. The remaining truck swerved to avoid the hole as a rush of air escaped through the opening. Dust and debris lifted off the ground, flying backward toward the hole.

"Breach!" Amelia cried. Our ears popped as the air pressure began to decline. "Okay, maybe that was a bad idea!"

I looked ahead, noticing a barrier rising up out of the pavement. For once, I wished every device *didn't* have a battery backup.

"Stay on the wall," Avro instructed, sounding calm considering the situation. Ahead of us, the barrier rose higher than our bumper.

The remaining truck lumbered after us, racing for the exit. The soldiers tore the doors off their vehicle, throwing them onto the deck. Their intention was obvious, climb over the rising barrier. They'd never make it.

"I don't know if I can hold it!" I yelled, leaning to the left as the vehicle fought to keep its wheels on the curving wall. The bridge's wall arched towards the exit as we neared the barrier. The tube curved just enough to keep the vehicle off the pavement. We flew over the barrier, the jeep barely passing through the shrinking gap.

"Brakes!" Amelia yelled, as we literally flew into the channel.

"Brakes?" I yelled back, "We're not touching the ground!"

The SUV leveled out before landing. I slammed on the brakes. The jeep skidded, spun, and came to a halt. We watched as the barrier locked shut, sealing the bridge with the two remaining trucks inside. From inside, headlights lit the tube like trains in a tunnel.

Though the barrier's rectangular window, we watched as the soldiers jumped from the trucks. They ran towards the barrier, trying to keep their balance as the bridge continued to wobble. One of the soldiers pressed his face to the barrier and pounded on the window. His eyes were bloodshot and blood poured from his nose from the lack of pressure. Another soldier pulled out his side arm, firing three rounds into the glass. Avro leaned out of our jeep, holding up the middle finger on his spacesuit's glove.

I turned the vehicle around and sped through the channel toward the spaceport.

A bead of sweat trickled down my face. "Let's not do that again," I said.

Chapter 27

CHAIN REACTION

We sped through the channels, following the signs to the MAV Terminal. With the first round of pursuers suffocating on the bridge, we expected reinforcements from the base to show up at any moment. We'd killed dozens of MDF soldiers during the riot and another dozen or more on the bridge. How many where left? Forty? Fifty?

We crossed into the spaceport's MAV terminal and Avro put a hand on my shoulder. "Stop the jeep," he said. "Amelia, pass me that gun."

Avro jumped out, turning toward the entrance. He opened a panel and found the manual override for the barrier that separated the channel from the terminal. The barrier clanged shut and Avro fired three rounds into the panel's battery.

"They'll breach the door but it'll buy us some time. And if we're lucky, they won't be bringing in any vehicles." Avro hopped back in and we raced through the terminal toward the waiting spacecraft.

The Martian Assent Vehicles rested in silos on the south end of the spaceport. The cockpits and cargo holds were accessible from inside. Only the vehicles' nose cones were exposed to the Martian atmosphere. Instead of seats and gates like the other terminals, this one had loading docks for accessing each spacecraft's cargo holds.

I slammed on the brakes, stopping at the first silo. A scaffold-like staircase led up to the cockpit. Avro sprinted up the two flights, yanking open the hatch. I backed up to the hold.

Our jeep's headlights illuminated the area. With the terminal's glass roof caked with dust, everything took on a reddish glow.

"Are you sure you don't need a key for this thing?" I yelled up to Avro.

"Nope, don't need one," Avro yelled back, leaning into the cockpit twenty feet above our heads.

"Do you know how to operate it?" Amelia asked.

"Let's just say I studied harder than most on that Martian transport," Avro replied. "You worry about rigging the bomb and I'll worry about getting it to sub-orbit, okay?"

"Roger that," I said, opening up the cargo hold. The hatch opened in sections like the door on the Tyson Space Telescope.

I turned on my spacesuit's flashlight, inspecting the hold. It was just big enough for the reactor and had several hooks we could use to secure it in place. The spacecraft's fuel tanks ran along the side of the vehicle, creating indents in the walls. The MAV used solid rocket fuel. If they had used liquid hydrogen and LOX, we would have siphoned it for the colony's energy reserve.

Amelia lowered the jeep's tailgate. "Do we need to lift this thing?" she asked.

"Shouldn't have to," I said, opening a utility panel on the silo. I slid out a truss, extending a cantilever arm over the reactor.

Amelia and I connected four carabiners to the reactor, hoisting it out of the jeep and into the air until it swung over our heads like a pendulum.

"This ain't so bad," Amelia said, steadying the reactor with a gloved hand.

"Thank one-third gravity," I responded. "Let's get this secured."

We pushed the reactor into the hold, fastening it to the floor with straps.

"Now for the fun part," Amelia said. "Time to rig the bomb." She grabbed the charges from the Jeep.

"How's it going up there?" I yelled to Avro.

"Almost got it," he called back. "This thing is designed for orbit but we need it to skim the atmosphere. Had to break several safeties for this to work. Hey, send Amelia up when she's done. We need to figure out the detonation sequence."

"I heard him," Amelia said. "I'll be up in a minute." She used duct tape to secure the breaching charges near the solid fuel boosters. Her feet stuck out of the cargo hold as she planted a charge on the far side.

"Do me a favor," Amelia said, sliding out of the enclosed space. In her gloved hand, she held a strange looking electronic device.

"What's that?" I asked.

"This is the trigger for the bomb. I need you to take this up to the cockpit and feed the cables back down." She handed me the trigger. A weave of fuses hung from the device like Rapunzel's hair. With the trigger in one hand and the fuses in the other, I climbed the stairs, finding Avro in the copilot's seat. I handed Avro the trigger and I fed the cables through a panel and down into the cargo holds.

"Got it," Amelia yelled, grabbing the fuses from below. "Let me get these connected and I'll be right up."

Amelia shimmied out of the cargo hold and closed the hatch. She then climbed the stairs to the cockpit and sat in the captain's chair. I watched for soldiers from the landing, leaving the experts to their work.

"How's it going?" she asked Avro.

"Almost done with the auto-sequence," he responded. "That should do it. The MAV is programmed to launch sixty seconds after we close the hatch."

"Okay, great," Amelia said. "Now let's get this detonator hooked up." Amelia held up the trigger in front of Avro, the fuses dangling out like a cobweb as they coiled downward to the cargo area below.

"What I am supposed to do with that?" Avro asked, examining the device.

"All we need is a current running through the wire to trigger the detonation."

Avro considered this for a moment. "Okay, the trigger needs current, but only after the ship reaches altitude."

"Correct," Amelia said.

"Can't be done. All circuits receive power during the countdown as part of the system check. Why can't you just set a timer?"

"We don't have a timer. I figured you'd program the MAV to do it."

"Really?" Avro said. "You thought I could rig a bomb with a spacecraft as the trigger?"

"Ah, yeah," Amelia said, "you're like the smartest man I've ever met."

"Guys?" I said from the stairs, "We're about to have company." At the far end of the terminal lights from a dozen flashlights bobbed up and down.

"You've got sixty seconds, max," I yelled. "You guys need to figure something out, and fast."

"A dead man's switch!" Amelia said. "Hand me that cable." We watched as Amelia added an extra length of cord to the trigger. "In the movies, when the villain holds the good guys hostage, he holds the trigger in his hand. If the heroes shoot him, the villain's hand releases the trigger and the bomb goes off."

"Oh no," Avro said, "I don't like this one bit."

"If you can't rig a timer..." Amelia said.

"What are you talking about?" I said.

"Shut up, John!" they both yelled at once.

Avro leaned out of the cockpit. "Get that jeep ready to move. I'll be down in a moment."

I jumped down the stairs in a single bound, closed the jeep's tailgate and tried to listen to Avro and Amelia's conversation.

Their voices were muffled but I didn't like what I heard. "No decent rockets.... Blast radius.... Radiation..."

"What the hell, Avro!" I yelled, looking at the lights bouncing in the channel. "They're almost on top of us!"

"Get in the jeep!" Avro yelled. "Passenger seat! And put on your helmet!"

I did as he asked.

Avro leapt down from the MAV's cockpit. When he got to the jeep, he grabbed Amelia's helmet. Like a basketball, he passed it up to Amelia on the landing. Avro put on his helmet, grabbed the two rifles and climbed into the vehicle.

"Take this," he barked, handing me a rifle and shifting the vehicle into drive. "Shoot people!"

"What about Amelia?" I said, as Avro pulled away from the silo.

"She'll be fine."

I looked back at the spacecraft. The hatch had closed and a blast shield rose from the floor, protecting the terminal from the launching spacecraft.

"Oh, no no no!" I yelled. "Is Amelia in that thing? How the hell is she going to be fine?"

Avro ignored my questions. "I said hold on!" he roared, hitting the accelerator and turning the vehicle south. In seconds we were going over one hundred kilometers per hour. Our headlights illuminated more MDF soldiers. They must have found another entrance. They raised their rifles. Avro jerked the wheel to the left toward a row of soldiers and they dove out of the way.

I pulled the trigger, not sure if I hit anybody, but they scrambled for cover as we sped past. Bullets clinked off the exterior of the Jeep as we twisted down the terminal's hallways.

There was a loud rumble behind us as the MAV's main engine ignited and the spacecraft shot up into the sky. Several of the troops stopped shooting and looked up. The spacecraft was visible for a few seconds as it blew the dust off the roof.

As the colony's last remaining power source screamed away, the soldier's expressions changed from anger to despair. I watched as one soldier kneeled, resting his hands over the back of his head.

"Ah, turn?" I asked, as we approached the southern wall.

"No time," Avro replied, pulling out his rifle and sticking it out the window.

"Turn the damn vehicle!" I yelled as we neared wall, realizing what Avro was doing. The wall wasn't a wall. It was a window!

"No time!" Avro bellowed and pulled the trigger. Dozens of holes dotted the window, weakening the structure.

The jeep crashed through the glass. Our windshield shattered, covering us with even more broken glass. Air blasted from the terminal, following us onto the Martian surface. With the pressure equalized, the storm rushed into the spaceport, filling the terminal with dust and wind, spelling a grim end to the soldiers inside.

The jeep was beat up, covered with bullet holes and missing the hood. But with the battery under the floor and the engine in the back, none of the vehicle's important systems appeared to be damaged.

Our spacesuits adapted to the environment. I could feel heat pumping though the suit, counteracting the subzero temperatures outside. The view ahead of us came into focus as my visor adjusted to the darkness.

"Do you mind telling me what's going on?" I asked.

"Amelia will activate the bomb manually," Avro replied.

"Manually? You two geniuses couldn't rig a timer?"

"Nope."

We bounced across the Martian landscape, our visors creating a scene extending a few hundred meters in front of us. Avro found the road leading back to the colony.

"Did you ever study the Cold War?" Avro asked.

"Not really, why?" I answered.

"When the Cold War began, spy satellites had just been invented, but digital cameras hadn't. The American spy satellite cameras used film. Can you guess how they got the film back?"

"The satellites re-entered the atmosphere," I guessed.

"Wrong," Avro said. "The satellites stayed in orbit but the film canisters were ejected. The canisters had parachutes but were never intended to hit the ground. Instead, an aircraft snagged the parachute out of the air with a hook."

"You're kidding," I said.

"That's exactly what happened," Avro said, cutting the wheel as we climbed the switchbacks on the canyon wall.

"I'm not questioning your history. I know what you want me to do."

"What we *have* to do," Avro responded. "In exactly ten minutes, Amelia is going to jump from that spacecraft. She has the drogue chute from the ascent vehicle's emergency kit, but the parachute will only slow her down to a few hundred miles per hour."

"What if we fail. What if I don't catch her?"

"We won't fail."

We crested the canyon wall and rumbled around the familiar remnants of the nine-o'clock dome. Avro cranked the wheel to the right, following a curved path around the circumferential. On our left, we passed the eight o'clock dome, then the seven o'clock dome. Moments later, our tarmac came into view. The Arachnid sat like a shadow, cloaked in dust.

Avro pulled up to the PDC's airlock. We jumped out of the jeep, leaving the vehicle on the tarmac. Avro raced towards the Arachnid, dusting the side door with his glove to reveal the handle.

"I'll meet you in the air," he yelled, climbing into his aircraft.

"Roger," I said, stepping into the airlock and closing the hatch.

I cranked the valve, drawing air in from the colony. Avro didn't need to communicate any more. I would make the initial capture, but since the Pelican couldn't land vertically, we'd need to make an in-air transfer.

The inner airlock door opened and I found Jackson standing in the lounge.

"What happened?" Jackson asked, jogging beside me as I ran down the hallway in my spacesuit. "Where are Avro and Amelia?"

"No time to explain but I think we just saved the colony," I yelled, not even bothering to take off my helmet. "If you can get the hangar doors open right now that would be a huge help. And head back to Central. Get ready to reactivate Project Bakersfield!"

I climbed into the Pelican's cockpit, gloved hands flying instinctively across the controls. The hangar door slid open and the dust flew in, peppering the aircraft.

A message appeared on my display, "Warning. Automated Hangar Landing System Offline." The hangar's landing sensors were caked and there was no time to clear them. I guess I'd be landing somewhere else.

"Here goes nothing," I said, activating the catapult sequence. The Pelican raced out of the hangar and into the storm. The turbulence jolted me in my harness as I accelerated to five hundred kilometers per hour.

I pulled back on the stick with my right hand, pushing the throttle with my left. The twin turbofans whined in my ears, thrashing the atmosphere with their teardrop-like blades. The aircraft's electric motors wined like a gyroscope spinning at full tilt.

"John, this is Avro, radio check, over."

"John here, I read you five by five."

"Set your radar to pick up Amelia's suit transponder: squawk 7700."

"Squawk 7700, roger."

The view from my cockpit brightened as I rose higher in the sky. I looked back to my displays, searching for Amelia's signal.

"Got her, she's at one hundred thousand feet. Velocity: six thousand kilometers per hour," I said. "She's still in the MAV!"

"Roger that," replied Avro, "Can you get any closer?"

"Negative, I'm approaching the Pelican's operational ceiling."

I rose above the storm. Sunlight streamed in through the canopy, almost blinding me before the visor polarized to compensate. The MAV streaked silently across the sky. Suddenly, the spacecraft's main engine cut off. The trail of smoke from behind it ceased. For a moment, it just coasted.

Maneuvering thrusters ignited from various orifices on the spacecraft's exterior. Avro must have programmed the MAV to move away from Amelia once she jumped. Maybe I imagined it, but barely, just barely, I saw something, or someone, separate from the spacecraft.

I had to shield my eyes when it exploded. The spacecraft morphed into a giant sphere of yellow and red light, brighter than the sun. My visor compensated further, leaving the rest of my view in pitch black.

"Oh shit," I said, more in amazement than fear. A cloud of radioactive and highly charged particles sprang from where the spacecraft had been. It worked! At least our plan to make a dirty bomb worked.

Whether this would subdue the storm, we could only hope.

I looked at my sensors. Squawk 7700 was still transmitting!

"I have her signal!" I called out. "Moving to intercept."

I held steady at fifty thousand feet and looked at my display, interpreting the data from Amelia's transponder. Her altitude ticked down from ninety thousand to seventy thousand feet.

"Parachute deployed!" a female voice said over the radio. "Avro? John? Do you read me?"

"I read you loud and clear!" I shouted.

In the distance, Amelia's bright orange parachute fluttered high above my position. Its shape resembled a giant ring, designed like a halo for deployment at hypersonic velocities.

I continued to read the data from my display. Amelia was falling fast but not losing much speed. "It's going to be close," I said.

"Tell Avro I love him," she said.

"You'll be fine, Amelia. Hang in there," said another voice from over the radio.

"Avro!" yelled Amelia.

"You did it, Amelia. Look at the clouds!" Avro said.

I checked my instruments. Amelia was three miles in front of me and ten thousand feet above. I pulled back on the control stick, attempting to gain what little altitude I could. Then I pushed the stick forward, forcing the Pelican into a dive.

"Avro, you're right! The clouds, they're receding!" You could hear a painful joy in Amelia's voice. I looked toward the horizon. A tidal wave of dust receded in all directions while mountain peaks broke out of the haze.

The sight was hypnotic, until Amelia's parachute whooshed past me. I looked at her transponder data as she descended past forty-seven thousand feet, traveling at almost two thousand kilometers per hour.

"On my way Amelia, put on those brakes!" I pushed forward on the throttle, looking for extra juice.

I descended past forty thousand feet and watched Amelia's parachute in the distance below me. "I'm catching up," I said.

Amelia descended past twenty thousand feet, her parachute continuing to grow in my field of view.

"Okay, Amelia, here I come!" I said, extending the Pelican's landing boom below the fuselage. The boom was designed to capture a landing assist cable on short runways. We sure hoped it would capture a parachute.

"I'm right behind you. Hope you like whiplash."

"Just catch me, dammit!" Amelia yelled.

Amelia descended past ten thousand feet and the ground came up fast. The ground! We could see the ground! For a moment I almost lost focus but quickly regained it as time ran out.

The parachute took up my entire field of view. It was huge, perhaps two hundred feet in diameter. The Pelican passed over the chute, the fabric bending as it rubbed the underside of the fuselage.

A vibration shook the Pelican and a green light flashed up on the display.

"Captured!" I shouted, yanking back on the stick to avoid driving my plane into a hillside. "Wahoo!" I shouted.

"Wahoo yourself," Amelia muttered. "That hurt!" I could hear the smile in her voice.

"Did it hurt more than jumping out of an exploding radioactive spaceship?" Avro asked.

"Yes, actually," Amelia responded. "You own me one hell of a massage!"

I tapped the dive brakes and leveled us out. Amelia pulled along behind me like a water skier. She turned herself around to face forward, holding on to the parachute cables like a water skier's rope.

We banked around and headed back toward the colony.

"Okay, Avro, form up," I called.

"Roger that. Decrease speed to three hundred kilometers per hour. Meet you at five thousand feet over the colony."

Avro transitioned from a hover to horizontal flight as I flew down over the canyon.

Amelia and I got our first view of the colony since the storm began. The nine o'clock dome looked worse from above. The dome's glass had shattered all the way to the zenith. The cleaning drones shot out of their bunkers, and we watched the first glints of sunlight off freshly dusted panels.

"Forming up," I said over the radio as we passed the Arachnid. "Slowing to three hundred."

Avro slipped his aircraft onto my six, flying next to Amelia.

"Well, howdy there, gorgeous," he said, in a fake Texas accent. "Nice of you to drop in."

"Hi-ya partner," replied Amelia. "Nice of you to stop by. What can I say? I guess I done fell for you."

Avro inched his aircraft towards Amelia with the side door open. He kept Amelia close, careful to keep her away from the thrusters.

Amelia reached out a gloved hand and grabbed a rail. "Contact!" she reported.

After pulling herself into the Arachnid, she connected her suit to the aircraft with a tether and released the parachute. The chute fluttered down towards the colony, settling on top of the suspension bridge that had finally stopped wobbling.

I watched through my port window as Amelia climbed into the

cockpit with Avro.

Avro looked over and gave me a salute. "John, I need to land ASAP. I'm running on fumes."

"Roger that. Safe landing you two," I said.

"You too. Good luck," Avro said.

"Why good luck?" Amelia asked, sounding confused.

"He has to land on the spaceport's runway," Avro explained. "The automatic landing system in our hangar needs repairs and the spaceport's terminal are out of commission."

"What happened to the spaceport?" Amelia asked.

"We depressurized it," Avro answered, with a smirk. "Along with the rest of the MDF."

"Oh, "Amelia responded. "That must have sucked."

I flew over the runway, looking for a clear place to land. The spaceport's runway was covered in dunes. The flight through the storm had drained the Pelican's batteries and I had minutes left before I became a glider.

I took a moment and looked around the colony. The solar panels were clean! Several drones were already retreating to their bunkers. I pictured Director Jackson with a big smile on his face and wearing his sunglasses again. Hopefully, he'd reactivated Project Bakersfield. With sunlight hitting the panels and energy pouring into the coils, the planet-wide storm would be over in a matter of hours.

I was afraid, terrified actually, of what would happen to me when I landed. Were there still any MDF soldiers left? If there were, would they shoot me on sight? If I were lucky, maybe they'd just rough me up since I would be coming in unarmed.

I thought of Marie and Branson. Marie would be so proud of me, her husband, the *hero*. Who would have thought? Branson would be almost five now. If he were here, I guess he'd be proud too. I pictured their smiles, smiles I'd never see again. I smiled back.

I thought back to that day in the simulator when I crashed into the San Francisco hillside. Looking to my right, I stared at the nearby hill. It was covered in solar panels glowing green and blue in the sunlight.

I returned my focus to the runway, thinking of Avro, Amelia, Kevin and Leeth. They'd poured their souls into me, building friendships forged in our shared experience.

A mile ahead, a flat stretch of runway caught my eye. It wasn't perfect but I figured I'd be able to get the aircraft down in one piece.

I switched my comm frequency to Martian standard. "MATC, this is Pelican Papa Delta Charley, requesting permission to land on runway one eight." Considering the circumstances, I expected Martian Air Traffic Control frequencies to be unmonitored. I was wrong.

"Copy that, Pelican, you are cleared to land on runway one eight. Just a warning, it looks like you have quite a welcoming committee down here." I chill ran down my spine. We'd put everyone's lives on the line not once, but twice, in the last few hours alone. We'd soon be faced with the consequences of our actions.

But then I recognized the voice, "Watson, is that you?"

"It sure is! I'll meet you at the MDF airlock."

"What about the airlock in the main terminal?" I asked, my fear slowing being replaced by relief.

"According to the folks here, you depressurized most of the spaceport with that jeep."

"Oh yeah," I said. "Sorry about that."

"Just get back in one piece, eh?"

I leveled the aircraft and lined up to the runway. The Pelican used a skid plate instead of landing gear, so this could be rough, but I couldn't be sure. I'd never landed on a runway outside the simulator.

The Martian dust softened the impact and the Pelican kicked up a spray of red fog as it cruised down the runway. I pressed the stick forward, driving the skid plate against the runway until I came to a complete stop.

The Pelican wasn't designed for taxiing but that didn't matter. There wasn't any place to park with the spaceport covered in sand dunes. I checked my suit to make sure it was operating and opened the hatch. I climbed out into the sunshine and began trudging across the tarmac. In the distance, several drones came out of their garages and began to plow.

The airlock's hatch slid open like the doors at a shopping mall. I stepped inside and closed my eyes, hoping I would be greeted with more appreciation than when I left.

When the interior door hissed open, I opened my eyes. Watson walked over and gave me a hug, slapping me on the back. A crowd of Harmony Colony's police and other people I didn't recognize started clapping, then cheering. One of the cops held a weapon captured from the MDF and another held one of Amelia's crossbows.

I walked forward, popping the seal on my helmet, lifting it off my head and tucking it under my arm. I walked through the crowd with Watson, people congratulating me by slapping me on the back. Apparently, Watson had spread the word about what we had accomplished and how we did it.

"John Orville," he said. "You just saved the planet."

"I had a little help."

I gave Watson a confused look. "How did you get here so quickly? I'm pretty sure the bridge is out of commission."

"I came with the reinforcements here," he gestured to the cops and other volunteers, "in a rover. We half expected a firefight but found only a half dozen MDF soldiers. They immediately surrendered, said they were the only ones left!"

"Thanks for coming to get me. What did I miss?" I said.

"There was chaos in the Alamo when you got away with the reactor. People knew what you were trying to do but no one thought it would work. When the spacecraft took off with the reactor inside, they thought that was it. They believed they had only hours to live. Grown men cried and people beat the walls in grief."

"That bad, huh?"

"But then we saw a light from up in the clouds. The storm parted like Moses and the red sea. People celebrated. It was like their home team just won the Super Bowl!"

"What about H3?" I asked.

"Look for yourself," Watson said, pointing to the window and at the Alamo. A hatch was open on top of the dome and a cloud of smoke billowed out. I followed the cloud upward, and at its tip, an MAV rocketed toward space.

"H3 had an escape pod?" I asked.

"He had it prepped after he met with you. The truth's getting out, John. You guys crumbled his empire like a house of cards."

Word spread to the Presidio that the storm had ended and Kevin led the people out as the barriers lifted. The colonists paused as they emerged from the deep, taking in the sunlight they never thought they'd see again.

With H3 gone, there was confusion about who was in charge. But within a few hours, a senior Red Planet executive issued a statement across social media.

"I, Fredrick J. Wong, will temporarily take over the leadership of Red

Planet Mining, Incorporated and its assets. Henry the Third's whereabouts are currently unknown. We will issue a formal statement in the coming sols. In the meantime, business as usual. I thank you for your resilience in these turbulent times."

To compensate the residents for the recent incidents, Wong promised all of Harmony's residents shares in the company. Not that the shares were worth much at the moment, but in time, we'd rebuild and the mining company would be onto its next great project. Maybe humanity's first intergenerational starship. I can dream right?

He also promised that all corporate decisions would be run by Council, giving the colony's residents some level or representation. "We're all in this together," he said. I guessed we'd find out.

After the drama at the medical station during the storm, Leeth was happy to be back at the clinic. Having seen his last patient for the day, he headed to the bar for a beer but was kicked out within minutes of arrival. Apparently, the bartender remembered him and was not in a forgiving mood, despite the circumstances of the day. Leeth had tried his best, telling the bartender, "Hey, man, I'm one of the heroes."

"Maybe," man said, nodding. "But you're still an asshole. Out."

Leeth had a dirty look on his face when he walked into Applebee's. Kevin had been the first to arrive, reserving our usual table. Watson and I followed soon after.

"Hey, nurse!" I called, directing Leeth to our table.

"You've been busy, mate. And making some new friends, I see."

"Leeth, this is Watson. Watson, meet Leeth," I said. They shook hands and Leeth took a seat across from me at the table.

Leeth put a hand up, flagging down the waitress while Avro and Amelia walked in, arm in arm.

"Well!" Amelia exclaimed. "The gang's all here!"

Leeth looked at Amelia and Avro. "So Amelia, you're still heading back to Earth on the next transport?"

Amelia winked at Avro. "Nah, I think I'll stick around," she said as Avro pulled out a chair for her.

I looked to the holovisions, expecting to see a baseball game or football game from Earth. Instead, *NewsFlash* reports played on every screen.

"I guess our story's getting around," I said, nodding towards the nearest display. We watched a replay of Avro and me flying up the canyon with Amelia in tow.

"Can't complain," Avro said. "Mars could use a few celebrities. I just didn't think it would be us."

A hand clamped down on my shoulder. Captain Daniels stood behind me in a freshly pressed uniform.

"Hey, listen up!" shouted the Captain, looking around the bar, and then staring us down one at a time.

Leeth slouched in his seat, not sure what was going on. Several other police officers gathered around our table.

"From now on, gentlemen… and lady," he said, looking at Amelia. "All your drinks are on us!"

The bar erupted into cheers and four pitchers of beer slammed down on our table. It was going to be a very good night.

John and Marie's adventures continue in *The Return of NASA.*
Summer 2016

ABOUT THE AUTHOR

Shortly after receiving his wings as a Royal Canadian Air Cadet, John dropped out of Aerospace Engineering at Carleton University to pursue a degree (and career) in Corporate Finance. Struggling to scratch his itch for science, his wife bought him a twelve-inch Dobsonian Telescope for Christmas (Jennifer got leather boots, to be fair). A few months later, John joined the Mount Diablo Astronomical Society, volunteering as many as four nights per week under California's cloudless skies. He soon began writing futurist essays for the club's magazine, *Diablo MoonWatch*, and later published his first book, *50 Things to See with a Small Telescope.* After doing a "What's up" speech on reusable rockets in 2012, John got the idea for this book and immediately began writing *The Martian Conspiracy.*